LINDA BYLER

LIZZIE'S CAREFREE YEARS

THE BUGGY SPOKE SERIES
book three

Good Books

New York, New York

LIZZIE'S CAREFREE YEARS

All rights reserved. No part of this book may be reproduced in any manner without the express written consent of the publisher, except in the case of brief excerpts in critical reviews or articles. All inquiries should be addressed to Good Books, 307 West 36th Street, 11th Floor, New York, NY 10018.

Good Books books may be purchased in bulk at special discounts for sales promotion, corporate gifts, fund-raising, or educational purposes. Special editions can also be created to specifications. For details, contact the Special Sales Department, Good Books, 307 West 36th Street, 11th Floor, New York, NY 10018 or info@skyhorsepublishing.com.

Good Books is an imprint of Skyhorse Publishing, Inc.®, a Delaware corporation.

Visit our website at www.goodbooks.com.

10 9 8 7 6 5 4 3 2 1

Library of Congress Cataloging-in-Publication Data is available on file.

ISBN: 978-1-68099-446-9
eBook ISBN: 978-1-68099-449-0

Cover design by Jenny Zemanek

Printed in the United States of America

To Debbie, Verna, and Mary

Memories are made of ridges,
of rivers and mountains,
of snow and ponds,
of ponies and cabins.
But most of all,
they are made of love,
which formed the best memories
of our childhood.

contents

chapter 1

The New School

The mountain was awesome in its beauty as Lizzie Glick walked to school with her sisters, Emma and Mandy. She wondered if she would ever become accustomed to it, rising above the river and the line of trees along its base.

There was a railroad track beside the river, before the mountain's steep ascent, and the train which wound its way along this track always gave its low, mournful whistle at certain points along the track. Lizzie had asked Dat why the train blew its whistle at the same place each time. Dat said the engineer blew the whistle before small towns or railroad crossings to let people know it was passing through.

The morning sun gave the mountain a yellow glow, and with the leaves having changed to flaming hues of orange, red, and yellow, it was almost unreal. Lizzie had never seen anything quite as beautiful or as awe-inspiring as the sight before her this morning. And, to think they lived here; she could walk to school every morning and see this.

Lizzie skipped a little skip of excitement. Her covering bounced a bit, the bow which was tied loosely beneath her chin swinging to the side. She reached up and pulled her covering straight, or at least it seemed straighter to her. It was so unusual to be wearing a covering to school, because where they had lived before, they didn't need to wear one until they were in the upper grades.

This was in Lizzie's first month of school in Jefferson County. They had all moved here from Randolph County the previous week. Lizzie was eleven years old, and lived with Emma, her older sister, Mandy, her younger sister, and Jason, her three-year-old brother. Her parents were called "Mam" and "Dat", which is Pennsylvania Dutch for "Mother" and "Father." But here in Jefferson County, their cousins called their parents "Mom" and "Daddy." They didn't pronounce "Daddy" the way Lizzie did. The *a* sound was more flat, which was the way her cousins spoke, because they all came from Ohio, where the Amish people's language was a bit different than the way it sounded in Pennsylvania. Lizzie loved to hear her cousins talk, the way they rolled their *r's*, using strange words that she didn't know the meaning of.

The girls were walking with their cousin, Edna, who was almost the same age as Emma. The older boys were walking ahead of them, but Danny, who was only six, tagged along with the girls.

Emma's dark brown hair shone in the sunshine. This morning they didn't wet their hair and roll it back in the way they had done in Randolph County. That was because there were different church rules, or "ordnung" here, so they were allowed to comb their hair more loosely, without rolling it. Emma's hair was so pretty—much darker than Lizzie's. She always wished she could have hair the color of Emma's, because lots and lots of people had hair the color of Lizzie's. Plain mousy brown. It really had no blond streaks or waves or even curls in it. It was just flat brown.

It was the same way with her nostrils. Emma's were round and small, like ordinary people's, but Lizzie's were long, flat, and slanted to the side. She spent lots of time in front of her mirror on her dresser, trying to hold her head so that people wouldn't notice them, but nothing helped. That's just how her nostrils were. Her uncle, Marvin, who was only a bit older, had the exact same problem, except it was different. His nose had a bump on the top, where no bump should have been. He often pressed hard on this bump with his thumb, but it stayed exactly the same.

Lizzie and Emma were not thin, like most girls who were their age. They were a bit chubby; actually, more than chubby, because Mam said it was time she put them on a diet. That hurt Lizzie's feelings terribly, although she didn't tell Mam, because Mam didn't say it to be mean to her. Emma and Lizzie both loved to eat, and Mam made lots of wonderful dishes they enjoyed. Mam loved to bake, too, making pies, cakes, cupcakes, and cookies for Dat and her appreciative daughters.

Mandy was small and thin, because she liked fruit and applesauce and Jell-O without cake and pudding to go along with it. She had beautiful large green eyes with yellow flecks in them, and her nostrils were normal, too. Her teeth stuck out in front the way Lizzie's did, so that made them look a lot alike. The only thing — Mandy was so thin, that she seemed to be about half Lizzie's size.

Their cousin, Edna, was a bit heavy, too. She had wavy brown hair, twinkling brown eyes, and the most adorable flat little nose. Her teeth were perfect; they didn't protrude one tiny bit, so Lizzie knew that was another thing she couldn't fix. Teeth grew either straight or crooked — you could never tell which way they would grow when you were a baby.

Mam had often told the girls their teeth were perfect. They looked like little rabbits, and rabbits were just as cute as a button. That was fine when they were small, but Lizzie was growing up, and sometimes she wished her teeth were straight. Weight was something she didn't worry about too much, because she didn't look too bad, she always thought. Besides, it was too hard to go without food. How were you supposed to have energy to walk to school or play baseball, or anything, really, if you didn't eat? There was no sense in going without good food.

They had to cross a fairly busy highway, which made Lizzie nervous. They all looked out for Danny, because he was only six. They looked carefully both ways before dashing across the road. The rest of the way to school was all downhill, not a steep incline—just a gentle slope leading down toward the river and the mountain. There were rolling pastures and houses dotted along them, until they turned a bend in the road and saw a small white schoolhouse tucked behind a hill. It was smaller than Lizzie had imagined.

There were a few boys there, throwing a baseball back and forth. Their cousins, Ivan and Ray, who walked ahead of them, had already put their lunchboxes inside and were running across the playground. They opened the gate carefully, causing Lizzie's heart to do a flip-flop, because she was nervous about meeting her new teacher. Edna had assured them she was really nice, although strict, so you could never tell, Lizzie thought nervously.

The teacher was so friendly, they had no chance to feel apprehensive about meeting her. They had barely opened the door, before she said, "Good morning!" in a loud voice.

Edna answered in the same loud voice, but Lizzie only spoke quietly. Emma smiled and Mandy only whispered, "Good morning," so Lizzie knew they were nervous, too.

The teacher's name was Barbara Renno. That was a name Lizzie had never heard of; Renno—not Barbara. There were lots of Barbaras in Randolph County, but not one Renno. There were Glicks, Fishers, Eshes, Kauffmans, Stoltzfuses, and lots of other Amish names, but not one Renno. So Lizzie thought they would probably meet completely different people, with different names and homes and personalities.

They sure were friendly. Everyone smiled and spoke kindly. Even the children Lizzie had never seen before walked over to the newcomers, smiling warmly. There were two girls in Lizzie's class named Salina and Becky. They asked Lizzie how old she was and when Lizzie told them, they were so excited, because they were almost exactly her age.

Salina did not really look like an ordinary girl. She had dark skin and coal black hair with lots of little waves in it.

Becky was black-haired, too, only her hair was straight. She had large brown eyes and a friendly smile. She lived just down the road a bit, almost at the river. They all lived together on a farm, with lots of children who were all dark-haired with brown eyes. Her sister, Sadie, was older, but was still in the same group of friends at school.

When the teacher rang the bell, the procedure was much the same as in Lizzie's previous school. The singing was much more boisterous; in fact, everyone sang so loud and with such rhythm that Lizzie almost had a giggling fit. She never once glanced at Emma, because if she would have, they would have had to laugh. That would not be polite on the very first day of their new school.

Once they were seated at their desks, Lizzie was delighted to find exactly the same arithmetic book they had used before. Even her spelling book was the same small yellow one that said "Fifth Grade" in black letters across the front. So she did not have to be afraid of not being able to do her lessons well, since the workbooks were much the same.

One thing was very different here. That was the huge cast-iron woodstove. It sat in the middle of the class-room, like a big black elephant. Before you came to the front door, you had to walk through a woodshed. There were three or four steps down from this room, which was filled with big piles of wood. The wood had bark on it and was cut in the proper size for the black wood-burning stove inside.

No one used coal in Jefferson County. Everyone heated their homes with wood, because there were lots of wooded ridges and sawmills, and the wood was very inexpensive.

Lizzie felt a bit awkward when the teacher tapped the bell for first recess. The children promptly got their lunchboxes from the shelves and proceeded to eat a cookie, or a small bag of pretzels. Lizzie said something to Emma about her lunchbox, and Edna informed them they called lunchboxes "buckets."

"Really?" Lizzie asked, raising her eyebrows.

"Why 'buckets?'" Emma inquired.

Edna shrugged her shoulders. "I don't know. I guess because Mom and Daddy always said 'bucket.'"

That answer was good enough for Emma, and she said nothing further. But after Edna went outside, Lizzie whispered quietly to Emma, asking if she was going to call her lunchbox 'bucket.'"

"Are you?" Emma asked in return.

"Not *bucket*!" Lizzie burst out. "A lunchbox is not a bucket!"

"Sh-shh!" Emma warned. "Someone will hear you."

So Lizzie wandered outside to watch as the older boys picked teams to play baseball. She leaned against the white wooden siding of the schoolhouse, putting one foot up against the concrete wall beneath it. She held a small plastic bag of potato chips in one hand and smoothed back her loose hair with the other. Strands of hair had already come loose from beneath her covering and were blowing in the breeze. That would have been considered terribly unkempt in Randolph County, but here it was quite ordinary.

Lizzie thought her hair looked much nicer, and it even felt a bit English. She had watched a few girls who had their hair cut in bangs at the grocery store, and thought that it would be so nice to have bangs. If she crossed her eyes upward, she could see her loose hair, and it seemed almost like she was English. *I had better never tell Emma that*, she thought wryly.

Lizzie was surprised to see the girls were being picked to help play baseball. She had often helped play, but thought maybe these girls wouldn't play, because their skirts were longer and they wore coverings. Ray called over to her, "Lizzie! Come on over!"

Lizzie shook her head. "No."

"Come *on*."

"I'm eating chips."

"Well, hurry up and finish them."

So Lizzie walked over and stood beside the other

girls, stuffing the last of her potato chips into her mouth. She crumpled the plastic bag, lifting her apron to put it in the pocket of her dress.

"Lizzie!"

Ray had already picked her! Lizzie was thrilled. *That was really nice of him*, she thought, as she hurried over to stand on his side. She couldn't wait to show these children how well she could play, because she actually could play baseball quite well.

The bell rang before they could play, but each team had the same amount of boys and girls, so it would turn out alright, Lizzie thought.

They had reading the second period, which kept Lizzie's mind fully occupied every second, listening to every new person read. She pretended to be studying her story and listing the new words, but she was actually watching each new pupil read. They were all shapes and sizes, with loud voices and quiet voices, low voices and high ones. There were tall children and small ones, and each one read in their own individual voice.

Her attention turned to Ivan and Ray, who were not studying or doing any writing. They were laughing with Jonas and Harvey, watching something outside the window. Lizzie decided big boys were all the same — it didn't matter where you went to school. They never behaved very well, because for one thing, they were bored, and for another, they knew they could worry the teacher. It seemed to Lizzie these boys were not too fond of Barbara Renno; but then, the big boys in her old school always made trouble for Teacher Katie, too. Not really serious trouble—just annoying little things that made her correct them in class.

Suddenly, Ray slid out of his seat with his ruler. He leaned over as far as he could and stuck it against the wooden baseboard of the floor. There was a sickening crunch that turned Lizzie's stomach, and she put up both hands to cover her mouth, her eyes wide in alarm.

The boys snickered and whispered, while Ray sat covertly back in his seat. Teacher Barbara turned slowly in their direction, keeping her white face absolutely impassive. She didn't say one word. She just walked slowly over and peered at the baseboard along the floor. She stooped and picked up the decapitated grasshopper, throwing it out the window.

"You could have caught it and took it outside," she said firmly, her mouth in a straight, tight line.

"Sorry, Teacher, but his time was up," answered Ray sorrowfully. Jonas, Ivan, and Harvey hid their wide grins behind their reading books, ducking their heads to keep from looking at one another.

Teacher Barbara resumed her class, turning her back as the boys laughed quietly. Lizzie had to smile in spite of herself, although she decided boys were the same wherever you went to school—they really were.

After they had eaten, they all went outside to play baseball. Their ball diamond was slightly uphill, so that Lizzie worried about making it to first base fast enough when it was her turn to bat. Emma had a good solid hit, but the pitcher caught it and threw it swiftly to first

base. Emma stopped running and turned back toward
home plate, her face flaming.

"That was a good hit," Salina said kindly.

"Yes, it sure was," Sadie chimed in.

"But I still made an out," Emma said shyly.

Lizzie's heart hammered in her chest and she felt
dizzy—she was so nervous. She hoped with all her heart
she would not strike out, because this was a new school,
and it was terribly important to her that everyone could
see she was a good ball player, especially for a girl.

She grasped the bat firmly, leaning forward slightly,
planting her feet solidly on the ground. Ivan was the
pitcher, and he smiled a teasing smile in her direction,
pitching a fast ball over the plate. Lizzie bit down on her
tongue and swung the bat with all her might. She twisted her whole body as the ball went sailing past, unde-
terred. *Oh dear*, Lizzie thought wildly. *I simply CANNOT
strike out.* Another pitch, which she let go to the
backstop, mostly because she was
losing her nerve. She was afraid to
strike at it, fearing she would miss it
like the first one.

After a slower pitch, Lizzie felt
the bat connect solidly with the
ball, which went flying in a high
arc over the pitcher's head. She
threw down the bat, flying
along the dusty grass
to first base. Her
covering lifted

off her head as the pins pulled dreadfully in her hair, but she kept running. Just as she reached the base, there was a solid "whack" as the outfielder threw the ball to first base. He reached over and tagged Lizzie solidly, just as her foot touched down on base.

"Out! Out!" yelled the opposing team.

"I am *not!*" Lizzie shouted, without thinking about being at a new school. She definitely was not out—there was no other way, because her foot was on first base when he tagged her.

"Oh yes, I got you," the first baseman said.

Lizzie did not even know his name, but he was absolutely sure she was out, and Lizzie was absolutely sure she was not.

"You didn't!" she yelled, her face turning a dark shade of red as her temper increased.

The boy looked embarrassed, because, after all, Lizzie was a stranger. He had never seen her before today and this was quite unusual—a girl yelling at him like that. So he just blinked his eyes and turned to look helplessly at the pitcher.

"You're out, Lizzie," Ivan said quietly.

"My foot was on the base when he tagged me," Lizzie informed him firmly.

The ball field became deathly still as everyone waited for Lizzie to give in.

Emma broke the silence, saying, "Lizzie, take your out."

"No!"

"Lizzie!"

"I'm not out."

So Ivan shrugged his shoulders and the first baseman shrugged his. "Okay," he mumbled.

So Lizzie ran back to first base, putting one foot firmly on it, and her other one toward second base. She didn't look at the boy on first base, because she didn't like him very much. He should not have been so insistent, because she wasn't out.

Another pitch, and Harvey hit the ball way up and out to left field. Lizzie raced to second base, relieved to feel the solid mound beneath her feet—and then she heard her team yelling for her to go back.

"Go back, Lizzie—he caught the fly! Go back!" Emma screamed.

But it was too late. The first baseman had already caught the ball, and she was quite fairly and quite thoroughly out.

Lizzie was horribly humiliated. She should have watched to see if anyone caught the ball. But she held her head high as she ran the full length of the ball diamond, back to home plate, and didn't say a word. There was no use.

Ivan's eyes teased her and the first baseman held his baseball glove to his face. Raw fury coursed through Lizzie as the boys looked knowingly at each other.

When the bell rang and Harvey said, "Proves it," quietly to Ivan, and he threw back his head and laughed, Lizzie bit down hard on her lip. She could not stand boys, hardly ever, and today she decided she would show them yet, somehow, someday. But she was also old enough to know sometimes it was best to be quiet when you were wrong.

Salina gave her a wide, kind smile before they were seated, which was a healing balm to her battered ego.

chapter 2

The First Snowfall

The new school was soon the bright spot of Lizzie's life. Every morning she hopped out of bed, anticipating another day of walking to school with her cousins. It was a different world, but a happy one, filled with new friends and places.

The air was turning into a chilly north wind as they all walked home from school on a Friday evening. They pulled their coats tightly around their bodies, as goose bumps chased each other up and down Lizzie's spine. The cold air turned their noses red, and Lizzie sniffed, wishing she would not have forgotten her handkerchief.

The gray clouds looked cold and menacing, almost as if there was an angry man inside churning up the gray and white colors to make them darker. For some reason it made Lizzie think about when Dat disciplined her for disobeying or misbehaving.

Lizzie was always getting in trouble. Emma hardly ever had to receive a punishment because she was not like Lizzie. Emma was just naturally a good girl who loved to wash dishes, clean up the whole living room, and sweep without complaining; she actually loved to go to the pantry, get the broom, and sweep a whole room. That was just how Emma was.

Lizzie sniffed again and looked over at Emma. Her nose was red, but she was smiling and talking to Edna.

"Aren't you cold, Emma?" she asked.

"Mm-hmm. Kind of," Emma replied.

"Let's walk faster. I'm all shivery," Lizzie said, a bit grumpily.

"It's going to snow!" Edna announced happily.

Lizzie spun around, her attention turned to Edna. "You think so? How do you know?" she asked, walking backward so she could see Edna's face better.

"It just feels like snow. Mom says if the cold goes into your bones, it's going to snow."

Lizzie was so excited. She loved snow, so it was almost incomprehensible to her, with the amount of hills that were all around their new basement house.

"Do you . . . I mean, do you . . . where do you go sled riding? There are so many hills!" She spread her arms wide, gesturing to all the slopes and ridges.

"Oh, we go all over the place! But the best place is right down past our house, past the barn. We start up at the sawmill," Edna said.

Emma, always the practical one, asked how they could get across the road safely.

"Can you get your sled stopped before you hit the road?" Lizzie asked, thinking about flying down that hill and the headlights of a car approaching in the dark.

"Oh, we have to take turns standing down by the road to yell back up the hill if it's safe to go across," Edna assured her.

"Wow!" Lizzie breathed, her heart skipping in excitement. "I cannot imagine how fast you must go across that road!"

"We do. And we always have to ask Debbie to go along. She loves to go sled riding, too."

Lizzie became quiet suddenly, because she still didn't know Debbie. They had met her once, on the day they moved, but she felt shy around English girls. She didn't even know if Mam would let her play with Debbie. They never had little English girls to play with before, so she didn't know if Dat and Mam would approve of it or not. It wasn't that she couldn't speak English well enough; she just wasn't sure if she wanted to become friends with Debbie, because she was allowed to dress much nicer and have her hair in bangs. It was something new to worry about, so Lizzie fell silent the rest of the way home.

·   ·   ·   ·   ·

That evening, just as Lizzie started carrying wood to fill the woodbox, she noticed little bits of wetness hitting her face. The air was gray and heavy, the cold hurting Lizzie's fingers as she carried armload after armload of wood. Mandy tailed along with Lizzie, but she only carried a few pieces at a time, because she was so thin and small.

Lizzie enjoyed carrying wood. She wished she'd be allowed to split the big chunks with an axe, like Dat did, but he never allowed her to use it. That irked Lizzie, because she saw no sense in being forbidden to split wood. She told Dat even if she missed the chunk of wood, the axe would only thump into the ground. He informed Lizzie that she could also hurt herself, sinking the axe into her toe. Lizzie thought that was the dumbest thing she had ever heard of—her toe wasn't even close to the axe head.

Dat would not budge about letting Lizzie split wood. She always had to sweep the wood chips away after they were finished, and she was allowed to put wood into the black stove in the living room, but she still wanted to split wood.

She held out her hand, palm up, and—sure enough!—the wet little splotches were real snowflakes. Tiny little ones, but snowflakes nonetheless. Lizzie turned her face to the sky, and suddenly she could see thousands of little whirling snowflakes.

"Mandy, look!"

Mandy turned her face up and gasped in awe. "Wow! Lizzie, look how many snowflakes there are!"

"Millions! Kajillions!" Lizzie shouted.

They leaped and bounced. They ran in circles, shrieking and laughing as the tiny flakes increased. They forgot all about carrying wood to fill the woodbox, and reveled in this wonderful surprise, so early in the season.

Dat came walking in the drive, on his way home from building his pallet shop. He looked tired and a bit preoc-

cupied, but lifted his head when he heard the sound of
the girls' joy. He smiled when he saw their jubilance, remembering the thrill of the season's first snowfall when
he was a boy.

"Dat! Dat!" Mandy shouted. "Did you know it's
snowing?"

"No. Really?" Dat teased her.

Mandy took Dat's hand and skipped beside him till
they reached the porch. Dat stood quietly beside his
boisterous daughters, watching the snow swirling in
from the northeast. He could tell that this snow would
not be just flurries. It might snow a foot or more. He
was glad they had the roof on the pallet shop, even if it
wasn't quite finished yet. He wanted to be making pallets before January, that was for sure.

As they entered the warmth of the kitchen, Mam was
standing by the sink, enveloped in a cloud of steam.
She was mashing potatoes, and the smell of frying meat
made Lizzie weak with hunger.

Emma looked up from putting knives and forks carefully beside their dinner plates.

"Hey! Emma, it's snowing!" Lizzie shouted.

Emma's eyebrows were drawn down in disapproval,
sniffing as she said, "Lizzie, don't be so loud. I know it's
snowing."

"Are you going to go sled riding with us?" Lizzie
yelled.

Mam stopped mashing potatoes, turning to look at
Lizzie. "Lizzie, quiet down. Go take off your coat and
help Emma finish setting the table. Hurry up!"

Lizzie sighed. There was no one like Mam and Emma to bring her down to earth. Her shoulders drooped as she hurried into the laundry room. She hung her coat on a hook, but it slid off, so she just let it lie on a heap below the hook. She threw her scarf across the hook and hurried back into the kitchen. It wasn't her fault she didn't pick up her coat, because she had to help set the table in a hurry.

She yanked open the cupboard door and started thumping the plastic drinking glasses into a tower. *Whack! Whack!* She carried them precariously across the kitchen and thumped them down at each place setting. Dat watched her from his seat at the head of the table, knowing why she was thumping them like that.

"Lizzie," he said quietly.

She stopped. "What?"

"Not so loud."

Lizzie said nothing, but the thumps definitely decreased in volume. Emma brought a steaming dish of macaroni and cheese to the table, which promptly made Lizzie's mouth water. Jason scrambled up on the bench behind the table, his curls bouncing as he scooted himself over to his plate.

Lizzie bent to bury her face in his curls. "Jason, Jason!" she sang to tease him. Jason giggled and reached up to slap her playfully. He was growing into a little boy, no longer a baby, and his talk delighted the whole family. He was smart for his age, speaking as clearly as a six-year-old child. He voiced his little opinions about everything, which often had Emma and Lizzie laughing uncontrollably.

When Jason was born, Lizzie thought he was the ug-liest baby she had ever seen. She used to be embarrassed by his curly hair, but now she thought he was adorable. His hair was curlier than ever, making his head appear much bigger than it actually was.

"Did you see the snow, Jase?" Lizzie asked. "Look out the window!"

Jason clapped his hands and squealed. His hair bounced as he kept clapping and asked, "Are you going to pull me on your sled?"

"Of course. As soon as the snow is thick enough."

After they had silent prayer, Lizzie piled mashed po-tatoes and gravy on her plate, adding a heaping table-spoon of macaroni and cheese. She bit into a crispy piece of fried chicken and passed on the bowl of green beans. Emma watched as Lizzie kept eating her fried chicken.

"Lizzie, you have to eat green beans," she said, always practical.

"I don't have to."

Mam looked at Lizzie and said, "Take some."

"I hate them."

"So?" Emma said.

"You should eat them, Lizzie," Jason said seriously. "They're good for you."

Mandy threw back her head and laughed, her mouth full of potatoes.

"Close your mouth, Mandy," Emma said.

Mandy and Lizzie looked at each other without smil-ing. Mandy closed her mouth and finished chewing, while Lizzie took a spoonful of green beans and plopped them

down hard on her plate. It was just an unspoken feeling
about Emma. She was actually bossier than Mam, and the
older she became, the greater the difference was between
Emma and Lizzie. Mandy was more with Lizzie now, and
they roamed the fields and fencerows, planning all kinds
of projects for spring. They only did the jobs they had
to do, while Emma washed clothes, learned to sew, and
helped Mam with everything she did.

Darkness settled over the supper table, and Mam got
up to light the gas lamp. They all sat in its soft glow,
enjoying their warm cherry cobbler with cold, creamy
milk as the snow swirled outside. Dat said they were as
cozy as hibernating groundhogs in their basement home.
Mandy said they weren't really like groundhogs, because only a part of their house was underground.

After the dishes were finished, Lizzie dashed outside
to see how much it had snowed. The grass was still
showing, so Lizzie knew it hadn't snowed enough to
go sled riding yet. The air had a quiet, solemn tone if
it snowed in the dark, Lizzie thought. You could hear
for miles—everything was so hushed. The snow whispered as it hit the grass—that's how well you could hear.
Lizzie was cold, so she wrapped her arms around herself
and shivered, but it was hard to go inside. She wished
she was an Indian. They lived in teepees with a real fire
in the middle, wrapped in blankets, so they were closer
to the snow in their houses than Lizzie was. It was sad
if you had to go to bed and sleep while the snow swirled
outside and you missed a whole eight hours of watching
the snow being driven in by a north wind.

"It's still snowing!" she announced triumphantly. "It's really coming down thick and fast!"

"And it's barely December," Mam said, glancing up from her hand sewing.

"Looks like we'll have a white Christmas," Dat said, looking up from his paper.

Lizzie threw herself on the sofa, grabbing her book that lay on the stand beside it. She tucked her feet beneath her skirt, settled herself comfortably, opened her book, and started to read. She had started to read a book called *Little House in the Big Woods* and it was such a cozy book. It made little warm circles around Lizzie's heart, to think how Laura and Mary Ingalls would have felt, playing under the eaves of their little attic of the log cabin they lived in. It wasn't really as exciting as some books she had read, but it was so intriguing, the emotions it stirred in her. She loved Pa and Ma and Baby Carrie, the house they lived in, what they ate, how they did their work, and everything.

She was reading about the dance at Grandpa Ingalls, when there was a hurried knock and the kitchen door burst open.

"Hello, Melvin Annie!" shouted Danny.

Edna, followed by Debbie, piled in the door, their hair covered with snow, scarves tied around their mouths.

"Hey, we can go sled riding," Edna said excitedly.

"May they go along, Annie?"

"It's bedtime," Mam said anxiously.

"Not yet," Edna burst out.

Dat looked up over his paper and Mam's eyes met his.

They both looked as they always did when they meant "No."

Lizzie threw down her book, scrambling to her feet. Mandy stuck her head out of the laundry room door, already getting her coat and scarf.

"Ivan and Ray made a track!" Danny said loudly.

Dat looked at Mam, as doubtful as ever.

"Can we go?" Lizzie asked.

"It's dark and cold out there," Mam said. "Don't your Mom and Dad mind if you're traipsing around in the snow?"

"Who? Mom and Daddy? Naw!" Danny said.

Dat burst out laughing. Mam shook her head in disbelief, as Dat grudgingly allowed them to go. Emma decided it was too late and too cold for her to go, so Lizzie and Mandy scrambled into their coats, boots, mittens, and scarves.

"One hour—that's it," Dat said sternly.

"Alright! We'll be home!" Lizzie called back.

She shivered with excitement as she fell into step with Edna and Debbie. Mandy squealed when her feet slid unexpectedly and she waved her arms to keep her balance. Debbie's feet slid out from under her and she sat down hard on her backside. The girls giggled and laughed as Debbie rolled around on her stomach. She was so small and round, she could not sit up, so she rolled over and pushed herself up. Her pants were completely covered with snow, but she briskly brushed it off, saying, "You guys!" and Edna burst out laughing.

"Come on!" Danny shouted, because he was way ahead of them.

"We're coming!" Lizzie yelled, as they all hurried along on the slippery macadam.

A soft, mittened hand crept under Lizzie's arm, and Debbie panted, "Let me hold onto you, please."

Lizzie swelled with pride, because Debbie trusted her to keep from falling. Debbie slipped and slid, giggled and sputtered as she struggled to keep going. She told Lizzie the reason she kept falling was because she had to wear last year's snowboots and the soles were much too smooth. Lizzie told her that you couldn't wear snowboots too long, because they got wet inside and then you always had cold feet, no matter if you started out warm or not.

When they reached Uncle Elis, there was a dark blur of movement and a sled shot across the road. Ivan and Ray were both on one sled, as they sped through the dark, cold night.

For the next hour, the night was filled with cries and shrieks of fear and excitement as the sleds silently sped down the hill. Danny stood sentinel at the bottom, making sure there were no cars approaching. After a while, he stopped watching because he was cold, so they all quit sledding. Debbie said her feet were cold, and Mandy looked quite pale, becoming more and more quiet as the hour went by.

The door of the stone house opened and Aunt Mary told them their hour was up. Lizzie wasn't cold, but she was so tired she could hardly put one foot in front of the other.

"Can you walk home with Lizzie?" Edna asked Debbie.

"Why?" Debbie wanted to know.

"Because I'm too cold and wet to walk home with you. And your house is close to Lizzie's," Edna answered.

"I guess I can. Lizzie, will you go home with me? I mean walk clear over to my house till I'm inside the door, 'cause my mom locks her door and when I ring the doorbell she might not hear me, and then what?" Debbie said, peering anxiously into Lizzie's face.

"Sure. We'll go along over. Come on, Debbie, we'll walk home with you," Lizzie said, feeling all kind and softhearted. She loved Debbie, she decided, and would gladly do anything she could to help her.

So they walked together through the soft, dark night, the snow falling around them in jeweled whispers. Snow was so magical, and Lizzie told Debbie so. Debbie lifted her head and stuck out her tongue, letting the soft flakes melt on it.

"Yeah, Lizzie, I love snow, too. But you know what is just as good as snow? Hot chocolate after you're done playing in it. I wish my mom would make hot chocolate, but she never does, because I make a mess. Does your mom?"

"We make our own," Lizzie said.

"Really?"

"Mm-hmm. Hot chocolate is just milk, sugar, and Nestlé Quik, or syrup."

"Pancake syrup?"

"No! Chocolate syrup!"

They both kept slipping and sliding, talking about snow and hot chocolate, until Mandy said she was so cold there were icicles on her nose. Then they had a serious conversation about icicles, because Debbie said an icicle fell on a man's head once and he died. Lizzie gasped in amazement, which started Debbie on the subject of skull fractures and concussions.

Before they knew it, they were at Debbie's door, and she was ringing the doorbell. It rang and rang. Debbie looked worriedly at Lizzie, saying, "See?"

The door was soon opened and Debbie's mother stuck her tousled head out the door. "You home? Come on in—take your boots off first," she said. So Debbie sat on the porch and pulled on her boots, as Lizzie said good-bye, dashing home as fast as she could through the slippery snow. She did not feel comfortable around Marlene, because she was so particular and big and black-haired. English people made Lizzie feel shy, so she was glad to be running through the slippery snow with Mandy, home to Mam and Dat and the cozy gas lamp in their basement home.

c h a p t e r   3

Christmas

The snow lay thick and deep, like a wondrous sparkling blanket over the cold landscape. The ridge on one side of the basement house looked like a picture book, because the whole side of it was covered with pine trees. The huge mountain about a mile away was covered with dark trees etched against white snow, which made an interesting pattern.

It was all so beautiful that Lizzie would often stand and stare, awed by the hills and trees.

Christmas was in the air. The neighbors were stringing lights around their bushes and shrubs. Lizzie had a poem to learn for the Christmas program at school, and Mam had gone to Marion, their new town, to buy gifts for the family. Actually, she had gone more than once, because they had some money left over from the sale of the harness shop. Mam was so eager about Christmas this year because she had more money to spend.

Lizzie desperately wanted ice skates. Her cousins all went skating, they told her, as soon as the ponds were frozen. Her uncles and aunts at Grandpa Glicks had all gone ice skating in the wintertime, so Lizzie was used to watching. Her one aunt, Miriam, could jump over barrels or sleds. She would skate as fast as she could, with long, low strides, until she hurled herself over the sleds. Uncle Samuel could do it even better and it thrilled Lizzie to watch them. Someday, she vowed, she would do everything they did, including skating backward.

She didn't know how much ice skates cost, but Mam said the good leather ones were very expensive. Lizzie told her she didn't want one other thing—not even a candy cane or Hershey's Kisses, if she could only have a pair of white figure skates.

Oh, how her heart thrilled to think of wearing white knee socks with white skates. Amish girls always wore black shoes and socks, which she never thought about very much. That's just how things were. But for some reason, girls were allowed to wear white knee socks to skate, and it was Lizzie's dream to glide across a pond as gracefully as Miriam did.

Mam was wrapping gifts in the bedroom when the girls came home from school. The door was tightly closed, but Mam stuck her head out to tell them where she was. Her cheeks were flushed and her eyes sparkled as she told them to stay out, trying to be stern.

"Am I getting ice skates, Mam?" Lizzie pleaded,

knowing full well Mam would never tell her.

"Now hush, Lizzie. I can't tell you. Now you girls get the house cleaned up and unpack your lunches, then Emma, you may peel potatoes while Lizzie and Mandy fill the woodbox."

She closed the bedroom door firmly, while Lizzie and Mandy hopped up and down in excitement. Lizzie took off her bonnet and twirled it across the living room, followed by her gloves and scarf. Mandy hopped on one foot and banged her lunch on the countertop. Emma frowned as she hung up her clothes in the laundry room.

"Pick them up, Lizzie!" she said scowling.

"It's Christmas, Emma! Wheee!" and Lizzie spun herself around the living room.

Emma smiled. Lizzie's joy was infectious, and she started singing, "We three kings of Orient are," and Mandy promptly joined in. "Oh, star of wonder, star of light," they all belted out, until Mam opened the bedroom door, shooing Jason out to the singing girls. He held his head sideways as if to inspect them more closely, then burst into song, way off key and without the proper words.

This was a happy season for the Glick family. The basement house was much warmer than their previous, rattly old house, and Dat and Mam were more relaxed. Mam was happy every day, because she loved living here in Jefferson County. Dat was so busy getting his pallet shop built, so he was almost never at home. When he was, he seemed a bit preoccupied, thinking and planning ahead about the machinery and the huge diesel engines it would take to run the equipment to cut boards and nail them into pallets.

The girls finished their song in a fit of giggles, because Jason did not know the words. He just stood in the middle of the living room floor and pushed out his stomach, lifted his head, and with his mouth wide open and his head of curls bouncing in rhythm, sang as loud as he possibly could.

Mandy wiped her eyes, while Emma and Lizzie sat on the sofa, weak from laughing. He looked like a little bandleader, putting his heart into every note, quite unaware of the girls' laughter.

"Oh, Jase," Lizzie gasped.

"I can sing," he announced proudly.

"You sure can," Emma agreed, which started them laughing again. Then Emma got up briskly and told Lizzie to get started carrying wood.

"I'm hungry. I'm going to eat something first," Lizzie told Emma.

"Supper will soon be ready. You can wait."

So because it was Christmas, and because Lizzie knew she should not eat Ritz crackers and cheese before supper, she didn't say anything, even if she would have loved to put two pieces of cheese between Ritz crackers. That was the trouble with white American cheese. It was sliced too thin; that was why you had to put on a half piece, broke in half again. Lizzie always wanted to put a whole slice on, which would actually be four slices on a cracker, but Mam didn't let her—it was too expensive and too fattening.

So she thought about crackers and cheese as she and
Mandy filled the woodbox. She wished they had so
much money that Mam would buy Pepsi, like Debbie's
mom. But she never did, because it was too expensive.
Besides, they didn't have ice cubes here, so what was
the use buying Pepsi? Lizzie always thought it was so
English to drink soda out of a fancy glass with ice clink-
ing around in it. If she ever got married, she would buy
pretty glasses and Pepsi.

After the woodbox was filled, Dat came home for supper. Mam was finished wrapping gifts for the evening, so
they all sat around the kitchen table and talked. Lizzie
told Dat he had better come to the Christmas program
at school, even if he was so busy, because he should hear
their poems.

Dat smiled tiredly, running his hands through his
beard. "When is it, Lizzie?"

"The day before Christmas."

"Which is?"

"Tomorrow!" Mandy squealed. Mam smiled knowingly at Mandy.

After supper, the girls all helped do dishes, because
Mam was going to make cookies that were put through
a press. She had mixed the dough earlier in the day, and
put it in a tight container. She set the container of cookie
dough on a bench on the front porch to chill it, which
made it easier to handle. Not everyone's Mam could
make cookies that were put through a cookie press.
Mam had a special talent to cook and bake, so everything she made tasted wonderful to Lizzie.

When Mam brought in the dough and lit the wick under the oven of the kerosene stove, the girls all scrambled around the kitchen table to watch. First, she spooned in some of the firm golden cookie dough into a shiny oblong tube. She screwed on the top, which had a round plunger-type handle that pushed down on the dough. The most wonderful part of all were the little plates Mam screwed on the bottom of the tube. There were stars, moons, crescents, or holly leaves. There were flowers or little bursts that looked like a pineapple.

They all took turns picking a design, and Mam used an entire tube of cookie dough for one pattern. Then Emma painted the top of the dough with beaten egg, using a small pastry brush. Only Emma was allowed to do that because she was the oldest, which actually irked Lizzie quite a bit. But because it was Christmas, she bit her tongue and didn't say a word. She knew she could paint the cookies as well as Emma. After all, she was only one year and a month younger. Mam had told her last year she was too "shooslich," meaning she went too fast, dribbling the egg beside the cookie. That made Lizzie feel bad, but she didn't know what to say, so she didn't say anything for a long time. This year she just didn't mention anything about wanting to paint beaten egg on the cookies.

They put red and green sprinkles on top of one cookie sheet, and tiny silver balls on another. Sometimes they put brown sugar and ground walnuts on top, or just sugar and cinnamon.

Mam's cheeks were flushed and her stomach was covered with flour. She always wore her "bake" apron, which was actually a tea towel with a band sewed along one side, which Mam tied in the back. Her sleeves were rolled up and her plump arms worked the cookie press, producing one perfect cookie after another. She pressed down on the press with the palm of one hand, holding the tube with the other, moving quite rapidly along the cookie sheet.

The kitchen was warm and cozy, with lamplight reflecting in the glossy varnish of the kitchen cabinets. The floor had little dots on the linoleum pattern, green and light brown mixed together, which matched the window curtains. There was a long braided rug on the floor in front of the sink, and one just inside the door. Lizzie loved their basement home, especially the kitchen, because it was so warm in cold weather.

·　　·　　·　　·　　·

After their Christmas program at school the following day, Dat and Mam talked quietly in the living room. Mam kept glancing to the kitchen table, where Lizzie and Mandy were using their new box of crayons their teacher had given them for Christmas. Emma was sweeping the wood chips away from the stove in the laundry room, getting the house all cleaned up for Christmas.

When Emma was finished, Dat said if they all came into the living room, he would read the Bible story about Baby Jesus.

Lizzie looked up, bewildered. "Why now?" she asked. He always read the Christmas story on Christmas morning, after breakfast, and then they were allowed to have their presents.

"Oh, just because; Mam thinks we should have the Christmas this evening," he said seriously, but Lizzie could tell his eyes weren't very serious.

"You mean, then we may have our presents tomorrow morning as soon as we get up? Before breakfast?" Mandy asked.

"Or tonight? Tonight! Right now!" Lizzie said, because she was catching on to Mam's surprise.

"Okay. Everyone quiet now," Dat said, as he cleared his throat and began to read. He read about Mary and Joseph, the trip to Bethlehem, and the tiny Baby Jesus being born in a stable. Lizzie loved this story. There was nothing to be afraid of and nothing in the story that gave her the blues. Lizzie was often afraid of God and fierce Bible characters, so she never enjoyed certain stories very much. But the Christmas story was different. Everyone was so glad that Baby Jesus was born; even the angels were so full of joy that they came down to the shepherds and sang to them. Lizzie thought it was no wonder these shepherds were scared, if the sky turned all bright like that and it was dark, during the night. They probably thought the end of the world was coming; but then, maybe the shepherds so long ago didn't know anything about the world coming to an end someday.

Lizzie hoped God would wait for a long time yet. She loved her life here in Jefferson County, because there were so many things to do. She was growing up now, and she wasn't quite as worried about things that could happen anymore. She and Emma hardly ever quarreled, since Emma helped Mam do her work, because that is what she enjoyed. So Mandy and Lizzie became best of companions, being close in age and so much alike.

Dat read about the three wise men coming to see Baby Jesus, with their strange gifts of perfumes and spices. Lizzie always thought they actually should have given Him diapers and baby clothes, because He didn't have any. She hoped Mary and Joseph could sell those expensive perfumes to buy baby things for Jesus.

Dat closed the Bible story, and Mam's eyes twinkled as she got up and hurried into the bedroom. She returned, carrying a brightly wrapped package and set it on Jason's lap. Jason looked surprised, looking first at the package, then at Mam, before he squealed excitedly.

Lizzie was so surprised. She thought this was one of the nicest gifts she had ever received. They were allowed to have their gifts on Christmas Eve, and did not have to wait till the next morning! It was unbelievable.

When Mam set a big square package on Lizzie's lap,
she whispered, "Thank you!" She was much too nervous
to say anything else, because she was so terribly afraid
it was not a pair of ice skates. She ripped the paper
greedily and in one second she saw the words "Canadian
Flyer." She jumped up, scattering paper, and held the
box of skates to her chest. She had really, truly, received
her very own pair of figure skates! Quickly, she sat
down again, struggling to open the heavy cardboard
box. After she had the lid open, she didn't know if she
would laugh or cry. Inside the box was a brand new pair
of woolly knee socks! They were white! She stroked
them lovingly, speechless with surprise. Surely this was
the best gift she had ever received.

There was a squeal of delight from Mandy, who had
received the very same Christmas gift. There was also
a pair for Emma, but she had a smaller package besides
her ice skates. It was a diary, to write in before she went
to bed. Emma was twelve years old now, so she was actually becoming a young girl; she was no longer a child.

Jason ran in circles, yelling hoarsely, holding a box
filled with plastic horses. He had a barn, so for his gift
Mam had bought lots of horses and their babies. He also
had a package containing a trailer to put his horses in,
which he promptly hitched to his old pickup truck.

Dat beamed, smiling at the children's joy. Mam sat
beside him on the couch, laughing at Jason's excitement.
Then she gave a package to Dat, which contained a soft
corduroy vest, lined with sheepskin. Dat said it was the
perfect garment to wear in the pallet shop, because that

way his arms were free to run the nailer. He tried it on, and Mam patted his stomach when she saw the vest was snug around it. He pulled in his stomach, standing as tall as he could, to show Mam he was not putting on weight. But he really was, Lizzie thought, laughing happily with everyone else.

Then Mam gave Dat a large glass jar filled with hot sausages. He just loved them, and he always bought one when he went away with a driver. She told him he was only allowed one or two every day, until they were all gone, but he was already on his way to the kitchen to open his jar of sausages. Mam shook her head, but she was smiling because it was Christmas.

Lizzie was putting the long, wide strings in her skates. She didn't understand why there were only hooks and no holes to put the strings through along the top of the skates, until Dat showed her how to do it.

"Here, put your foot out," he said. So Lizzie stuck out one foot, and Dat helped her put on her skates. They pinched horribly, because they were so narrow.

"Ow! Ouch!" she winced. "They're too tight."

"I doubt it, Lizzie. Stand up on them."

So Lizzie stood up and, much to her delight, they weren't tight on her foot, just hard and firm around her heel and ankle.

"Now, when you lace them, this is what these hooks are for," Dat said, as he firmly laced her skates around her leg, criss-crossing the strings around the hooks.

"O-hh," said Lizzie. "Now I understand."

"Now put on your other one."

So Lizzie put on her other skate, as Dat helped Emma. Mandy watched carefully, then sat on the sofa and did her own.

Lizzie stood up, and her ankles wobbled, because she was standing on one thin silver blade. For a moment, despair coursed through her. How in the world would she ever learn to glide across a frozen pond? It was hard just standing on the wooden floor with the back of her knees propped against the sofa.

"This is going to be impossible," she groaned.

"Oh, no," Dat said. "Skating isn't hard at all. You'll take a few tumbles, don't you worry, but you'll be fine. All you do is put on your skates and put one foot in front of the other, and you'll learn."

"Are you going to teach us?" Emma asked.

"Maybe. If I have time."

Then they all went out to the kitchen and Mam made hot cocoa. They ate all the Christmas cookies they could hold, and salted peanuts and Hershey's Kisses wrapped in red and green foil. They even had a large cut-glass bowl filled with sweet, cold grapes, purple and green. There was another pretty bowl with tangerines and bananas, and they were allowed to eat anything they wanted.

Lizzie unwrapped her chocolate candy and popped it into her mouth. The sweetness melted on her tongue, and she washed it down with a sip of hot chocolate. Then she tasted a green grape, which puckered her mouth because it was so sour.

Emma said you should eat fruit with crackers or

peanuts, not chocolate candy. So Lizzie ate a handful of salted peanuts and tried a purple grape, which was absolutely delicious.

"You're right, Emma," she said smiling.

Emma smiled back, and Lizzie's heart was filled with warmth. Everybody had such a happy, Christmasy glow, that even the gas lamp seemed to have little twinkles of happiness around it. Lizzie didn't say anything, but she figured they were rich now, because they had tangerines and grapes and Hershey's Kisses. She wished she could give some to Baby Jesus. He would like that—she just knew He would.

chapter 4

Learning to Skate

The temperature dropped steadily for a week after Christmas. Every morning Lizzie checked the thermometer on the porch post, shrieking with excitement when the red line of mercury was down almost to the 0° mark. Dat had told her if the temperature hovered around 0° for a week or so, the ice would probably be thick enough on Hetrick's pond.

Edna had told her that after the ice was five inches thick, there were people skating on that pond almost every evening. They built a huge bonfire, roasted hot dogs and marshmallows, and took Thermoses of hot chocolate and straw bales to sit on. Lizzie's eyes shone with anticipation. She could not imagine how terribly thrilling that would be, because she had never skated before. It was partly fear, because she imagined the ice being extremely smooth. How she would ever stand upright on those narrow silver blades and actually go on that slippery surface was beyond her.

She pondered over this while washing dishes in the morning, while doing her arithmetic in school, and even on their walks home. She started chewing her finger-nails again, and biting her lower lip until it became sore and irritated. She so desperately wanted to be a good skater someday, because she had read a book about skaters in Holland who skated for miles on canals. In the book, the girls' skirts flowed out in a graceful billow of light-colored fabric and their hands were daintily cov-ered with a fur muff. The boys wore tall black hats and sometimes they held hands with the girls, so Lizzie knew there was nothing more thrilling in her entire existence than ice skating with a whole group of people.

Then one evening when they came home from school, Lizzie had just started carrying wood to fill the wood-box, when she caught sight of Edna and Danny racing up the road. Lizzie quickly finished carrying her wood and met them in the drive. Edna's face was flushed, and she was breathless, laughing and gasping as she told Lizzie there was a skating party that evening at Het-rick's pond.

"We have to go tell Debbie yet. Be ready when she comes to your house at six o'clock," she panted.

"Oo-oh!" was all Lizzie could say, because she was too excited. She dashed into the house, calling for Mandy at the top of her voice.

"What?" Mandy looked up, her big green eyes open-ing wide.

"Hey! Hey, there's a skating party. We're allowed to skate now, because the ice is thick enough," she said.

Mam looked a bit doubtful. She said Dat should go along with them to check and make sure. Lizzie told Mam that Edna said Mr. Hetrick wouldn't let children skate on his pond unless he checked the ice himself, and, besides, he should know because he was as old as the hills and had lived there his whole life, right beside his pond.

So when Dat came home for supper, Mam didn't say much about letting the girls go skating. Dat just smiled, asking if the big boys were going, and told them to be very careful with the lantern.

Lizzie could not eat one bite of supper. Mam had made Creole beef, which was elbow macaroni cooked with spaghetti sauce and lots of ground beef and cheese. Normally, Lizzie just loved it. But her mouth was so dry and her heart beat so fast, she simply could not eat, so she didn't.

Promptly at six o'clock, there was a loud knock on the kitchen door. It was Debbie, dressed in layer after layer of warm clothing, but her head was bare, her black curls bouncing around the plaid scarf around her neck. She was carrying a huge metal Thermos and her skate strings were tied together, so one skate hung down her back and one down the front.

"Hello, Mrs. Glick," she said politely.

"Why, hello, Debbie! How are you this evening?" Mam asked with a smile.

"I'm well—thanks!" she said.

"You have a big Thermos there," Mam said, nodding at the Thermos in her hand.

Debbie giggled, a soft little sound. "Yeah, Mom put hot chocolate in there for everyone. Well, at least for me and Emma, Edna, Lizzie, and Mandy." She giggled again.

Mam laughed with Debbie, because Lizzie knew she couldn't help it. Debbie just was like that; she made you feel like laughing with her short, round, brown little form topped with that curly black hair.

Mam handed the girls a paper bag containing chocolate chip cookies and cheese curls. Lizzie was pulling on her red yarn mittens, when she saw Mam give Debbie a cookie.

"Mm-mm, Mrs. Glick. These are so good," she said warmly.

"Thank you, Debbie," Mam beamed down at her. "The girls have a bunch more in the bag."

After they had tied their skate strings and slung them over their shoulders, they headed out the door, shivering in the frigid night air. The stars were brilliant in the night sky, the snow sparkling, catching the starlight it seemed. Dogs barked in the distance and traffic hummed steadily on the highway. But they were not crossing the highway today; they were turning toward Uncle Elis, who lived at the foot of the ridge. The road past their house twisted and turned along little pinecovered hills called ridges, winding its way through a little group of houses that could not have been called a town at all, mostly because there weren't enough houses to

make one. But when they walked through, it seemed as
if it was a town, because the porch lights were on and
they were so close to the road.

After they passed through the group of houses, there
was a flat stretch of road, but to the left a road turned
off and went straight up over a huge hill.

Lizzie told Edna that a horse could never pull a buggy
up that hill. Edna said of course they could—they did all
the time, because someone Amish lived up there. Lizzie
said she was glad she didn't live up there. Then Debbie
said her Thermos was getting heavy; she didn't know
why someone else couldn't carry it for a while.

"Here," Emma offered. She took the Thermos, but
they all had to stop walking while Debbie stood in the
middle of the road and shook her hands to warm them.
After that she had to carefully retie her scarf before she
was ready to move on.

"Debbie! *Come on!*" Danny yelled, quite impatiently,
because they were almost at the pond.

Lizzie thought that was rude of him, and pitied Debbie.

"Go on awhile!" Debbie yelled crossly. So Lizzie
guessed they must have known each other for a very
long time, acting the way they did—almost like she and
Emma.

They rounded a bend in the road, turned downhill,
and suddenly there was the pond. It glistened in the
starlight, with skaters dashing across the smooth surface
like dark birds dipping in the wind. A fire crackled on
the bank close to the gate in the fence, which was close

to the road. There were straw bales to sit on, and blankets for whoever became too chilly.

Lizzie was breathless now. Her nose tingled from the cold, and her cheeks actually hurt, but it was a good hurt. It meant she could actually go out into a very cold night with only her cousins and friends, so she must be growing up.

They all sat on the straw bales, chattering and laughing as they strained and groaned to take off their boots. Debbie informed them that she was wearing five pairs of socks. Edna put her hand over her mouth to hide her smile, because Debbie was being very serious.

"I don't believe it, Debbie," Danny said.

So she started pushing away layers of socks. Red socks, green ones, striped ones, and blue ones, until her bare brown feet shone in the firelight.

"There," Debbie said firmly.

Danny just shook his head like a wise little owl, and didn't say anything as Debbie put all those socks back on her feet. Lizzie and Emma looked at each other and burst out laughing.

"What's so funny?" Debbie asked.

"Oh, nothing. Well, you!" Lizzie laughed.

"Well, I showed Danny how many pairs of socks I was wearing, didn't I?" she said with a smile.

"You know what, Debbie? Your feet are going to sweat because you have way too many pairs of socks on. Then your feet will get cold," Dannie said loudly.

Ivan and Ray swooped in on the bank and walked through the snow with their skates on, plopping down

on the straw bales, panting for breath. They barely
noticed the rest of the group, because they were playing
games on the ice, which meant they had to be careful.

Edna stood up first, making her way carefully down
the snowy embankment to the ice. Debbie and Mandy
clung to each other for support, as did Lizzie and Emma.

When they reached the pond, Edna stepped out
gingerly. Lizzie watched as she stood up straight for a
second, before putting one foot forward, then the other,
moving slowly away from them, staying close to the
bank. Lizzie shivered. She knew she must step out on
that ice sometime, so it may as well be now. For one
wild moment, she looked back at the straw bales, wishing with all her heart she could just go back there and sit

down, never even attempting to try skating. She knew she couldn't do that, either, so she put one foot on the ice. Immediately, that one foot went straight ahead, as if it had a will of its own, causing Lizzie to sit down hard, because her other foot was still in the snow. Half of her was on the ice and the other half was in the snow, so she rolled out of the snow and sat down on the ice. She wasn't hurt one tiny bit, so she laughed with everyone else.

Now she was determined to get up. She got on her knees, then put one foot down on the ice. Debbie came over to lend a hand, so Lizzie put one mittened hand in hers and pulled herself up. She leaned forward too far, and her feet slid backward, causing her to fall flat on her stomach.

"Ooof!"

"Whoa!" Debbie's arms waved as she tried to keep her balance, but Lizzie had thrown her completely off, and she sat down hard on her backside. Lizzie looked back at her, and they both burst out laughing uncontrollably. Lizzie lay on her stomach, shaking all over, helplessly caught up in her amusement, while Debbie propped herself up with both hands, her head thrown back, her legs stuck out in front of her, whooping with merriment.

This was so much fun. Lizzie decided then and there she was no longer afraid of the ice. If it didn't hurt any worse than this, there was really nothing to be afraid of. So she rolled over, sat up, and tried to get back up by herself again. To her surprise, it really was possible.

This time she did it much slower, straightening herself by
degrees, making sure her skates didn't slide one way or
another, which was not really too difficult. She learned to
turn the blades in very slightly to control their movement.

Now she was standing straight, and her feet stayed
right where she wanted them to stay.

"Can you stand up okay?" Edna asked, skating over.

"Looks like it," Lizzie said with a grin.

"Now, just move one foot and then the other, kind of
like walking, but more like sliding," Edna informed her.

So, tentatively, Lizzie put one foot forward. It took
all the effort she could manage, because her other foot
wanted to go in another direction. She managed to pull
it along, but the foot she had put forward first just kept
going, and the other one lurched along behind it, which
made Lizzie's head bob in little jerks.

She moved her arms, trying to get her feet to work
together, which helped immensely. She could move both
feet in unison now, if she used her arms to propel herself
forward a bit.

"Great! Great!" Debbie shouted.

"Keep going!" Edna yelled.

Lizzie was so excited, she forgot all about the big
boys' game, lurching out toward the middle of the pond.
She was learning to control her feet by working with the
movement of her arms, when—SLAM!—she was hit
from the front by a very large, dark figure that was going at an alarming rate.

Lizzie had a distinct feeling of flying through the air
before she landed hard on her hip, her head hitting the

ice with a sickening thud. She clenched her teeth in a grimace as pain exploded through her head. She literally saw stars, or at least little jaggers of white light danced in front of her eyes.

She heard everyone shouting, Danny the loudest of all. The dark figure crept over, saying, "Are you alright, Lizzie?"

Lizzie lay on her back, the unrelenting cold of the ice hurting the back of her head. She blinked her eyes a few times before saying hoarsely, "I . . . I think so."

"I'm really sorry. I was looking over my shoulder."

Lavina and Esther skated over, fussing over her, helping her sit up. She felt dizzy and a bit confused, but she wasn't hurt seriously. She reached up and smoothed back her hair, straightening her scarf, shaking her head to clear it.

"I . . . I guess I could have watched where I was going," she said, feeling very ashamed of herself.

"I guess I could have, too," Ivan smiled wryly.

"Okay," Lavina said in her matter-of-fact way. "We're going to put a line on part of the pond and you kids have to stay in that line. Otherwise, we're going to have wrecks like this all the time."

For some reason, Lizzie felt like crying now. For one thing, she was only a small "kid" to Lavina and Esther, and she admired them. She wasn't so much younger, only five or six years. So she sat on the ice, her head bowed, her hip hurting painfully, and wished she was five years older and could skate well. They would all sit on the bank and watch her cut a graceful figure eight or, even better, skating backward and bowing and dipping, her skirts floating around her.

She gritted her teeth and thought, *Just wait—I will skate well someday. I won't be just a bother on the pond and only be allowed to skate in a roped-off area.* She thought of her aunt sailing across five sleds, and resolved to learn to skate, and learn to skate well.

She watched as Emma and Mandy struggled to stay on their feet. Mandy was doing quite well, but Emma soon got tired of it, saying her feet were cold.

"Let's all go sit on the straw bales a while," Edna suggested, so they all trooped up the snowy incline and plopped on the bales. Lizzie was able to pull herself up much better the third time, making her way safely to the bank. She smiled ruefully as everyone talked about how Ivan should have watched where he was going.

Debbie poured steaming cups of creamy hot chocolate, while Emma opened the bag containing cookies and cheese curls. Shivers of cold chased each other up and down Lizzie's spine, but the blazing fire made her face feel hot. The cocoa burned her tongue, but the chocolate chip cookie was so cold her tongue cooled as soon as she took a bite. They laughed and talked, warming themselves by the fire, then Lizzie said she was going skating again.

Mandy followed, so together they made their way down the snowy bank.

"Lizzie, I can skate!" Mandy said.

"Can you? I didn't even see you. I guess I was too busy with falling," Lizzie said wryly.

"That wasn't your fault."

"I meant the first two times I fell."

"Give me your hand," Mandy said.

So they stepped out on the ice together. It was much easier if they hung on to each other's hand. Together they stepped out, slowly measuring the length of each glide, as they learned how to control their movements.

"This is so fun," Mandy said, smiling widely.

"Oh, Mandy, we have to come here every night, if Mam and Dat let us. I want to learn to skate really, really well."

"Me, too!"

"Hey, we're skating and talking at the same time!" Lizzie yelled.

"We can definitely skate!" Mandy responded.

Around and around they went, their confidence increasing as they became accustomed to the feel of the ice and the small blades beneath their feet. They talked about Ivan bumping into Lizzie and whose fault it was.

Mandy was staunchly loyal to Lizzie. Whatever she did, Mandy thought she could do, too. That was why Mandy thought it was all Ivan's fault, because she would never have blamed Lizzie for being somewhere she wasn't supposed to be. Lizzie knew it was partly her fault, but she didn't say that to Mandy.

"You know what hurt me more than falling, though?" she asked.

"What?"

"That Lavina said we're kids!'"

"We didn't used to be allowed to say that, remember?"

"I know."

"Oh, well. I guess we are little kids."

"I guess."

Solemnly they skated around their allotted circle until Danny told them it was time to go home; everybody was getting tired. Lizzie was disappointed, but she knew it was getting late. She sat on a straw bale, yanking her skates off, her mouth pinched in a straight line. She did not want to go home at all.

"Where are my snowboots?" she yelled grumpily.

"Boy!" Edna said. "I don't know."

"Where are they?" she asked again.

"Here." Emma threw them toward her. They were ice cold and lots of snow was clinging to the sheepskin on the inside.

"Who put my boots away from the fire?" she asked, shaking her boot up and down vigorously.

"Nobody had your boots, Lizzie. That's where you put them in the first place," Emma said.

"Hurry up! I'm cold," Debbie said.

So because it was Debbie, and because Lizzie knew Emma was right, she smashed her cold feet into her frozen boots, yanking on the zipper as hard as she could. She sniffed, because she desperately needed a handkerchief. Her whole body ached from her fall on the ice, and the fire was turning into blackened ashes, so, quite suddenly, the magic was gone.

Her toes felt as if they were frozen into blocks of ice. Her zipper remained only halfway up on her boot, and pinched her leg horribly. She stopped to swipe at the troublesome thing, catching her thumbnail on the jagged edge. She fell behind the others, sniffing and being miserable.

The cold penetrated the insulation of her coat and goose bumps broke out on her back. Lizzie trudged along, head bent wearily, wishing she could be home in her bed instead of trudging along this winding, snowy road.

"Hurry up, Lizzie!" Emma called back.

"My feet are cold!" Lizzie yelled.

"We'll wait up," Debbie said, stopping to let Lizzie catch up. So they all trooped home together. Somehow, it wasn't quite as cold if she walked with the whole group. She couldn't help being cheered immensely when Danny asked Debbie if her feet were cold. He was sure she would say yes, Lizzie thought to herself.

"No, Danny. My feet are warm," Debbie answered.

"You think I should wear five pairs, too?" he asked doubtfully.

"Not if your feet sweat!" Debbie answered.

When Danny swung his mitten across Debbie's sleeve and Edna laughed her hearty laugh, Lizzie's heart was warmed again. She would tuck this wonderful evening away, hoping to remember it as long as she lived — cold, frozen snowboots and all.

chapter 5

Growing Up

Many magical evenings
followed in quick succession,
while the cold snap held through the month
of January. There was always starlight, cold frosty
air, a crackling log fire by the frozen pond, straw bales,
and hot chocolate. Lizzie learned to roast a hot dog to
perfection, crispy and blackened on the outside and
scalding hot on the inside. When she put the sizzling hot
dog on a roll and slathered ice-cold ketchup on the top,
it was one of the best foods she had ever tasted.

The only problem with the frozen pond was too many
skaters digging their blades into the smooth surface.
It became scarred, with deep ruts where the big boys
played hockey. Sometimes it snowed, too, causing the
ice to become soft on the surface.

Lizzie always loved snowstorms, but since she had
learned to skate, snow worried her, because it ruined

their skating. She would sit in her desk at school, watching out the window in despair as the snow was driven in from the northeast.

Skating was so much more fun than sledding, because Lizzie and Mandy had learned to skate fairly well. Emma could skate, too, but she didn't enjoy it as much. Some evenings she stayed home, helping Mam finish the dishes, sweeping the kitchen, and picking up toys that Jason had strewn across the living room floor.

Lizzie was glad that Emma liked to do housework, because then she and Mandy could leave without helping with the dishes. Sometimes Mam made them do dishes anyway, saying it wasn't fair to Emma if they never helped. Emma would agree with Mam, but Lizzie could tell that Emma truly did not mind doing dishes.

Lizzie and Mandy could both skate well enough to help play Freeze Tag. That was a game they never tired of. Two people were "it" and if you were caught, you had to "freeze," or hold perfectly still on the spot where you were caught.

Lizzie learned to dig in the figures of her skates, dodging people, often falling hard in the attempt. Her knees were often torn open, bleeding onto her socks, but she dabbed at the minor injury with a cold, wet handkerchief and went on skating. She learned to skate backward, her arms flying on each side for support. Mandy was quite good at this, because she was so small and competitive. Whatever Lizzie could do, Mandy did, too, often excelling in difficult maneuvers on the ice.

But one day in February, Lizzie heard the icicles dripping during the night. The covers on her bed felt damp and much too heavy, so she threw the comforter off her shoulders.

"What are you doing?" Emma growled.

"It's too warm in here," Lizzie whispered.

So Emma helped fold the comforter down, and they both fell asleep again. Lizzie dreamed she was flying across the ice on her skates and skated into a warm pool of water, soaking her feet up to her knees.

While they were getting dressed for school the next morning, Lizzie told Emma what she had dreamed. They laughed about it. As warm and drippy as it was outside, that's probably what would happen if they went skating, Emma assured her.

Emma watched as Lizzie combed her hair.

"Lizzie, do you remember when we lived in our other house, how tightly Mam would comb back our hair?" Emma asked.

Lizzie smiled into the mirror, because Emma stood behind her. "Oh, of course. She used to plaster our hair down with water and roll it so tight, our eyes were slanted. Then on Sundays, she'd slather that awful gel stuff on yet. Eww!" Lizzie shuddered.

Emma laughed. "You used to hate it worse than I did."

"I'd much rather comb my hair loosely like this," Lizzie said, turning her head to catch the lamplight. "Did you notice my hair is not completely straight anymore? It's a bit wavy if I comb them a certain way."

"I noticed," Emma said kindly. "But, Lizzie, you shouldn't comb your hair quite as loosely as you do. It

looks almost fancy. It's a wonder Mam doesn't say anything about it before you go to school."

"Oh well, Emma. It's not really *that* loose," Lizzie
answered, frowning at Emma.

"Whatever you think," Emma said, shrugging her
shoulders.

Lizzie finished combing her hair in silence. Emma
pinned on her apron, asking Lizzie to straighten it in
the back. There was a small piece of cloth sewed to the
waist of their dresses, called a "lebbley," and their black
aprons had to be spaced evenly on each side, as was
their custom.

"Yesterday your apron was so crooked I couldn't even
see your 'lebbley,' Lizzie," Emma informed her.

"So?"

"Well, you could let me straighten it for you."

"I can do it myself. Besides, I don't even care much
what I look like here in Jefferson County. Nobody
really cares as much about clothes here. It's much more
relaxing," Lizzie said, sniffing.

"I agree," Emma assured her. "But you looked so
sloppy yesterday in school, I was almost embarrassed.
Your hair looked a fright. I mean, I don't want to be unkind, Lizzie, but you should hold still and be a bit more
quiet. We're not exactly little girls anymore!"

Lizzie narrowed her eyes at Emma. She had a straight
pin in her mouth, because she was pinning her black
school apron, so she didn't say anything immediately.

"Emma, we're not old yet. I don't want to have to
grow up right now and start worrying about what I look

like. There's too much to do yet, like playing baseball, going sledding, and skating," Lizzie said, holding a straight pin to the lamp to see why it wouldn't pierce the fabric of her black belt apron.

"I'm twelve now, Lizzie."

"Well, good."

"You'll be twelve this year."

"What does that mean? I have to like washing dishes and sweeping the floor? Emma, I'm not like you. Why can't I have fun with Debbie and Edna for a long, long time?" Lizzie asked, her voice squeaking in frustration.

"You can, Lizzie."

"Okay, then."

Emma sighed, turning to hang up her flannel night-gown. She shook her head wryly, because there was no use trying to persuade Lizzie to act a bit more grown up. Lizzie thought she was fine exactly the way she was, although Emma thought she was too noisy in school, often speaking her mind quite loudly.

As they splashed through the slush on their way to school, Emma hung back a bit, because Lizzie was stomping her boots into the shallow ditch beside the road. Bits of slush and water flew in every direction, splattering anyone who was close to her.

"Stop it, Lizzie," Edna said. "You got my socks wet."

Lizzie laughed and skipped ahead, trying to catch up with Ivan and Ray. They were talking, never noticing Lizzie trying to catch up with them. Emma watched as Lizzie sneaked up behind them, stomping her boot into the slush, splattering their pant legs with cold, wet snow.

"Hey!" Ivan yelled.

"Cut it out!" Ray growled.

Lizzie stomped again, splattering more cold, wet snow across their legs. Ray put down his lunchbox, grabbed a handful of wet snow, grabbed Lizzie by the shoulders, and rubbed the snow into her face. Lizzie shrieked and tore out of his grasp, stopping to shake the water off her face. It ran down her chin, soaking her coat, so she rubbed a coat sleeve across her face in an effort to dry it. Her face was red as a beet, her bonnet pushed to the back of her head, her hair a disheveled mess, and the day hadn't even begun.

"Lizzie!" Emma scolded.

"What?"

"Behave yourself."

Edna was scowling at her and Emma looked embarrassed. Mandy walked quietly behind them, but her eyes were twinkling at least.

"That makes Ivan and Ray mad if you splash slush on them," Edna told her sourly.

That made Lizzie feel terrible. No one smiled—not even Mandy, so she figured that wasn't a good thing to do this morning. She pressed her mouth into a tight, straight line and fell back behind everyone else. That was just the trouble with getting older, she thought bitterly. There were always these unspoken guidelines of what was nice behavior and what wasn't. Who was to say what was grown up and what was childish? Emma? Emma couldn't always be there with Lizzie to remind her to behave herself her whole life long. And that Edna had nerve, telling her Ivan and Ray didn't like slush splashed on them. How did she know? Everybody was mean this morning. Even Mandy was sober and serious.

So Lizzie walked behind the others, thinking sad thoughts about growing up. It wasn't one bit fun. She still had five years before she was sixteen years old and had to go to the singings with the youth, so what was wrong with being sloppy and loud if she wanted to be? She didn't even like boys one bit, and she certainly was not going to get married until she had taught school for a very long time. Well, she liked Ivan more than most boys, but he was her first cousin so she couldn't marry him. Besides, she was only eleven. That Emma, talking like that this morning. It just gave her the blues.

She wondered what was in her lunchbox. She stopped, put it down on the road, and snapped open the lid. Her little red and black plaid Thermos was on one side, but she didn't have time to open the lid and see what it contained. There was a thick sandwich, with two slices of bread, filled with ham, cheese, mayonnaise, and lettuce. That cheered her immensely, because it looked so good. Mam had made a banana nut cake, which was so delicious. Lizzie had eaten two pieces for supper. There was a piece in a Tupperware container, a jar of peaches, and a small plastic bag with barbecue potato chips.

Why peaches? Mam knew she didn't like peaches. She decided she was going to pack her own lunch. One sandwich was never enough, anyway. If she ate all of her barbecue chips at recess, then she had only one sandwich and a piece of cake the rest of the day, because she was not going to eat her peaches. The juice was alright, though, because she would pour that over the banana nut cake.

She clicked the lid of her lunchbox and straightened as Edna called back, telling her to hurry up. They were all waiting, so she walked a bit faster.

"What were you doing?" Emma asked.

"None of your business," Lizzie answered, her chin held a bit higher than usual. With that, she walked past everyone else, not saying a word.

Her arithmetic assignment only made her feel worse. There were twenty problems of long division, which Lizzie was not very good at. She could have received better scores if she would have taken more time, check-ing her work by multiplying. She always did this the first fifteen minutes, but it just took too long, so she didn't check all of them.

Salina always had better arithmetic scores, because she bent her dark head diligently over her work, never looking around or turning around in her seat like Lizzie did. No matter how hard Lizzie tried, she very rarely had a better score than Salina.

Teacher Barbara told the class the only way to really become adept at long division was to do the problems repeatedly, meaning they would be getting long division assignments for quite some time. This depressed Lizzie to the point of unshed tears. Her humiliating walk to school was bad enough; now all this long division to toil over for most of the day.

She glanced at the clock, then down at her tablet. She loved school paper — that dirty-colored, cheap paper with blue lines running across it. Every lesson was a new challenge on a sheet of her school tablet, so she sighed, straightened her shoulders, and went to work.

She forgot all about her walk to school as she figured numbers, jotting swiftly with her pencil. Suddenly, her head jerked forward as an object hit the back of her head. She looked straight at Teacher Barbara with a bewildered expression, then turned in her seat to see who had thrown something against her covering.

Jonas and Ray were grinning openly, but bent their heads quickly under Teacher Barbara's intent gaze. Lizzie turned around slowly in her seat and resumed her work. *Who had thrown something*, she wondered. Surely the teacher must have seen her head jerk forward.

And then, without warning, another object hit her head again. This time it wasn't quite so hard, so she kept her

composure. There was a loud snort from the back of the
room as one of the boys tried to keep from laughing aloud.

There was stone silence as Teacher Barbara raised her
head from her answer book.

"Jonas!"

Jonas was not laughing now, and neither was Ray.

"What is so funny?"

"Nothing."

The teacher glared sternly at the boys, saying, "Don't
let it happen again."

Order was restored once more, and Lizzie had completely forgotten about being hit when—bang!—another
small object caught her completely off guard. Her head
went forward as she fought to conceal her surprise, but
Teacher Barbara was busy and did not notice.

Now she could no longer concentrate on her division
problems. What should she do? If she raised her hand
and told the teacher what was happening, she'd be labeled
a tattletale by the boys, and she certainly did not want
that to happen. If she turned around and smiled at them,
she could just hear Emma say, "Lizzie, behave yourself."

She actually did not know what to do. She chewed the
eraser on her pencil nervously, hoping with all her heart
it wouldn't happen again. She glanced down and saw a
tiny piece of a pink eraser under Salina's desk. So that
was it! Someone was throwing erasers at her—either at
her or someone else.

Slowly she went back to work, but her concentra-
tion was broken by wondering when the next piece of
eraser would hit her. She thought if Emma and Edna

hadn't been so strict and sour on their walk to school, Lizzie probably would have turned around and at least let the boys know she knew they were throwing bits of eraser. That was what she wanted to do. But since she and Emma had talked about growing up, Lizzie felt a bit bewildered. She really didn't know what was the right thing to do. She knew Emma was partly right, because she should act her age—maybe just a bit more, anyway.

Another piece of eraser hit her shoulder, and Lizzie knew without a doubt she could not finish her arithmetic this way. So she turned around in her seat and glared at Jonas and Ray.

"Stop it," she mouthed, her eyebrows drawn down severely.

Then Ray stomped his foot in the aisle, and Lizzie knew exactly what he meant—Lizzie splashing slush on the way to school.

Her face flaming, she turned with a sniff and sat up straight, staring blankly at the blackboard, seeing nothing. She was so embarrassed, because now she knew for sure they were trying to hit her and it was all her own fault, because she had been too sassy and bold on the way to school.

If she would have been in first or second grade, she would have put her head in her arms and cried. But she was in sixth grade, an upper grader now, and she couldn't do that.

Another piece of eraser hit her covering.

A hot anger coursed through Lizzie's veins. Self-righteous and being a tattletale or not, she could not let this go on. So she raised her hand, feebly at first, but straighter as her resolve strengthened. Those boys were just going to have to learn that she wasn't the silly little girl they thought she was.

"Lizzie," Teacher Barbara said.

"Uh, someone is hitting me with small pieces of eraser," Lizzie said quite clearly.

Silence settled over the classroom, as the pupils raised their heads in bewilderment. For one thing, it was very different for Lizzie to be tattling on anyone, because she was always the one to be mischievous.

"Who is it?" Teacher Barbara asked, in a voice that made Lizzie shiver.

Silence.

"We will not have any recess at all until someone comes forward and says what is going on," Teacher Barbara said, in the same terrible voice.

Lizzie felt so bad, because it was all her fault. If she wouldn't have acted so smart on the way to school, this may never have happened. Now the whole school would get no recess and it was all her fault. Lizzie panicked, raising her hand again. When the teacher raised her eyebrows at Lizzie, she blurted out, "It was Jonas and Ray."

"Was it?" Teacher Barbara asked.

The boys solemnly nodded their heads. Ray didn't look too repentant, and Jonas wasn't very worried when Teacher Barbara told them to stay in at recess.

Lizzie watched the water drip from the eaves. Brown patches of wet grass were showing between piles of cold, dirty snow. The realization that skating was over for the year, coupled with what she had done to Jonas and Ray, made her heart feel as heavy as she could ever remember.

She bit her lower lip, her chin cupped in her hands, as she watched the water dripping. She guessed this was just how life was. There was no use being sad, even if she felt like crying. You had to deal with changes and challenges as they came.

It was her fault in the first place, but it was not entirely her fault that Jonas and Ray had decided to throw erasers. And it was Teacher Barbara's decision to say the whole school had to stay in at recess—not hers.

She wasn't crying, but she rubbed her eyes to clear her vision before returning to her division problems.

.   .   .   .   .

At recess, all the girls crowded around her. This was quite unexpected for Lizzie, because she figured everyone would feel sorry for Jonas and Ray, thinking she was a tattletale.

"That was exactly the right thing to do," Emma said.

"It's good for them. They shouldn't get away with that. It's just horribly distracting," Salina said, in her grown-up manner.

"Serves them right!" Edna said airily. "They know better than to throw erasers. She'll probably send a note home for Daddy."

Lizzie ate her barbecue chips and didn't say much. For once, there wasn't much to say, because she felt bad for the boys. It wasn't completely their fault.

.   .   .   .   .

On the way home, Lizzie hung back, because she felt ashamed of Ivan and Ray. They hadn't said one word to her the rest of the day, so she knew they were unhappy because she had tattled.

She jumped when Danny came up from behind her. He put his mittened hand on her arm and said, "Do you feel bad, Lizzie?"

Lizzie looked down at Danny's anxious green eyes, peering out from beneath the brim of his straw hat. She shrugged her shoulders miserably.

Danny pulled himself up to his full skinny length. "Well, Lizzie, I'll tell you one thing; this was a lesson for Ray. You know why?"

"Why?" Lizzie asked quietly.

"'Cause!" He stopped and lifted one knee, propping his lunch against his leg as he opened it.

"Here—you want a Grandpa cookie?" He unwrapped a package of soft, chewy sugar cookies, covered with brown sugar frosting. "You want one?"

"Mm-hmm," Lizzie answered. She bit into the sweet frosting, smiling at Danny as he smiled back at her. Lizzie's heart was warmed by his gesture of friendship.

"You know why it's good for Ray?" he went on.

"Why?"

"Because. You know my rabbits I have?"

"Mm-hmm."

"Well, two of them got out. They can't open their own doors, mind you—not even close. Well, they got out, and I still think it was Ray. He fed my rabbits that night, because I had to go away with Mom and Daddy. He

says it wasn't him, and Daddy said it wasn't, and I have
to be quiet about it. Well, this proves it; if he doesn't get
caught letting my rabbits go, he gets caught throwing
erasers. That's what he gets," he said staunchly, taking a
huge bite of his Grandpa cookie.

He chewed solemnly, his cheeks bulging, and swallowed, looking closely at Lizzie. "They won't be mad for
long. Ray says you're a good skater."

"He did? He said that?"

"Yep!" Danny announced proudly.

So Lizzie was cheered immensely as she finished her
walk home from school. She waved good-bye to Danny,
thinking how the Grandpa cookie and a bit of praise
helped her otherwise difficult day. And, tomorrow she
would pack two sandwiches in her lunchbox.

chapter 6

Springtime on the Ridge

Lizzie's eyes followed a large formation of Canada geese flying in a V across the sky. It was a mellow evening; warm air with a slight breeze was stirring the bare branches of the trees. The buds were showing red, pushing through the little funny-looking knobs that would turn into leaves.

The sound of the geese honking always reminded Lizzie of the playground at school. Everyone talked or shouted a bit differently, yet it was almost all the same. She shaded her eyes with her left hand, squinting as the slanting rays of the sun shone directly into her face.

There was no more skating now, so Lizzie and Mandy had wiped down the silver blades of their skates, put them back in the box, and stored them on the top shelf of the closet. They felt a bit sad, but the warmth of the spring air was wonderful in a different way.

Lizzie turned toward the ridge, which rose behind
Uncle Eli's sawmill and Dat's pallet shop. It was covered thickly with trees, although one spot almost directly
behind the shop looked darker green, so Lizzie wondered if they were all pine trees. She had to talk to Edna
about it and ask her if they ever went up to the ridge
and explored it.

Lizzie was proud of Dat's pallet shop. Uncle Eli and
the boys had helped Dat, planning and building a long,
low building with concrete loading docks. They had
gone on trips with a heavy truck, bringing home huge
pieces of heavy equipment that cut boards, smoothed
them, and cut holes in them—not really holes, but a
huge bite out of a board. That piece of machinery was
called a notcher. Dat put a board in it and "ka-chunk,"
it bit out a piece of the board. Mandy told Lizzie she ate
corn-on-the-cob like a notcher, and they laughed until
the tears streamed from their eyes.

There was another piece of equipment called a cham-
fer, which took a smaller, smoother bite. That was so a
person who drove a forklift in a warehouse could slide
the prongs of the forklift under the pallet easier.

That's what pallets were for. Huge stacks of boxes
were loaded on a wooden pallet in factories or warehous-
es, and forklifts loaded or unloaded them. Pallets came
in all different shapes and sizes, depending on what they
were for. Dat was always happy when he had plenty
of orders for tractor and trailer loads of pallets. When
Lizzie heard a huge truck go past the house, she knew it
was either a load of Dat's pallets or logs for Uncle Eli.

The most fascinating piece of equipment was the
large nailing machine. It had steel boxes of nails on the
top, which constantly rocked back and forth, allowing
only the proper amount of nails to fall through, into the
"chucks" or tubes that clunked down on the boards of
the pallet to nail one whole row at a time. The girls liked
to watch the men nail pallets with this machine, going
"ka-chunk, ka-chunk" steadily across it.

The only thing about Dat's pallet shop that Lizzie
didn't like as well as the harness shop was not being able
to help him. There were always men working, so there
wasn't much a girl could do. Sometimes after supper
Lizzie would go with Dat to sweep sawdust from under
the saws, but she was not allowed to help during the
day. Lizzie knew it was because Mam had told Dat in
no uncertain terms that the pallet shop was no place for
a girl.

Mam was like that. Once her nostrils flared and her
cheeks turned red, with her mouth in a straight, firm
line, she meant what she said. Lizzie guessed Dat would
let her try using the notcher, because it looked so easy.
But no, not when Mam acted so bossy. Dat told her
she put the foot down. Lizzie knew very well what that
meant.

"Lizzie!"

She jumped. "What?"

"You have to hurry up and get that wood carried.
Mam isn't feeling well and there's all the laundry to get
in," Emma called.

"Well, okay, but you don't have to startle me so badly," Lizzie answered.

Emma shut the kitchen door, and Lizzie hurried to the woodpile. *This carrying wood gets really boring,* she thought sourly. That was one thing about summer—she didn't need to carry these endless armloads of wood.

The kitchen door opened and Jason came out, wearing a brightly colored head scarf. "I'll help you!" he said proudly.

"Jase, who put that scarf on you?" Lizzie said laughingly.

"I did. By myself," he said, grinning.

Lizzie looked at him, wearing a scarf on top of his riot of brown curls. His shirttail was hanging over his blue denim pants, and he wore a pair of Mandy's bedroom slippers. He shuffled through the wood chips, collecting little pieces of bark and sawdust on the furry pink slippers. He bent over, straining to pick up a large piece of wood.

"U-nnhh," he groaned.

"You're too little," Lizzie said with a smile.

"Ah, no—you watch." His face turned bright red in color as his arms strained to lift the chunk of wood. He grasped it firmly against his chest, before his feet slid backward on the loose sawdust and he fell, pinching his fingers under the chunk of wood. He cried and yelled, sitting beside the wood, his pants covered with sawdust, the bedroom slippers flung a short distance away. Lizzie kissed his cheek, blowing on his fingers to cool them, murmuring that everything would be alright. She cra-

dled his curly head against her coat, knowing he would
stop yelling after a while. Jason was actually quite brave
for a three-year-old toddler, Lizzie always thought.

As suddenly as his crying had started, it stopped. He
pointed to the driveway and Lizzie turned to see what he
wanted to show her. Edna and Danny were hurrying up
the drive, their arms swinging in their haste to reach her.

"What are you doing?" Lizzie asked.

"Do you want to go along with us to explore the ridge
behind the pallet shop?" Edna asked, panting.

Lizzie's eyes grew wide. She could hardly believe
Edna was allowed to go by herself. "Edna, are you sure
your mom doesn't care?" she asked hesitantly.

"Not if you and Mandy go!" Danny piped up before
Edna had a chance to answer.

"Well . . . I mean, what would we explore? Can you
get lost on the ridge?" Lizzie asked.

"Nah," Danny said confidently. "All it is, is a pine forest and a clearing in the back. We're not allowed to go
farther than the monkey vines."

"Monkey vines? What in the world is a monkey
vine?" she asked, her eyebrows raised in concern.

"Was he crying?" Edna asked, pointing to Jason.

"He fell," Lizzie answered quickly, before returning to
her question about monkey vines.

"I dunno what a monkey vine is. Just a vine that
hangs down from the trees, and you back up and run
like crazy and fly through the air," Danny shouted.

"Not so loud, Danny. Lizzie, go ask your mom," Edna
ordered.

So Lizzie opened the kitchen door, pulling Jason along. "You can come in," she told Edna.

So they all piled into the kitchen, finding Mam sitting on the old swivel rocker, looking tired. Lizzie could tell by the heightened color of Mam's cheeks that she was not in a very friendly mood. When she didn't say 'hello' to Edna and Danny, Lizzie's hopes sank, because she knew she would not be allowed to go to the ridge tonight.

Sure enough, Mam started shaking her head before Lizzie finished her sentence.

"No."

Just flat no, not even an explanation. Lizzie felt her temper rise, and, before she thought about the conse-quences, she blurted out, "We're *never* allowed to do anything in the evening, 'cause you're always tired and grouchy!"

"Lizzie, now stop it. If you would have gotten the wash in and carried your wood before this, maybe you could go. And don't talk back to your mother like that," Mam said tiredly.

"Mam, please—it's so nice out tonight," Lizzie whined.

"No!"

And Lizzie knew the subject was over; there was no use. She walked out with Edna and Danny, feeling so embarrassed and sorry for them because she was not allowed to go.

"Your mom's *mad*!" Danny breathed.

"Danny! Melvin Annie's just tired," Edna corrected him. She turned to Lizzie and adjusted her scarf, jutting her chin forward to tuck the knot in farther.

"Well, now go get your work done, Lizzie, so you can go tomorrow night," she said.

"Is Debbie allowed to go?" Lizzie asked.

"She probably won't get home from school in time."

"Oh."

"See you!"

"See you." Lizzie turned dejectedly, walking around to the back of the house to the clothesline. It was hanging full of line after line of dry clothes, rocking gently in the evening breeze.

Tears pricked at her eyelashes as she tied the strings of the pocket apron that contained the clothespins. She jerked on the strings, tying it so tightly she could scarcely breathe. Yanking at a blue towel, she thought how unfair life was. She hadn't known Edna was going to want to go explore the ridge. How could she have known she was supposed to hurry with the wood?

Staggering under a huge basket of dry towels, Lizzie burst into the kitchen. "Somebody pull out a chair," she gasped. Mandy hurried to slide one beside the table, and Lizzie plopped the heavy basket on it.

"Whew!"

"Why didn't you tell me you were getting wash in?" Emma asked, turning from the sink where she was peeling potatoes.

"I can do it!" Lizzie chirped brightly, watching Mam from the corner of her eye. She started folding wash with vehemence, hoping with all her heart it would help her get to the ridge the following evening.

.   .   .   .   .

Rain blew across the roof of the little basement home, dripping from the eaves, water gurgling down the spouting. Trees swayed as the April showers came from a dark, dreary sky. Even the yellow dandelions cowered under the deluge, and Lizzie couldn't tell the difference between the blades of grass and the dandelions.

Her chin was cupped in her hands as she stared across the lawn. They'd just never get to the ridge, she thought darkly. Either there was work to do or the weather was not nice. Now they were living in Jefferson County with all these exciting things to do—and here she sat.

Mandy came over and watched the rain with Lizzie. "It'll clear up and we can go tomorrow evening," she offered kindly.

"If Mam doesn't think of something for us to do, you mean," Lizzie answered.

"Or Emma."

"No, Emma doesn't mind. I talked to her last night. She said the only reason I had to get the wash in was because Mam wasn't feeling well all day. But we have to carry the wood."

.   .   .   .   .

So the following evening, the wood was carried in double quick time. It was a beautiful evening, even if the wind blew in quick little gusts, chasing old brown weeds and leaves left over from winter. It was one of those days where it seemed like spring, but the wind was determined to put forth a blast of cold north wind, as if to remind people that winter was not yet over.

The wind didn't bother Lizzie at all, because they could finally go explore the pine woods on the ridge. Mam was feeling better, smiling as she made sandwiches for their lunchbox, because they were taking supper with them.

She put bologna and mayonnaise on one side of the bread, put a thin slice of cheese on top, and added lots of light-colored, crunchy lettuce. Lizzie never tired of those sandwiches, marveling at the fact that they were allowed to have bologna *and* cheese *and* lettuce on one sandwich. They were so good.

Mam put two sandwiches in their lunchbox, two apples, and two bags of potato chips. Lizzie was concerned about the fact that there were only two sandwiches, but Mandy said she could easily have half of hers.

So they ran down the driveway, their lunchbox between them. Lizzie could hardly walk fast enough to Uncle Eli's, so sometimes they ran until she was gasping for breath. Mandy could run a lot longer than Lizzie without running out of breath.

Edna and Danny were ready, charging out the sidewalks, excitement shining from their wide eyes. "Hey, guess what? Ivan and Ray are going along, too!" Danny said.

"No, they aren't, Danny. Where did you get such a stupid idea?" Edna said, sniffing.

"Oh, yes, they are. After they shut the sawmill down and have supper, they're going to. Ray said," he snorted.

Edna shrugged her shoulders.

They started up the hill past the barn, skirting the large piles of logs behind the sawmill. Edna informed them they were never, ever allowed to play on the log piles because if one log rolled, the whole pile could come tumbling down and kill or seriously injure someone. Lizzie remained in awe of those huge piles of logs long after Edna said that.

They had to go up a steep bank, somehow. Danny scrambled up, grabbing handfuls of weeds and digging in his shoes until he made it. He stood on top, looking down at them, eyes shining. He looked doubtfully at Lizzie and Edna, saying, "Mandy can easily make it up here, but I don't know about you two," he said.

"Danny, if you don't stop acting so big, I'm going to stomp on your straw hat!" Edna shouted, glaring at him.

Danny grabbed his straw hat, smashing it down farther on his head, as if that would protect him from Edna's anger. He adjusted his pants, hitching up his suspenders, and eyed them again. "Well, you're both pretty good-sized!"

Lizzie was furious. Her weight was a bit of a sore subject lately, because she was going on twelve years old. Somehow, she cared more than she had when she was younger.

"I can get up that steep bank if you did, you skinny little thing," she told Danny. She stepped back, taking a head start, and charged up the embankment. She easily made it up halfway, but could go no farther. Her feet kept sliding, so she grabbed tufts of weeds, digging in the toe of her sneakers. It took every ounce of strength, willpower, and all the pride she had, as puffing and grunting, she clawed her way to the top.

Edna and Mandy cheered before Edna tried. She had a false start at first, but she also made her way up. Mandy grinned, her head thrown back, then she scrambled up, as light and nimble as a deer.

"Good for you, Danny. We made it," Edna announced triumphantly.

Danny didn't hear her. He was already headed into the tall, dead brush that bordered the pine forest. Lizzie followed hesitantly, because it looked a bit scary to her. She had never seen brush and weeds that tall, and what if they got lost?

"We need a trail or something we can follow. How do we know where we'll end up? Or how are we going to know how to come back?" she asked.

"By the time we're through these weeds, we'll know where we walked coming back, I'm sure," Edna said.

"Just follow me," Danny said airily.

So they did. First they fought their way through the unpleasant brush, jaggers from thornbushes tearing at their coat sleeves. Little bits and pieces of thistle seed and other loose objects that fell from the brush stuck to their eyes and mouths. They snorted, wiping their eyes, trying to get rid of the bothersome things.

"This isn't fun!" Mandy said emphatically.

"Where do you think you're going?" Edna demanded.

"We're almost to the pines!" Danny yelled.

Lizzie pushed her way through the brush, determined not to complain, because she so desperately wanted to see what the ridge looked like. The woods smelled wet, like rain—only the smell was mixed with an earthy scent, much like the garden when Dat plowed it. If she was watching closely, she could see little shoots of green plants pushing through the dead brown undergrowth.

A tiny creature scooted from under a crumbling log. Lizzie shrieked with surprise, grabbing Edna's sleeve.

"It's only a chipmunk!" Danny said.

"Oh. Well, how was I supposed to know? I've never traipsed around in a woods before!" Lizzie said, indignant because Danny acted as if he was a seasoned traveler in the woods.

"They're cute!" Mandy said.

"Yeah," Edna agreed.

The brush was getting thinner and easier to travel through. Suddenly they stood at the edge of the pines. The weeds were only small here, almost as if someone mowed the grass in the summertime. And the smell! It was the most wonderful scent, almost spicy—it was so pungent with the odor of pine needles. Lizzie could see the sticky pine tar covering the outside of the trees, shining on the grooves of the bark. She reached out to touch it, to see if it was sticky.

"Don't get pine tar all over your hands. It's hard to get off," Edna offered.

But Lizzie could not resist touching it. It felt cold and slippery, but sticky at the same time. She smelled it, but all she could smell was pine scent everywhere, so she couldn't tell if it was the pine tar or the needles.

Suddenly they burst through the grass and the first row of trees. Lizzie was absolutely stunned. She had never seen anything like this. All her senses tried to absorb it all at once, but it was too much to comprehend. Her mouth dropped open, and her eyes widened, but not one sound came out. As far as she could see, there were pine trees. The lower branches had no pine needles on them, so the bare branches looked like little ladders; they were so close together. The whole floor of this wonderful pine forest was covered with a thick layer of rust-colored pine needles. It was so soft, it felt like she was walking on a mattress of some sort.

The part that was best of all was the wind tossing the tops of these trees, gently but powerfully, back and forth. Lizzie's ears were filled with a soft, gentle sound, almost like a sigh, as the wind sifted through the pine needles. It was a sound unlike anything she had ever heard. It was almost mournful, but so steady and sweet that it stirred her soul. Her heart swelled to hear this

sweet sound, smell the wonderful scent, and see this unbelievable pine forest stretching out in front of her.

"*This is great*!" Danny declared, every vein in his thin neck protruding as he spoke at the top of his voice.

"Imagine what all we can play here!" Mandy's voice squeaked with excitement.

"Indians!"

"We'll be Indians!"

"We'll build teepees, make feathered headdresses . . .!"

"First, we have to clean up the vines."

"We need a rake."

"We need a hammer."

"We need to tell Debbie!"

Everyone was talking at once, and Danny was racing in circles, grabbing pine branches, and scooting up trees. They were quite beside themselves with joy and excitement.

Lizzie plopped down in the middle of the soft pine needles and opened her lunchbox. The climbing and this outdoor atmosphere made her hungry. So they all ate their supper in a circle on the soft floor of the pine forest. They planned who would live with whom and talked about Indian names. Danny said Ivan could make a neat bow and arrow, and Lizzie said she would make headbands out of construction paper at school.

"We need a name for our forest of pines," Edna said.

"Lovely Acres," Mandy said shyly.

"Of course! That's exactly what we'll call it. We can be the Glick-Miller tribe, living in Lovely Acres!" Edna said.

"That's not very original," Lizzie said.

"What can we call our tribe?" Mandy asked.

"Pine Indians!" Danny shouted.

"Pine?" Lizzie wrinkled her nose. "Just plain 'Pine?'"

"Pine Cone?"

"Pine Cone Indians!"

"That sounds stupid."

"What then?"

"Pine Needle Indians?"

"No!"

"Pocahontas Indians?"

"Pocahontas was just one girl—not a whole tribe."

"How do you know?"

"It's in the history book. I remember. She saved John Smith's life, then she married him, went to England with him, and died. I pity her. That's sad."

"No use being sad now. She's long dead," Danny snorted.

"Stop talking about Pocahontas. That's too sad," Mandy said.

"Well, we still don't have an Indian name."

Everyone sat in a circle and thought. Lizzie picked up a pine needle and examined it closely. She chewed her fingernail and thought. There were Shawnee and Sioux and Dakota Indians, but they were all out West. She wondered what kind of Indians lived in Pennsylvania ridges.

"We could be the Monkey Vine Indians!" Danny said.

"Monkey Vine?"

"No!"

"Not Monkey Vine! We're not monkeys!"

Lizzie noticed the sunlight slanting through the pines and expressed her fear about darkness overtaking them. Mandy's eyes were big and scared, but Edna assured them they would easily be able to follow their trail home.

After they had cleaned up the paper from their lunch-boxes, they easily found the trail, as Edna had said. The whole way home, Lizzie tagged behind, her thoughts filled with Indian names and the sweet smell of the pine needles. She thought she had never heard anything quite as lovely as the sound of the wind in the pine branches. Except—just maybe—her Aunt Becca when she played the harmonica.

chapter 7

Playing on the Ridge

As early spring turned into warmer days of early summer, Lizzie knew without a doubt that this was the very best time of her life. Everything was fun — everything! Even working at home was fun, because they did everything as fast as they could so they could run down to Uncle Eli's and play Indian on the ridge with Edna and Danny.

The pine forest was cleaned with rakes; dead branches were cleared away and put on a huge pile. They were not allowed to burn anything, Uncle Eli said, so they just carried all the debris to the very edge of the pines, and that is where it had to stay.

They begged Uncle Eli for slabs of lumber or leftover pieces of pallet lumber to build teepees. They had tried for about a week, using different sizes of lumber, even tying them to trees. The whole pine needle-covered hill

was on a slope, so it didn't matter how hard they tried —
the teepees leaned downhill. Finally they were success-
ful; they actually built a fairly good teepee, using black
plastic as an outer covering.

Lizzie was so proud of that teepee, she could hardly
believe they had actually done it. Her heart was so light
when they were coming off the ridge that evening that
she ran ahead of everyone else, tumbling down the steep
slope at the bottom and waiting on an old stump for the
rest to catch up.

The next evening, after a windy day, they raced to
Lovely Acres to the teepee.

"Awww, no!" Lizzie wailed, covering her eyes in
despair.

"Awww!" Danny wailed.

"It was the wind."

"I told you it wouldn't work."

"What are we gonna do?"

"Not have a teepee, evidently!"

"We could rebuild."

"No!"

Lizzie walked slowly through the pines where the
"perfect teepee" lay in shambles. She could see it was
just too weak with those thin poles, and with the uneven
terrain, teepees just didn't work.

"We have to do something different," she announced.

"What?" Edna asked.

"We have to build cabins, instead of teepees, and be
pioneers instead of Indians," she said, surveying the
damage.

"How can we build cabins?" Mandy asked.

"Slabs!" shouted Danny.

"Slabs! That's it! There are hundreds of slabs on the burn pile!" Everyone started talking at once, all excited about the prospect of building cabins with slabs. Slabs were the outer slices of logs, mostly covered with bark. That was really the most exciting part—the cabins would resemble actual log cabins!

"Let's just nail the slabs to trees, for cornerposts, because we aren't strong enough to dig the poles for the corners," Edna said.

"Let's ask Ivan and Ray to show us how," Lizzie suggested. "Do you suppose they would?"

"We can do it ourselves," Danny said emphatically.

"Where are we going to get our nails?"

"From the pallet shop!"

"Dat isn't going to let us," Mandy warned.

"We can ask. Let's all go down to the sawmill and ask Uncle Eli and Dat for whatever we need," Lizzie decided.

So they all marched down the trail, through the weed patch, and down the steep slope. It was so noisy at the sawmill, with the huge diesels chugging and the saws grinding through the logs that there was no chance for them to talk to anyone.

Uncle Eli stood at the saw, his blue shirt opened at the neck, his stomach stretching the buttons in the front. He was whistling and singing, as he always did at his job. When he spied the children, he threw up his hand and waved, a broad grin spreading across his face.

Lizzie knew what he would say: "Here come the babies!" because that's what he always said. He loved the children, and they loved him, because he always had a twinkle in his eye and a big smile.

He pointed to the clock on the office wall, meaning they should wait till five o'clock, the time when the sawmill shut down.

So they all sat on a log, away from the men working, until Uncle Eli had time to talk to them. The saw whirred, sawdust flying out the huge pipe and down over the sawdust pile. The rough lumber was put on rollers, carrying it away from the saw, until a worker picked it up and stacked it. Sometimes another smaller saw cut the boards into exact lengths for pallet lumber.

Uncle Eli finished the last log, flipped a lever, and everything slowly ground to a halt. The saw blade went slower and slower until it stopped, so he went to the diesel room to shut it down, too.

Quickly Danny leaped up, following his dad. "Daddy, Daddy!" he yelled.

"Can you wait till the diesel stops?" Uncle Eli said with a laugh, rumpling Danny's hair.

"Daddy! We need slabs! A whole bunch of slabs, to build cabins up on the ridge. Please, Daddy?"

"Oh, now, why would you need cabins?" Uncle Eli teased.

"Teepees don't work," Edna said.

"They fall over," Lizzie finished.

"So you need a bunch of slabs, do you? And how are you going to get them up to your ridge?" he asked, tilting his hat to the back of his head and running his hand across his brow.

"We'll get them up somehow," Danny assured his dad.

"If you can get them up, you can have the whole pile," Uncle Eli said, smiling.

They all jumped, clapping their hands and shouting in unison, then raced off to find Dat.

"Bunch of Indians, no doubt," muttered Uncle Eli, shaking his head, but his eyes were twinkling, the crows' feet at the corner crinkling as usual. He loved his children, always chuckling at their antics, never being harsh or strictly admonishing them. It just wasn't his way.

Dat was not quite as easy to get along with. He was a good Dat, but stricter than Uncle Eli, taking life more seriously. So Lizzie's heart fluttered a bit nervously, because she was afraid Dat would not let them have all the pallet nails they needed. She ran along with the others, though her fears were kept to herself.

Dat had also shut down his diesel, and was sweeping shavings when they burst through the door.

"Dat! Can we have a bunch of nails to make cabins?" Mandy shouted.

Danny and Edna didn't say anything, because it wasn't their Dat. Dat didn't stop sweeping right away, but when he turned to look at them, he didn't look tired or grouchy, which was a big relief to Lizzie.

"Why?"

"To make cabins!" Mandy said.

He didn't say anything for a while, then he turned and pointed to the nailing machine. "You can have all the nails you find scattered under the nailer. But don't you ever try to get any while the nailer is working," he warned.

"We won't, Uncle Melvin—don't you worry," Danny said, almost reverently, because he was so relieved to find a source of materials for building the cabins.

Lizzie found an empty box, and they dropped on all fours, crawling under the nailer and producing fistfuls of nails. This was so exciting that Lizzie could hardly stand it. She could only imagine the neat cabins they would build.

And so the work began in earnest. Every evening that they were allowed to, they painstakingly dragged slabs of lumber up over the steep trail, and through the narrow paths between the pine trees, before dropping, exhausted, on the soft pine needle-carpeted forest floor. It was a labor of love, though, especially for Lizzie. She learned that spring and summer that if you persevered, or worked as hard as you could and kept trying even if things went wrong, you could do almost anything. And work she did, dragging slabs and pounding nails until her hands were blistered and her back hurt in the evening.

They had one rule, and that was to be home before dark. As soon as the sunlight slanted in long, dust-filled shafts through the pines, they instinctively knew it was time to pack up for the evening and return to their homes.

The quiet slope was now dotted with crude-looking little huts. They were three-cornered or sometimes five-cornered, depending how the pine trees were situated. The bark was on the outside, and it really did resemble a log cabin. The roofs were made of black plastic tarp, which was often pinned together to make the ends meet from one tattered piece to the next. It was too hard to make real doors, so pieces of black plastic suited them just fine.

They scrounged every old piece of furniture from their homes, begging for little tables, old chairs, blankets, and dishes.

Debbie and her little sister, Jeanie, joined them on Saturdays, contributing lots of good food. Often they brought bottles of Pepsi, which was a rare treat for the rest of the children, because their parents didn't buy soda, like English people did. So Lizzie always tried to have Debbie or Jeanie live with her, so she could have Pepsi.

They brought lots of sandwiches, cupcakes, cookies, and little containers of pudding or peaches. Plastic jugs of water to drink or wash dishes with were kept in each little hut.

One warm day, after they had worked exceptionally hard, they were so hungry when lunchtime came that they could hardly wait until all the food was ready. They were having a picnic that day, spreading everything on a clean cloth in the middle of the community.

Debbie's mother had packed seven sandwiches for the two girls, which they were to share with the rest of the group if they wanted any. Jeanie was little and round, as was Debbie, and she was hungry, not wanting to share any of the seven sandwiches. It caused great concern, because they never had any serious disagreements. They hardly knew a moment's anger among themselves, so no one really knew how to resolve this serious matter.

Jeanie sat cross-legged on the blanket, her mouth pinched in a firm line, resolution written all over her little round features. Her hair was straight and lighter in color than Debbie's, but her skin was tanned to a nut-brown color, too. Her eyes were small and a bit slanted, giving her a unique look all her own.

"Debbie, Mom said. Five for me and two for you," she said, her eyes flashing indignantly.

"Jeanie! It's embarrassing! Why would you even need five sandwiches? It's just ridiculous—you can't eat five," Debbie pleaded.

"Two for dinner, one for snack, and two for supper," Jeanie insisted.

Edna rolled her eyes and sighed. Mandy blinked her big green eyes, saying nothing. Lizzie was mad at Jeanie, because she felt she was being greedy. She knew Marlene had packed three sandwiches for each girl, and one extra, which she was hoping Debbie would offer her. Debbie's sandwiches were always much better, because her mother bought expensive bologna that was so delicious.

The argument continued, Debbie pleading and Jeanie refusing to budge. Everyone was becoming irritable and hungry. Finally Edna said, "Jeanie, give three to Debbie and you can have four."

Jeanie shook her head.

Then Debbie lost her temper, saying she had had enough. "I'm taking you home, Jeanie, and I'm telling on you!" This caused Jeanie to open her mouth and howl with indignation, the sound disrupting the usually peaceful atmosphere of Lovely Acres.

Danny had grabbed his sandwich earlier and perched on a low branch of a pine tree. He was so thin, and like many thin children, food was not one of his top priorities. He just ate to keep going; nothing ever really tempted him or interested him too much, as far as food went. So he was quite puzzled at this disruption, especially since it was only about sandwiches.

So, like a wise little owl he kept quiet, watching the exchange between the two girls become more heated. Suddenly he could take it no longer, so he burst out, "Ach, 'Deppie,' all because of a stupid *sandwich*!" His English was not very good, because he was only seven.

But the way he said it, knowing a sandwich to him was nothing to argue about, just struck Lizzie and Mandy as funny. They looked at each other, knowing how hilarious Danny was, on his perch in the pine tree, and burst out laughing.

Soon the little pine forest echoed with the sound of the girls' mirth, Edna joining in, and finally even Jeanie had to smile in spite of herself. Danny only looked bewildered, shrugging his shoulders.

The whole thing was soon resolved by cutting all the sandwiches in half, putting them all together on a plate in the middle of the blanket, and they could all share.

It turned out to be a wonderful day. One family became sick, with the "fever and ague," like in the Laura Ingalls book, and the other family had to help take care of them. They mixed all kinds of bitter berries and weeds to make medicine, like real pioneers.

Then they needed to make some repairs, and discovered they were out of nails. Everywhere they looked, there were no nails to be found. They remembered the last amount they got from under the nailer didn't last very long, so they all debated about what they should do.

Edna was busy cleaning up, scraping the foul potion that had been their medicine out of a bowl. "Well, I'm not going for nails. It's not my dad," she said.

"Me, neither."

"Or me."

"I'm not going."

"Then I'll go," Lizzie said, because she was the one who wanted the nails most. There were lots of boards coming loose, making everything look sloppy, and she did not like their neat little cabins to be falling apart like that.

So everyone watched as she marched resolutely down through the pines by herself. She hated asking Dat for new nails, but she knew it was the only way to fix the cabins.

When she reached the pallet shop, she heard the chugging of the diesels and the 'swish-swish' of the nails rocking back and forth in their steel boxes on top of the nailer. Lizzie opened the door and peeped in. *Hmmm*, she thought, *that's unusual.*

There was not a soul around, yet the nailer was going. She stuck her head through the door, looking to the right, then to the left. She looked at the huge steel boxes, rocking on top of the nailer. "Swish, swish."

Lizzie's heart raced. She could climb up on that little stack of pallets beside the nailer and when the one metal box came down, she could grab a handful. Dat would never need to know. Quickly she clambered up on the stack of pallets, making her way carefully to the nailer, waiting breathlessly until the box was tilted just the exact angle she needed to reach a handful.

"Swish." Lizzie grabbed, and was rewarded with a huge handful of nails. She filled her pocket, and quickly grabbed another handful. She tiptoed across the pallet and climbed down as fast as she could, turning swiftly, and raced for the back door. Just as she slipped out she heard Dat coming through the break room door, but she had not been detected.

"Whew!" she breathed. "That was close!"

She scrambled up the steep embankment, the sharp nails in her pocket banging against her leg. She never stopped to fix the discomfort, because she did not want to be seen. She just kept going.

Just as she was about to enter the pine trail, a movement beside the trail caught her eye. First, she thought it was another chipmunk, but its movement was too long and slithery. Then the eyes of a snake stared straight at Lizzie. It was the most awful stare she had ever encountered. It was so cold and sinister, shivers ran up her spine, and she screamed, all alone at the edge of the pines.

The snake must have been just as terrified as Lizzie, because it slithered off into the tall brush beside the trail. Lizzie kept screaming until she realized no one would hear her, so she started crying. She felt so awful. She knew the reason she had seen that snake was because her pocket was bulging with stolen nails.

Once, when she was younger, she had taken a bottle of orange soda from Dat's harness shop. She had tried to persuade herself it wasn't stealing, but she still had to tell Dat in the end. This time, she was sure God had sent that snake. She had so much fun playing on the ridge that she often forgot about God and the devil and the end of the world. But that snake reminded her of what she had done wrong. It really wasn't that different from Eve, being misled by that snake.

A great and awful fear fell on Lizzie's shoulders. She could not — she absolutely could *not* go back down to the pallet shop and tell Dat about her pocketful of nails in front of the workers. Especially not in front of Ivan and Ray, because they would tease her unmercifully if they found out. So she sniffed and moaned under her awful load of guilt, making her way up the trail to Lovely Acres.

Every shining moment of the day was overshadowed by fear, and all Lizzie wanted to do was go home and

tell Emma. She always knew what was right and what
was wrong.

She didn't say much when she came back, being subdued and quiet. She dumped the nails in an old coffee can,
saying nothing. Mandy asked her what was wrong, so she
told her she had a stomachache and wanted to go home.

"You ate some of that medicine, Lizzie," Edna gasped.

"No, not for real. I just don't feel good. Besides, I saw
a snake on the trail, coming back up."

"A real one?"

"Just a little one."

"Do you want to go home?"

"Yeah."

Since it was getting late, they cleaned up, chattering
and laughing as usual. All except Lizzie, who was furiously blinking back tears. All she wanted to do was sit
on their bed with Emma in the soft glow of the kerosene
lamp and ask her if it was actually stealing to take two
handfuls of nails. She already knew what Emma would
say, but Emma would tell her what to do. That was the
nice, safe thing about having a big sister who was good.
She could help Lizzie a bit when she did crazy things
she should not have done. And Emma was so easy to
talk to, because she fully understood that Lizzie was not
the same as she was.

Dat and Mam didn't always understand that. She
wondered where you could buy a book for parents
to read about things like that, because Mam and Dat
needed one.

chapter 8

Serious Matters

Emma stood in front of the mirror, a soft pink towel wrapped around her shoulders. Her hair tumbled down her back in sleek, wet disarray as she struggled to make an even part in the middle of her head.

Her nightgown hung to the floor in soft, satiny folds. Tossing back her hair, she turned to look at Lizzie, who was curled on the bed, her face turned to the wall. Emma ran her fingers through her yellow plastic hairbrush, extracting all the loose hair, then tossing it into the yellow wicker wastebasket.

Lizzie was filthy. Her dress had dark smudges of pine tar on the back, and the hem was so soiled it was darker in color than the rest of it. Her legs were grimy with black earth—actually so stained that Emma could see the white line where her sneakers had been. Her hair was loose and straggly, with only a few remaining hairpins holding her hair in place. Her covering was long gone, Emma figured. She could not for the life of her see how Lizzie could stand to run around that woods, getting herself so dirty.

"Lizzie, it's your turn to take a bath. You may as well wash your hair right away," she said quietly.

"Mandy's in the tub," came the muffled reply, as Lizzie shifted her weight to be more comfortable.

Emma's eyes narrowed, and her mouth took on a firm look, as she surveyed the significant mound that was Lizzie. She certainly was not getting any thinner, which didn't seem to bother her at all. Emma had been watching her weight lately, because she would soon be thirteen years old, and it bothered her to be as chubby as when she was younger. But not Lizzie. She took three sandwiches in her lunch to school, more than the eighth grade boys, and Emma was terribly embarrassed by this. She wondered how to approach Lizzie about going on a diet so she wouldn't be offended. Oh well, sometimes you just had to tell someone what you thought, and if they flew off the handle, then they just did. Besides, Lizzie was her sister, and they told each other almost everything.

"Lizzie, you're so filthy. You're going to make our nice yellow bedspread as dirty as you are."

"Mandy's in the *tub!*" Lizzie yelled.

"Oh." Emma turned to check her complexion in the mirror. It was still smooth and soft, but lots of her friends were getting pimples and other blemishes on their faces. She could not imagine how that would be, having to put up with those nasty red spots on your face.

Lizzie stirred, sitting up on the bed. She wiped both eyes with the palms of her greasy hands, blinked, and sighed a ragged sigh. She coughed, scratching under her chin as she cleared her throat—almost nervously, it seemed to Emma.

"You're really grouchy, Lizzie," Emma ventured, though not unkindly.

"So? You were staring at me, and I guarantee you were thinking how fat and grubby I look," Lizzie said sourly, scratching her ribs.

"Quit scratching yourself."

"Maybe I have lice."

"I wouldn't be surprised."

Lizzie was planning on pouting, showing Emma all the disapproval she possibly could. But somehow they happened to look at each other exactly the same way, catching the humor in each other's eyes, and burst out laughing.

"Lizzie, go take your bath. Then we can talk."

So Lizzie yanked open her drawers, gathering her underwear and clean nightgown before shuffling off to the bathroom. Mandy was finished, sitting at the kitchen table, eating a dish of orange Jell-O. Lizzie could have gagged—that's how much she despised that slippery, low-calorie stuff. *Skinny Mandy*, she thought, feeling no better about her own size. She just didn't feel happy. Not one bit. She tried to tell herself it wasn't just because of the two handfuls of nails from the pallet shop. That was just silly. God really hardly noticed two handfuls of nails.

After her bath, she felt better, so she went to the kitchen, where Mandy was finishing her Jell-O.

"Mam, I'm going to bed. I'm really tired tonight."

Mam looked up from the book she was reading. "You do look tired, Lizzie. You play, or work—whatever it is—too hard up there on the ridge. I wish you wouldn't drag up those heavy pieces of lumber, because you could ruin your back."

"They're not that heavy, Mam. Don't worry."

Mam smiled, saying, "Good-night, Lizzie."

"Good-night, Mam."

"You're going to bed already?" Mandy asked, licking the back of her spoon.

"Mm-hmm."

"'Night."

"'Night."

Lizzie went off to her and Emma's bedroom, flinging the towel off her head. She yanked the hairbrush through the tangles, grimacing horribly, because the snarls were just awful.

"Ouch! Ow!"

"Lizzie, use conditioner, then it wouldn't be so hard to

get those snarls out," Emma said.

"It takes too long," Lizzie growled.

"Well then, suffer, because it would make a big difference if you would use some."

"It stinks."

"Hah-ah!

"Mm-hmm. I can't stand that slimy stuff."

They fell into a companionable silence, Lizzie brushing her hair and Emma reading a Trixie Belden book, lying on her stomach on the bed.

"Emma?"

"Hmm?"

"Do you think . . . do you suppose if a person would take two handfuls of nails out of a nailer, if their dat told them not to, do you think . . . I mean, do you even imagine God would have such a fit He would punish you a few minutes later?" Lizzie asked, chewing on her lower lip.

"What in the world are you talking about?" Emma asked.

"Put your book away, so you can hear what I'm saying," Lizzie said.

So Emma folded a corner of the page down to hold her place and slapped the book shut. She rolled over and sat up, pushing a pillow behind her back.

"You took nails out of Dat's nailer?"

"Well, Emma, now you have to listen. It was this way. Our cabins are looking kind of tumbledown and we were out of nails to fix them up. Nobody else would go get nails. So I went." Lizzie stopped, took a deep breath, and stared at the ceiling. "There's a spider."

"Get him, Lizzie. I hate spiders!"

"No, let him go. Those little black ones are cute."

"Then what?"

"Then I went. And there were no nails loose under the nailer, the kind we're allowed to keep if we pick them up. So I crawled up on a half stack of pallets and took two handfuls of bright, shiny new ones out of the steel box that rocks back and forth."

"And Dat said you're not allowed to?"

"Yes."

"Then what?"

"Then . . ." Lizzie paused. "You're not going to believe this. Then I saw a real snake, looking straight at me. Emma, it wasn't e-even funny. Snakes' eyes look exactly like the devil, and I was so afraid and so guilty, 'cause I stole, so . . . Did God put that snake there, or what?" she finished miserably.

"I don't know," Emma said wisely. "But probably the snake wouldn't have bothered you or made you so afraid if you wouldn't have been guilty about stealing."

"Do you still think taking something from your Dat is *real* stealing, not just taking? Remember the orange soda in the harness shop?" Lizzie asked.

"Yes, I do. Well, Lizzie, you will never learn. As much as you suffered about that soda, what's the difference?

Dat said you can't take those nails, and you did, so you stole *and* disobeyed," Emma finished.

"Should I tell Dat? He's going to be upset with me. And I'm so afraid he won't let us play on the ridge anymore that I just *can't* tell him. See, Emma, Dat isn't like he used to be in the harness shop. He's so busy and so tense or something, that he doesn't even have time to think about a few nails. He will never ever miss them. One teensy-weensy bit of nails towards the thousands of millions they use every day," she said.

Emma picked at the tufts of the yellow chenille bedspread, saying nothing.

"Emma, don't you ever do one thing wrong?" Lizzie burst out.

To Lizzie's surprise, Emma slowly and sadly nodded her head. And to her absolute astonishment, a tear slid slowly under her dark lashes, landing on her cheek, which turned a shade darker because of her shame. Slowly, Emma raised miserable eyes to Lizzie's and whispered, "Yes, Lizzie, I do. I doubt if I feel one bit better than you do."

"Emma!" Lizzie was so bewildered.

"Lizzie, I am honestly not one bit better than you. Remember how I always used to think I was? Well, maybe I was somewhat, but if you promise, cross your heart, you won't tell anyone, I'll tell you what I did."

"I won't. Promise—cross my heart," Lizzie breathed.

"You know I'm not very good at arithmetic in school? And you know how good Salina is?"

Lizzie nodded.

"Well, I copied four answers from her paper by looking over her shoulder. It was long column adding, and I
always get them wrong—or a bunch of them, anyway. So
I looked," Emma ended, quite ashamed of herself.

"Did you use the answers on your own paper?" Lizzie
asked.

"Yes. I should tell Teacher Barbara what I did, and
Mam, but I dread it so horribly that I just don't."

They sat in silence, Emma steadily picking at the
chenille tufts, and Lizzie staring at the hairbrush in her
hand.

"You always pray, Emma. I'm sure God has already
forgiven you. You're usually a good girl," Lizzie said.

"Oh yes, of course, I prayed. But why does it still
bother me so much?" Emma asked.

"I hardly pray right," Lizzie said.

"You should."

"I know, but . . . I can't understand, Emma. I always feel self-conscious on my knees. Almost like I'm
ashamed of God, or like someone will come in and see
me. Just like when you're in the bathroom. Why do I
feel that way?"

"You always were like that," Emma said.

"I know. So I don't pray very much."

"Did you ask God to forgive you for taking the nails?"

"No."

"Why not?"

"I don't know, Emma. Do you think He would even?
Would He if I didn't tell Dat?" Lizzie asked.

"I think so."

"How do you know?"

"We can't really know. We can't see God or know for sure. We just kind of depend on Him."

There was a long silence as the kerosene lamp glowed softly and steadily, casting a long shadow behind it. The little black spider crawled slowly across the ceiling, stopping and starting for reasons all its own. Lizzie drew her fingers through her hair, pulling it out and away from her face. She thought about God, wondering if He knew she wished she would not have taken the nails. He probably did. But should she tell Dat? She was so horribly afraid he would make them stop playing at the ridge. Everyone would blame her. Maybe he would let the others play anyway, and just make her stay at home for a few weeks. Or one week. Or maybe just two or three days. That wouldn't be so bad.

"I'm going to tell Dat," she announced.

Emma gave her a steady look. "Are you?"

"Yes. Right now."

"Lizzie, wait. If you do, then I have to tell Teacher Barbara. I just can't!" Emma wailed.

"Emma, you don't have to. What she doesn't know won't hurt her. If she knows nothing about it, and Salina knows nothing about it, and you probably still had some wrong, then don't worry," Lizzie said, trying her best to help Emma.

"But God knows—that's why my conscience is so bothered," Emma said.

"God might not care. He might not be the one who makes you feel so miserable. What is a conscience, anyway?"

"I don't know exactly. But if something bothers you, I think you need to do what is right."

"I know!"

"What?"

"Write her a letter!"

"Why?"

"Well, it's much easier to write than looking someone square in the face and telling them you did something dumb like that," Lizzie said stoutly.

"Looking at answers isn't dumber than taking those nails!" Emma said, a bit huffily.

"They're both dumb, that's for sure," Lizzie said gloomily. She threw herself down on the bed and put her chin in her hands. They could hear Dat and Mam conversing in low tones as Mam rocked Jason, the rocker squeaking with each backward movement. She still had the blue platform rocker with the carved swans' heads for arms, and it only squeaked on the way back, not forward. It was so peaceful here in Jefferson County, since Dat was making more money. They did not have to worry that Mam and Dat would argue in the evening, because they had very little to worry about.

Mam had told the girls they were planning to build a house on top of the basement house. They would live upstairs, and their basement would be just that—a basement. Mam was so happy, because they could have a large, new home, and she could have new windows that kept out the cold. She so loved African violets, and she told Emma she would fill the east windows with them.

Lizzie remembered when times were not as good. She

was always nervous, worrying about their conversation in the evening when she was trying to sleep.

She heard Dat's soft laugh, so she sat up and told Emma she was going. She opened the door quietly and slipped into the living room. Dat smiled at her, putting down his paper. She held his gaze, walking over to the sofa, and sat down beside him.

Very seriously, she said, "Dat, I took two handfuls of nails out of the nailer. I'm sorry."

"I saw you," Dat said, just as seriously.

"You did?" Lizzie couldn't believe it.

"Yes. And . . . I figured any girl who climbs up a stack of pallets and reaches into those moving nailer boxes has more nerve than sense. That was really not a smart thing to do, Lizzie."

Lizzie searched Dat's face. His eyes were deep gray-blue and serious, but not quite strictly serious enough to be angry. His mouth was not held in a straight, thin line; it was almost smiling, but not quite. So Lizzie was happy, because she figured he was actually kind of proud of her for being so capable of doing something almost dangerous without fear.

"It wasn't scary. I wanted the nails too badly."

"You are one determined person," he said.

"I . . . I won't do it again," she said, pleating the folds of her housecoat as she watched his face.

"Why didn't you ask me?" Dat questioned.

"You weren't there."

"I was in the break room. Did you forget there's a window in it?"

"O-oh. There is," Lizzie said slowly, as it dawned on her.

Dat threw back his head and laughed. Then he reached over and put his arm around her shoulder, squeezing her arm, because he just couldn't help it. Lizzie punched his arm with her fist and said, "You think it's funny!"

Mam smiled at them from her rocker, saying, "Lizzie, I'm just glad you told Dat about it. At least it bothered you. Good for you!"

"Yeah, I guess," Lizzie said, almost shyly, as her lashes swept her cheeks.

"Don't do it again, okay? One thing, it isn't safe, and how can we make a profit on our pallets if you take all the nails?" Dat asked.

"We don't take them *all*."

"Just about."

Lizzie made a funny face, because now he was teasing her. He smiled and she told them both good-night.

"Aren't you going to eat cheese and pretzels with me?" Dat asked.

Lizzie desperately wanted to, but she pitied Emma all alone in their bedroom, feeling so worried. "No, not tonight."

She closed the door firmly and twirled her way to the bed. She flung herself down and said, "Emma, he wasn't even mad! I think he was actually amazed that I climbed up that stack of pallets."

"Do you have to stay home from the ridge for a while?" Emma asked.

"No."

"Boy, he must have been in a good mood!"

"He was."

They lay in silence until Emma got up, opened the nightstand drawer, and got out her pink rose stationery. She put it on one knee and began to write.

Lizzie watched her, thinking how much Emma was growing up. She didn't look like the same ordinary, chubby little girl she used to be. Her neck looked thinner and her eyes seemed bigger and farther apart. Maybe that's what dieting did—just gave you a long, skinny neck and bigger eyes.

Well, Lizzie was not going to go on a diet anytime soon. That was too hard. How in the whole world could you drag slabs of wood to the ridge, pound nails, and carry wood without lots of good food? Mam thought Lizzie should lose weight, because she said if she'd try, she would buy diet soda for her. That almost persuaded Lizzie, but still . . . what was one can of diet soda if you were only allowed one sandwich with it? And that Roman Meal bread Mam and Emma ate was so thin and full of seeds, you might as well go out and stick your tongue in the birdfeeder. Same thing. No, she most certainly was not going to go on a diet.

Emma bit her lip, erased, and muttered to herself. "Here," she said, handing the letter to Lizzie.

Dear Teacher Barbara, she read.

I looked over Salina Renno's shoulder, and copied some of her answers for long column add. I am very

sorry. I promise never to do it again.
Your loving pupil,
Emma

"Your loving pupil?" Lizzie asked, raising an eyebrow.

"Well, it will help if she thinks I love her. I do, too," Emma said.

Lizzie started giggling. She shook quietly, trying not to hurt her sister's feelings. Emma watched, trying to be serious, too, but Lizzie's giggles caught on and before they knew it, they were both laughing uncontrollably.

Emma gasped and wiped her eyes. "Lizzie, why are we laughing? It isn't even funny," she said.

"Well, E-Emma, you . . . didn't have to . . .!" and Lizzie's giggle fit only increased. After they quit laughing, Lizzie told Emma it really was a very nice letter — there was nothing wrong with it at all. She just didn't really think of Emma as quite that loving to her teacher.

After Emma had tucked the letter carefully into a pink envelope and wrote "Teacher Barbara" on it, she sighed. Then she got out a thin white scarf and tied it over her head before she turned the kerosene lamp low, got on her knees beside the bed, folded her hands, and said her prayers, quietly and devoutly.

Lizzie watched. Maybe next year she would be good like Emma. It was just an unspoken fact of their lives. Emma covered her head as Mam instructed her, knelt, and prayed, while Lizzie just rolled over and thought her prayers to God — if she remembered. Neither girl was self-conscious or judgmental of the other; it was just how they were.

After Emma had blown out the lamp, covered herself, and was comfortable, Lizzie asked, "Do you feel better?"

"Oh, my, yes!" Emma said.

"Do you want me to give it to Teacher Barbara?"

"Will you?"

"Mm-hmm."

Lizzie figured if she could climb up a stack of pallets, she could give a letter to the teacher. The floor was a lot flatter.

chapter 9

The Twins

Emma told Lizzie very seriously one evening that Mam was going to have another baby soon. Lizzie watched the leaves on the silver maple bend and sway, some of them dancing almost ridiculously in little cross currents of air. She felt a sickening thud way down in her stomach. A sadness fell over the warm summer evening, mostly which caused her to feel guilty, knowing how much Emma probably anticipated this event.

Lizzie did not like newborn babies. To tell Emma that outright would never work, because she would be appalled. Emma did not understand things like that. She loved to learn to sew, whistling under her breath, which proved she loved what she was doing. Anywhere there were babies, Emma was watching the mothers, hoping to have a chance of holding one.

Lizzie bit on her thumbnail, mustering all the bravado she could, saying, "Really?" It came out in a high-pitched, false quaver, and Emma looked at her sharply.

Lizzie pulled up her knees, covering them tightly with the skirt of her dress and her gray apron. She stretched her big toe, followed by all the rest of them. She wondered why it was easier to stick your little toe out so much farther than the others. Probably because it was way out on the end. But then, so was her big toe, and she couldn't stick that one way out. Toes were funny things.

"Lizzie, talk 'chide,'" Emma said.

"Chide" was a Dutch word, meaning "right" or "decent," anything proper or good. It was a familiar phrase, but tonight it angered Lizzie. Why did Emma have to spoil a perfectly good summer evening by saying they were going to have a baby?

"I did. I mean, are we really going to have another one? Jason is still a baby, sort of. And besides, he's finally cute, and now we don't have to have more, do we?" Lizzie asked.

"Lizzie, you just aren't normal! Why don't you like babies more? You should be ashamed of yourself," Emma said.

"I guess," Lizzie said slowly.

"You could grow up and be glad. It's a blessing to have children," Emma told her. "Quit stretching your toes."

"No. I like to stretch them."

"Lizzie, when Mam goes to the hospital, you have to help me clean up the house and listen when I say something. Mandy and Jason are better than you are sometimes."

"Well, Emma, you . . . Okay, I will. But you are not
allowed to be so bossy. If you don't make me do things
I don't want to do it's not half as bad. Like take out the
garbage in the dark and stuff like that."

Silence fell over the yard as twilight approached.
Mandy was in the back yard, throwing a plastic ball for
Jason to bat with a large, plastic baseball bat. Lizzie
could hear his shrieks of excitement as he tried to whack
the ball. She felt so sorry for Jason, thinking of a new
baby, but she said nothing.

Maybe she wasn't normal, like Emma said. Oh,
she knew she was normal as far as her brain, because
schoolwork was not hard, but maybe not normal where
babies were concerned. That was something new to worry about, seeing that Emma seriously thought so.

She watched as the lady who lived across the street
opened the door of her breezeway and let out three of
her white, long-haired cats. They were as beautiful as
cats go, but Lizzie didn't care much for cats, either.

The cats padded their way around the yard, lifting
each paw delicately, as if the green grass might stain
their perfectly white feet. The lady turned, going back
into her house.

See, Lizzie thought, *that's just the thing with cats and
babies.* Cats could get run over and killed, and babies
could fall off the couch or choke on their bottle, or get
a fever and have to go to the hospital. They could die.
Sometimes babies screamed for a very long time, their
faces contorted into a most awful-looking thing. Some
babies opened their mouth so wide you could easily see

their tonsils, which were bright red and looked like a
kidney bean. They just were not something Lizzie was
very happy to be thinking about.

She sighed, looking sideways at Emma. "Emma, do
you think it will be a boy or a girl?" she asked, trying to
sound normal and enthused.

"Probably a brother for Jason would be best."

"Mm-hmm."

The conversation ended again, because all Lizzie
could think of was Jason's huge red face and swollen
eyes when he was a baby. But she kept quiet, because
that was not a nice thought. God made every baby
special, so she shouldn't even think Jason was homely
when he was a baby, but Lizzie still hadn't figured out
how to think other thoughts if one like that came into
your mind.

Emma slapped at a mosquito. Darkness was approaching and the sound of the night insects chased all
thoughts from Lizzie's head. She watched the fireflies,
slapped at another mosquito, and sighed again.

"Let's go in."

"Okay. Mam probably wants me to bathe Jason
anyway."

.   .   .   .   .   .

And so, on a midsummer's evening, as the heat gave
way to the coolness of night, Lizzie was startled when
Mam knocked quietly on their bedroom door. She was
dressed in the clothes she wore to go away, and smelled
of the best talcum powder she used when she was going
somewhere important.

"Emma."

Emma sat straight up, completely at attention.

"What?"

"Dat and I are going to the hospital." She came over and put her arms around Emma, then gathered Lizzie in at the same time. There were tears in her eyes, but she was smiling bravely as she told them to be good for Esther. She was going to stay for a few days.

Mam's covering shone white in the glow of the lamp, and her dark hair looked sleek and clean. She told the girls there were special treats in the pantry for their meals, and Emma could show Esther how to start the gas motor to do the laundry.

"Bye, Mam," Emma whispered.

"Bye, girls," Mam said softly.

"Bye," whispered Lizzie.

Mam closed the door softly. They heard Dat talking in a low, serious voice, then the kitchen door closed, and a car engine started and backed down the gravel drive.

An overwhelming feeling of loneliness crept over Lizzie. She just couldn't bear the thought of Mam feeling weak and crying because her baby wouldn't sleep. Why did they need another one?

"Mam seems almost like an angel," Emma said.

"Why?"

"I don't know. She just does."

"She smells good."

"I know."

They lay together in silence, till they heard the kitchen door open as Esther and Lavina come in, talking softly.

They lit a lamp, carrying it across the living room to Mam and Dat's bedroom, before closing the door, preparing for the night.

Lizzie felt worse and worse. She felt so bad, a huge lump rose in her throat and a lone tear slid sideways across her nose. She swiped at it angrily, feeling guilty because of the disturbing feeling about babies. Besides, she was too old to be crying, just because Mam and Dat went to the hospital. She squeezed her eyes shut as tightly as she could, trying to push the threatening tears back inside her eyes.

Emma sniffed loudly and sighed. The last thing Lizzie remembered before falling asleep was wondering why Emma sniffed.

. . . . .

The next morning she felt bewildered, hearing a strange voice talking to Dat. He said something and there was a loud exclamation of "Melvin!"

Then Lizzie heard Dat's genuine laugh of happiness. Emma jumped out of bed, Lizzie at her heels. They threw open the bedroom door and hurried across the living room and into the kitchen.

"What? What is it?" Emma asked, quite beside herself in excitement.

"Emma, we have twins! Two babies! Girls!" Dat said, smiling broadly.

Emma put both hands up to her mouth, her eyes opening wide in total surprise. "Twins! Dat!" she shrieked, after she found her voice.

Lizzie stood behind Emma and stared at Dat, her mouth falling open. She was completely speechless. Twin babies. Two of them. Her emotions were so mixed up, she sat down weakly and let her arms rest limply at her sides. Mandy came quietly from the living room and stood at Lizzie's side.

"What?" she asked.

"Mandy, we have twins! You have two baby sisters. They have dark hair and look exactly alike. They're identical twins, meaning they look almost perfectly the same," Dat beamed.

Mandy blinked her big green eyes, unable to concentrate so early in the morning. "You mean . . . two babies at one time?" she asked softly.

"Yes. They're tiny, but both doing well. Mam has to stay in the hospital for a few days, but they'll soon be home."

"But . . . but we have only one crib," Emma said, practically.

"They'll easily fit in one, as tiny as they are," Dat assured her.

"What did you name them?" Lizzie remembered to ask, finding her voice.

"We're not sure yet. What do you girls want to name them?" Dat asked.

So they all sat around the kitchen table, discussing names. Dat wanted to name one after his sister, but Mam insisted on naming one after her mother, Mommy Miller, who had passed away recently. Dat thought, too, one should be named Katherine after her mother, but Susan didn't rhyme very well.

"Sarah and Susan," Emma suggested.

"No, one has to be Katherine," Dat said.

Lizzie didn't say much. Dat would probably name his baby Susan, whether it rhymed with Katherine or not, because that's how he was. If he insisted on something, usually that's how it went, because he was Dat. Lizzie thought Katherine and Katrina would be so cute, but it was too English. Katrina was an English name.

Amish people picked old-fashioned Bible names, mostly, or named their babies after a relative, as they had done in the Old Testament. It was considered custom to never stray too far from plain Bible names, although some different names were acceptable, too.

So Lizzie didn't say what she thought about Katrina, because that name was much too fancy for Dat.

After breakfast, Lavina and Esther scrubbed and cleaned. The gas motor hummed continuously as they washed bedding, baby clothes, and rugs. Emma swept and dusted while Esther washed windows. They even waxed the kitchen floor, which seemed a bit unnecessary to Lizzie. Who would notice the shine, anyway?

After lunch, they all took a rest, with drinks of grape Kool-Aid on the porch. Lavina was swinging on the porch swing, her brown arms slung across the back.

"It's *hot*!" she exclaimed. "We should go to the river!"

"We never went swimming," Emma said.

"I'll take you. You would love it," Lavina said.

Lizzie narrowed her eyes, pleating her apron with her fingers. She was not going to go to the river, that was for sure. She could not swim, and that current would take you clear to the ocean, Debbie had told her. And besides, if she was still not drowned after being carried along by the river's current for miles and miles, she most definitely would be by the waves in the ocean.

She had a picture in her history book of five men in a rowboat in the ocean on great swells of water, leaning way back to steady their craft. That picture was branded in Lizzie's imagination, so Lavina may as well forget it. She was not going swimming.

As they sat on the porch, the familiar figure of Debbie came hurrying across the yard. She was laughing with delight, having heard about the twins.

She grabbed Lizzie's hands and twirled her around. "Whee! Lizzie, you have two sisters at once!" she said, laughing. "I can't wait to see them!"

Lizzie laughed at Debbie's enthusiasm, assuring her they would be home in a few days. Debbie flopped on the porch swing, fanning her face with her hands.

"It's hot."

"We should go to the river with a picnic lunch," Esther said.

"No!" Lizzie said loudly.

"What's wrong with you?" Debbie asked.

"I can't swim."

"We can teach you."

"No. Not in the river."

Debbie's brown legs were covered with mosquito bites. She had so many, they looked like chicken pox or the measles. She would sit and scratch them until they bled, then pick at the scabs. That was just how Debbie was. Lizzie and Mandy often told her not to pick the scabs, but she would anyway.

So now she pulled up one leg, picking at a mosquito bite.

"Don't, Debbie."

Debbie wet her finger in her mouth and rubbed it across the mosquito bite. She looked at Lizzie and told her the river wouldn't hurt her. They always took big black tractor tire inner tubes, so there was nothing to be afraid of, because there was no way you could drown with an inner tube.

But Lizzie refused to budge. Besides, Mam was in the hospital with two babies, and that was enough to think about in one day, without learning to swim in that horrible, brown, frightening river.

.   .   .   .   .

The blue station wagon pulled into the gravel drive two days later. The house was spotless, dusted and shining, as Mam walked slowly through the kitchen door. She looked pale and so thin, Lizzie could hardly believe it was Mam. She sank weakly onto the sofa and smiled a tired smile in the girls' direction.

Dat and Lavina each carried a small pink-covered bundle. Lavina was so excited she was almost on her tiptoes as she lifted a corner to peep at the tiny baby underneath.

"O-oh!" she squealed.

Emma hurried to take Dat's baby, lifting the corner of her blanket. She became completely speechless. Lizzie

ventured over far enough to take a peek from a safe
distance.

She saw a very small head covered with heavy black
hair. Two perfect little half moons were closed across
dark red cheeks, with a tiny nose and mouth perfectly
aligned underneath. Lizzie was amazed to see the black
hair was perfectly straight—it was not curly at all. That
was a tremendous relief, because there was just no way
you could comb a girl's hair if it was as curly as Jason's.

Slowly, she sat beside Emma on the couch, peering
into the second pink blanket. It was simply a repeat of
the first baby—a perfectly formed little head covered
with black hair. Not one curl in sight. Lizzie sighed, gaz-
ing at Dat with disbelief in her eyes.
"They're cute!" she said softly.

Dat smiled back, including
Mandy in his attentive concern.

He was always careful to make sure everyone felt included when there was a new baby. Jason was seated on his lap, looking as if he could burst into tears, as he was so bewildered.

Lizzie's heart went out to Jason in that moment. She loved him so much—curly hair, big frightened eyes, and all. She got up and walked over to Dat, saying, "Come, Jason—do you want to see the babies?"

He climbed down off Dat's lap and followed Lizzie, peeping into the blanket to meet his new sister. He looked closely, then peered up at Emma, saying, "They look like monkeys."

Everyone burst out laughing, including Mam, until Jason became self-conscious, trying to hide his eyes.

The days that followed were all a blur of babies, bottles, loads and loads of laundry, and a very tired Mam. Lizzie even helped, rocking these tiny little ones and giving them a warm bottle of formula whenever she was needed.

She still did not like it when they cried. She soon found out that these small, petite babies could cry just as loudly as Jason did when he was tiny. And when they cried in full volume, their tonsils looked like kidney beans, too.

But she did learn to hold a baby, deciding

which end was up, even feeling comfortable rocking them. Emma was a much better helper, because Lizzie tired of it so easily. But Mam told her she did good and she would be a good mother someday, which made Lizzie feel so very much better about babies in general.

Sometimes even Mam was confused about which baby was Katherine, and which one was Susan, so she put a pink safety pin on Katherine's blanket and a blue one on Susan's.

Dat shook his head, saying, "Five girls. We have five girls," as if he was trying to believe it. "Poor Jason."

Mam spent plenty of time including Jason in her care, telling him stories and singing to him while she rocked babies. Often Lizzie found Mam with a twin on one arm and Jason on the other, fully relaxed, enjoying her children. Emma was the one who swept, mopped, dusted, and yelled at everyone to put their stuff away.

The basement home was getting full, no doubt about it, so Dat set about drawing serious plans for a new house, which only increased everyone's excitement.

chapter 10

The River

The thermometer on the porch reached ninety-five degrees one day. There had been no rain for a while, parching the grass in the yard and curling the corn-stalks in the field beside it. Every morning the sun rose, a huge orange ball, waiting to heat up the earth as noon approached. The heat shimmered over the macadam road and the stifling humidity felt as if you had to move the mountain to breathe easier.

Even the twin babies were dressed only in a diaper and a little white tee-shirt. They were still so tiny, Lizzie could hardly see they had grown at all in a few weeks' time. But Mam put a cookie sheet on the kitchen scales, carefully folding a blanket on top before balancing each baby to see how much they weighed.

"Oh, yes, Lizzie, they're gaining," she said, expertly flipping Katherine onto her own blanket. "Only a few ounces, but they're doing alright."

"Mam, their legs are so scrawny. I can't see how they can be gaining," Lizzie said, worriedly, spanning one little leg with her fingers.

"They are—don't you worry. Do you want to give Katherine her bottle?" she asked.

"Do I have to?"

"Unless you can get Mandy to. Emma's washing."

"I was going to ride Dolly."

"Lizzie, aren't you a little too heavy for that pony?"

Lizzie shrugged her shoulders, taking Katherine from Mam. "Where's her bottle?"

Mam brought it, and Lizzie held the nipple against the tiny little mouth. Katherine sucked greedily, downing an ounce in no time, then Lizzie had to hold her over her shoulder to burp her. She hated burping babies, because they scrooched way down in an uncomfortable little ball, and made funny grunting sounds, sucking on their fists, doing anything but burp. Lizzie rocked and rocked, patting the baby gently on the back, feeling more and more upset.

"Mam, she doesn't burp," she said loudly.

"Here, Susie's asleep. I'll finish her," Mam said.

"Not 'Susie,'" Lizzie said sharply. "Susan."

"No, I like 'Susie.' We'll probably call Katherine 'KatieAnn,' like my mom," Mam said.

Lizzie sniffed indignantly, slamming the screen door on her way to the barn. Mam was so plain. Emma, Lizzie, Mandy, Susie, Katie. Every name was so Amish, except Jason. She did not like any name especially, except Mandy.

Dolly nickered as Lizzie walked up to the fence. She caught her halter, murmuring hello to her old pony. Dolly was almost blind now. Dat had showed her the spots in the dark black part of her eye that had turned white, meaning there was no vision at all. But that didn't matter to Lizzie; she loved Dolly just the same.

Slipping the bridle over Dolly's head, she slung the reins across the pony's neck, before hopping onto her back. Dolly was small and fat, so it wasn't hard to slip onto her round back. They headed out to the trails in the pasture, walking carefully among the dips and rocky places.

There was just something so special about riding. Lizzie loved the smell that wafted up from the pony and the heavy mane bobbing in front of her, with the delicate ears pricked up to hear Lizzie's command. She loved to reach back and stroke Dolly's sleek haunches as they meandered along the pasture trails.

She stopped Dolly under a maple tree to let her rest. Flies swarmed around them in the morning heat, bees droned in the bushes beside the barbed wire fence, and birds called to each other from the fencerow.

Lizzie was content and relaxed, feeling at ease with her world once again, after the twins' birth. Mam could easily take care of them by herself, which was an immense relief. They didn't cry as much as Jason had, so Mam didn't even get the blues at all.

The only thing that worried Lizzie was thinking about these babies walking. How would they ever keep them off the road?

There was a loud shout from down by the barn, and Lizzie looked up to see Debbie yelling and waving from the fence. She urged Dolly back to the barn, even trotting for a while, until Dolly stumbled, so Lizzie pulled her back to a walk.

"What?" Lizzie asked, when she was close enough.

"C'mon, Lizzie. Lavina and Esther are taking us to the river for a picnic. We're going swimming 'cause it's so hot," she said excitedly.

Lizzie's stomach lurched. She had always wanted to learn to swim, but she really did not want to try in the river. It was the current that scared her, the unrelenting steady flow of that deep water, all headed in one direction, taking whatever it could carry along to the ocean. She did not want to admit to Debbie that she was afraid, but she was terrified of that current.

"Did Mam say?" she asked.

"She said you and Mandy can go. Emma has to stay here," Debbie said.

"Emma would probably rather stay here anyway," Lizzie said, hopping off Dolly's back, unbuckling the leather chin strap and pulling off the bridle in one swift motion. She patted Dolly's neck before she went off to find the water trough in the barn.

"You sure Mam said we can go?" she asked again, half hoping Mam would say no.

"Yeah, Lizzie, I *asked*," Debbie said impatiently.

So Lizzie and Mandy found themselves in the kitchen, spreading mayonnaise on slices of bread, carefully arranging bologna and cheese on top. Debbie leaned against the counter, eating a piece of cheese and exclaiming over the molasses cookies.

"Mmmm, they look *so* good!" she said, rolling her eyes.

"They are good," Lizzie assured her.

"Who made them?"

"Emma."

"Emma?"

"She loves to bake. She even made a chocolate jelly roll."

"Wow!"

Lizzie had learned to love Debbie whole-heartedly. She was almost like a sister to her, like Mandy, except sometimes even better. They played on the ridge together, skated, and went sled riding. Everything they did with Uncle Eli's children included Debbie, and often her

younger sister, Jeanie, too. Mam and Dat both loved
Debbie, too, never disapproving of her because she
was English. Mam told the girls they must never think
they were better than others, English people as well as
Amish. "God made us all different, and yet we are the
same," Mam would say wisely, nodding her head. So
Lizzie never thought twice about accepting Debbie into
their lives.

Of course, their lives were different in lots of ways.
Debbie went to a huge elementary school near Marion, where they learned the Pledge of Allegiance and
had gym classes, with huge crowds of English children. She had a television set to watch, all the Pepsi
with ice cubes in it she wanted, and fancy food she
heated in the oven that came already made, out of a
box. When she went away, it was in her mother's fancy gold car.

But there was nothing Debbie liked better than a
ride with Dolly in the cart, or eating Mam's homemade
chocolate cakes. "She would live with us if we would
let her," Lizzie often told Mam. But Mam didn't allow
her to be there all the time, mostly because the girls
had work to do. But most days, for a few hours, Debbie was included in their days unless she had other
plans.

Their lunches were packed, swimdresses and towels
rolled into a canvas tote bag, and they were off with
Lavina, Esther, and Edna. The sun was so hot, they had
to wear sneakers to walk to the river, because the black,
bubbly tar hurt their feet too much to go barefoot. They

chattered together about the depth of the river, how cold the water was, why it was brown, and how soon you couldn't touch the bottom.

Lizzie hung back, feeling sick to her stomach — she was so afraid. Along with the fear, she had a deep determination not to let it show, because no one else seemed to be even one tiny bit frightened or nervous. So she kept it to herself.

They walked past the empty schoolhouse, grass growing tall along the fence. There were about eight or nine huge workhorses in the pasture surrounding the little white schoolhouse, so the grass stayed cut, almost like a lawn. After they passed the school, the macadam stopped, leaving only a dirt road. Lizzie was glad for her sneakers then, because the huge gravel would have hurt her feet worse than the hot black tar.

They passed the Swarey farm, the large red barn standing close to the dirt road. The big white house with a green roof was situated behind the barn and corncribs, up a gentle slope, surrounded by large poles with white purple martin houses on them.

They rounded a curve and the river was in plain sight, running swift and deep beside a cool green line of trees on the opposite bank. The grass was all mowed perfectly by an English man on a riding lawn mower on their side of the river, because the Fish and Game Commission owned the land. They kept everything very nice, even log privies and a dock to tie a boat. Willow tree branches hung almost to the water's surface, swaying and bending in the hot summer breeze.

"Let's eat first!" Debbie suggested. "I'm hungry. I only had one piece of cheese at Lizzie's house."

"No, Debbie," Lavina said. "If we go swimming too soon after we eat, we could get cramps."

"Not if you walk around first."

But Esther and Lavina insisted. So they went to the hot, insect-infested privies and changed. It was so hot inside, it felt like an oven, because there were no windows, only light-colored corrugated plastic. Swarms of houseflies, wasps, bees, and other assorted insects banged and buzzed against the plastic.

Lizzie hung back nervously as they made their way to the river, watching as Lavina and Esther waded into the clear water. Debbie ran in, full force, flopped on her stomach, and started to swim out into the current.

Lizzie gasped. "Debbie!" she screamed, without thinking.

Esther and Lavina looked sharply at Lizzie. "Shhh!" they warned her.

Lizzie felt terrible. There was Debbie, paddling out way, way too far, and all she had meant to do was save her. Then Lavina and Esther had to act like that. She was so humiliated that she sat down on the grass, wrapping a towel around her shoulders and pouted. *Okay, then, let Debbie drown*, she thought. It didn't help matters one bit to see Mandy wade at the water's edge. Esther helped her out into deeper water, splashing her to help her become acquainted with the cold river water. Mandy's eyes were big and scared, Lizzie could tell, but she bravely ventured in deeper with the bigger girls.

Debbie was paddling around happily, almost in the middle of the river. She looked relaxed and happy, floating on her back, before flipping over and swimming back in.

"Lizzie, come on in. The water isn't a bit cold," she yelled.

"What's wrong with you, Lizzie?" Edna asked. "Didn't you ever go swimming at all?"

"No!" Lizzie yelled.

"Never?"

"No! Where would we have gone? We had no place to swim," Lizzie answered defensively.

"Well, we didn't know that," Lavina apologized. "No wonder you're scared."

"I am not scared!" Lizzie shouted, getting up and stomping off to the privies, the towel flapping behind her like a robe. She slammed the heavy log door of the privy and sat down, wishing she was at home. Why didn't she tell Debbie she had a headache or a backache, or anything other than coming here to this horrible place?

She watched the bees trying desperately to find their way out, some of them having died weeks ago. She wondered why the insects didn't have more brains in the first place and watch when the door opened, then fly out to freedom, instead of killing themselves by flailing their delicate wings against the plastic. They were stupid. After a while the thought entered her mind that maybe she was the same. She refused to let go of her worries and fears, not even thinking about the possibility of enjoying the river if she would let Esther and Lavina help her.

Mandy was a lot smaller and skinnier, and the river had not washed her away. She had to stop being afraid if there was nothing to be afraid of. She was too embarrassed to go back out, so she stayed where she was, her chin in her hands, wondering what to do, or how long a person could survive in two hundred degrees with a bunch of half-dead insects.

After that, another thought entered her mind. The only thing keeping her in this little prison was her pride. That was dumb, too. So she got up, pulled the towel around her shoulders, and walked resolutely across the freshly mown green grass.

"Here! Here! We're over here!" Debbie called, waving both hands to catch Lizzie's attention. They had come out of the water, and were spreading a tablecloth on a rustic-looking picnic table. Lizzie waved and hurried over. *Good, they're going to eat, so I don't have to worry about going swimming right away,* she thought.

Lavina was unpacking everyone's lunch and mixing up the food, so they were allowed to pick whatever they wanted. Lizzie chose Aunt Mary's sandwiches, because the bread was homemade. It was sliced thicker and was more chewy, with a thick brown crust. They piled three

pieces of chopped ham in the center, with a generous
spread of mayonnaise, which was the best sandwich
Lizzie had ever tasted.

They drank cold grape juice from paper cups and ate
thick wedges of Aunt Mary's cherry pie. Potato chips,
molasses cookies, Grandpa cookies with caramel frosting, Oreo cookies, cheese curls, tiny sweet pickles from
a pint jar, and cheese popcorn. It was a picnic fit for a
king, and Lizzie told Debbie so.

Debbie laughed. "Kings would never eat food like
this!" she said.

"You don't know."

They all decided if a king was really hungry, he would
eat this food, which made Lizzie feel better. To her, nothing was better than picnic food, like sandwiches and
potato chips, eaten outdoors.

They sat around the picnic table, talking about all
kinds of subjects, watching boats if one made its way
up or down the river. Sometimes, a small boat without a
motor would go past, men rowing it with oars, their fishing poles sticking out the back.

After an hour was up, they all headed back into
the water. Debbie splashed in as usual, but Edna and
Mandy stayed with Lizzie. The water swirled around
her ankles first, which was surprisingly warm. Lizzie
had thought the water would be much colder. After the
water was above her knees, she could tell the current
was not as strong as it looked. It just went past so slowly
you could barely tell it was moving.

After she discovered that, nothing would hold her back. Before she knew what had happened, the water was up to her neck, and she was bouncing along on her tiptoes, her arms held out, almost as if she was swimming. It was a most lovely feeling. She had never been in water this deep, so she was amazed at how light she felt.

They splashed, kicked, and laughed as the hot afternoon sun bore down on the river. Lizzie was still a bit cautious about getting her head wet, because she most certainly was not going under water; she didn't care what Debbie and Edna said.

She was astounded when Mandy pinched her nose tightly with her thumb and forefinger, dipping her whole head underwater. When she lifted it, water streamed from her hair and into her eyes, which were held tightly shut. Debbie clapped her hands and cheered, while Mandy wiped the water from her eyes, laughing.

If Mandy can do it, so can I, Lizzie thought. She held her nose, but forgot to take a deep breath. When she lowered her head and the water rushed around her ears, she was so shocked at the caved-in feeling, she gasped. Suddenly, her mouth and nose were filled with river water. It felt as if a whole gallon of cold water was running into her throat, and it smelled like mud and fish.

She came up, spluttering and coughing. To her chagrin, everyone started laughing, pounding her back until she almost fell in again. It was awful. Water ran out of her nose and she could not catch her breath. She gasped and coughed, water flying in every direction as she struggled to keep her footing.

"What happened?" Edna asked.

Lizzie shook her head, continuing her coughing.

"Were you trying to be a fish? Are you sure there are no minnows in your ears?" Esther teased.

Even though Lizzie felt like crying, she laughed bravely with the others. She would have to remember to take a deep breath. She looked out over the surface of the river, amazed that the water could seem so friendly. It did not scare her anymore, even if she swallowed some. That was her fault, not the river's, because she had forgotten to hold her breath.

"Minnows can't get in your ears, can they?" she asked, after she had caught her breath.

"No," Lavina said. "Stop telling her that."

"Are you going to try going underwater again?" asked Edna.

"Not today," Lizzie said, shaking her head.

But by the time the afternoon was over, she had ducked her head under the water twice, without swallowing any. She was so happy about learning to like the river that she could hardly contain her joy.

As they packed their food back into the containers, Lizzie told Debbie she didn't know which was the most fun, skating or swimming, playing on the ridge or sled riding, riding Dolly or driving her in the cart.

"Debbie, I mean it; since we live here, there are so many fun things to do, I can hardly stand it!" Lizzie said, emphasizing her point by throwing her arms wide.

"Do you like to live here?" Debbie asked.

"Oh, I love it. There are so many things to do, a day is hardly long enough. But you know what, Debbie? There is one thing we didn't do yet this summer," Lizzie said, catching her tee-shirt and tugging.

"What?"

"Build a tunnel in the hay!"

"Yay!"

"We forgot!"

So the walk home did not seem long, even if they were hot and tired. They planned the tunnel and the house at the end of it, what they would call it, and what kind of food they would have to eat.

As they walked closer to Debbie's house, she became very serious.

"What about Jeanie?"

"She's too little."

"Mom's going to yell at me if we don't let Jeanie play, too."

"What are we going to do?"

After discussing the matter seriously, they decided Debbie would ask her mother if she could spend the night with them. They would not mention the hay house at all. Besides, Dat had not told them they were allowed to sleep there. He was pretty particular about his barn and haymow, so they better not plan anything for sure before Dat said it was okay.

"Bye!" Debbie waved as she turned into her short drive.

"Bye, Debbie!" Lizzie and Mandy waved back, saying good-bye to their cousins as they crossed their own yard.

"Thank you for taking us!" Lizzie shouted.

"You're welcome!" Edna yelled, walking backward to wave at them.

Lizzie hopped and skipped for a short time, because she didn't know how else to express her happiness. She guessed if she didn't skip, she'd just have to turn a cartwheel, and she was far too old for that. Surely she was having the best summer of her life.

Grape Kool-Aid
&
Chocolate Cake

Lizzie and Mandy had more chores in the summertime, because there was the yard and garden work. Mam's garden had lots of weeds in it this summer, which really wasn't her fault with the twins being born and all.

Two days a week, a girl named Sadie Peachey came to help with the work. She hoed the garden, picked and canned tomatoes, mowed the grass, and cleaned flower beds. Sadie was a hard worker, and Emma often worked with her, learning things like canning pickles, or turning basket after basket of beautiful red tomatoes into a thick juice.

Lizzie hated working in the garden. For one thing, the soil had lots of stones in it. Big round ones. Actually, big enough to toss to the side where they had to haul them away with the express wagon. Stones that weren't really big enough for that just annoyed you when the edge of the hoe hit them, sparks flying from it, the impact hurting your hand on the hoe handle. If it was an old hoe that had a rough wooden handle, you always got a splinter in the palm of your hand.

Lizzie would yell, dropping her hoe, and would try to pick out the splinter with the nails of her thumb and forefinger. Often she ended up banging the screen door, complaining loud and long to Mam, who extracted the splinter with a tweezers. Lizzie would try her best to make it sound as horrible as possible, but usually Mam clamped her mouth firmly, slapped a Band-Aid on the small hole where the splinter had penetrated, and Lizzie found herself back out in the garden hoeing.

It was just not right, Lizzie often decided. The sun was so hot it made you feel like dropping down and never, ever hoeing one more time in your life. The long rows of string beans irked her, because no one really liked them. Beans were just something you ate because they were vegetables, and, of course, they were good for you. The same way with pickles. They were so unnecessary. Sour, disgusting things. The only way a pickle tasted good was if it was buried under a pile of sweet Lebanon bologna, cheese, and mayonnaise. And Mam always canned quart after quart of those little saccharin pickles that turned olive green and salty after a while. Dat ate so many of them, with tomato soup, cheeseburgers, or hot dogs; Lizzie could not believe they were very good for his stomach.

The thing about those saccharin pickles that irked her most was Mam's odd notion that you could only pick the small ones. A saccharin pickle was supposed to be small. What in the world was the difference? Why couldn't you wait to pick the cucumbers until they were big, then cut them into pieces? They went a lot farther that way and you didn't need to pick them every other day. But no, Mam said they turned mushy in the jar if you did that; it was better to pick them small.

So besides hoeing, picking cucumbers was just as bad. The stalks were thick and long, with large prickly leaves that gave you a rash if you picked them too long. Plus, the little green cucumbers were exactly the same color as the leaves, so it was impossible to find them all. Then, if Mam helped and she found too many big ones, she scolded Lizzie thoroughly, which hurt her feelings terribly even if she knew it was partly guilt, because she could have done better.

So there were very few things about a garden that made any sense to Lizzie. Corn-on-the-cob was about the only thing she would grow if she ever married and had her own garden. That was so delicious it almost made up for string beans and pickles.

Red beets weren't quite as bad as pickles, because you let them grow together in a nice long row. Then one day when the beets were big enough, Mam pulled them, trimmed off the tops, and washed them in a big bucket under the spigot in the yard. The fun part was peeling them after they were cooked. Some of the small ones you could squeeze with your hand, and that was it— they were peeled. Mandy and Lizzie peeled red beets at the sink in the basement for a long time, because Mam canned lots of them for pickled eggs. Dat loved them, sprinkling salt and spreading mayonnaise on each half.

So when there was gardening to be done, Lizzie was almost always reluctant to start. This morning was no different. Mam was tired, since the twins had not slept well, and she had school sewing to do as well. Emma was washing, whistling over the steady whir of the gas engine that powered the washing machine, happy as always, loving every minute of her time doing laundry.

But Mandy and Lizzie were not happy, because Mam had given them instructions to hoe around the tomato plants and clean the area where the string beans had been.

School would be starting next week, so the garden work was winding down, but they still had to clean part of it, which Lizzie thought was absolutely unnecessary. Why couldn't the weeds grow for a little while? The frost would soon kill them. Besides, they wanted to make a house in the hay so Debbie could come over to sleep overnight.

Lizzie flopped down in a kitchen chair, moaning to Mam that it was too hot to hoe. Mandy asked why the weeds couldn't grow for a while.

"Because," Mam said tiredly, heating yet another bottle on the stove.

"Well, we wanted to make a hay house, Mam," Lizzie said. "Debbie wants to come over once yet, before school starts."

"Did Dat say you could?" Mam asked, putting her smallest finger into the saucepan to test the temperature of the baby's formula. She always used her smallest finger. Lizzie never knew why.

"Yes, he did. If we don't rip any baling twine off the bales," Mandy said happily.

"Isn't it too hot up there?" Mam asked doubtfully, pouring the warm milk into a bottle.

"Not if we open both barn doors."

"Then someone will fall out."

"Hah-ah, Mam."

Mam fell silent, reaching for KatieAnn and settling herself in the blue platform rocker.

"Mam, is Debbie allowed to come over tonight? And . . . please, please, please, would you make a chocolate layer cake with white icing for her? You know how she loves it," Lizzie asked.

Mam's eyes narrowed. She watched Lizzie for a while before she sighed.

"Alright, Lizzie, it's a deal. I'll let you have Debbie over and I'll make a cake, but what about you moaning and groaning about working in the garden? It just isn't right, the way you two run around having fun while Emma works almost all the time," she said, running a hand through her uncombed hair.

"Mam!" Lizzie burst out.

"What?"

"You know it's not fair to accuse me and Mandy of not helping Emma. If I went out there and *offered* to help her, she would never let me. She is so different, Mam," Lizzie wailed.

"She loves to wash," Mandy chimed in.

"I suppose you're right, girls. But I'm always afraid I'm not raising you two as I should. I have never seen two girls who are eleven and nine years old, run around and play like you do with Edna and Debbie. How are you ever going to learn responsibility?" she finished.

"Mam, Emma thinks about getting married lots of times. She told me the other evening she can't wait till she has a house of her own. She wants an old farmhouse with patchwork quilts on the bed and a *whole* pile of children. I don't even think about things like that."

"Me, neither!" Mandy said, rolling her large green eyes for emphasis.

Mam started by smiling, then shaking quietly with laughter, and finally throwing back her head, opening her mouth, and laughing a real, deep genuine sound of merriment, which the girls had heard very seldom since the twins' birth.

"You two!" she gasped, wiping her eyes.

Lizzie and Mandy giggled appreciatively, because if Mam was in such a good mood they probably would not have to hoe weeds.

But they were wrong. Only after the gardening was done, were they allowed to make a hay house, and Mam was firm. So it was after lunch by the time Mandy and Lizzie could even start on the house in the haymow. It was stifling under the tin roof of the barn, so they slid back the huge doors on each side. A nice breeze soon cooled the interior, so they started to work. They lifted heavy, prickly bales of hay, piling them in a neat square in the farthest corner, so they could build a tunnel to the house.

When Debbie came over late in the afternoon, she found Lizzie red-faced and disheveled, her face shiny with sweat, hay sticking from her hair, with red scratches all over her legs. Mandy didn't look much better, except her face was not quite as alarming in color.

Debbie giggled. "Look at you!" she laughed.

"What?" Lizzie asked.

"You're so red!"

"You would be, too, if you built this house."

Debbie giggled again. Lizzie and Mandy showed her through the tunnel and into the nice square house built of hay bales. Debbie was so thrilled, because her mother had said she could stay for the night. They planned where the imaginary couch, bed, stove, and table would be, then ran down the steps to ask Mam for sheets and quilts. They were not allowed to have anything woolly or anything the hay would stick to. But, since it was summertime and the nights were warm, they didn't need a lot of covers.

"Oh, you made a chocolate layer cake, Mrs. Glick!" Debbie squealed.

"Yes, I did, Debbie. Just for you," Mam beamed.

Mam loved Debbie so much, and Debbie loved Mam, calling her "Mrs. Glick" until Mam told her to call her "Annie." Debbie just was like that—so easy to love. For one thing, her soft, little, round form, tanned as dark as an autumn walnut in the fall, topped with a mop of naturally curly black hair, was just the most endearing sight. Besides, she had a great sense of humor. Topped with her soft giggle, she was just the most captivating little person.

Sometimes Mam was grouchy and even Debbie was hard on her nerves. Then she would send her home, saying she had stayed long enough, and Lizzie and Mandy would feel bad for days.

But that was how Mam was, and Debbie never stayed away very long at a time, always knowing Mam would be friendly the next time she appeared at their door.

They carried all the sheets and old quilts, old pillows, and flashlights up the stairs and into their hay house. They spread them carefully on piles of soft, prickly hay, tucking the corners under.

"This looks so cozy!" Debbie said, rolling into the center of the freshly made bed. Instantly all the corners came flying up and the cozy-looking bed went flat.

"Debbie!" Lizzie yelled. "You ruined it."

Sheepishly, she climbed off hurriedly. "I didn't know."

"Well, loose hay is not going to work for our bed — that's for sure," Lizzie said with a sigh.

"I'm sorry."

"No, that's alright, Debbie. We just need to use something that works better."

"Like what?"

"I don't know."

"How about a mattress?"

"How could we ever get a mattress through this tunnel?"

"We can't."

They sat in a semi-circle, their chins in their hands, chewing on pieces of hay. Lizzie was tired, dirty, and so warm she seriously doubted if she would ever cool off again. This was so depressing, working so hard, and now they had no decent place to sleep.

"I know!" Debbie shouted. "My camping mattress!"

"Of course! We'll pump air in after it's in the house!" Lizzie yelled.

So while Debbie hurried home, Mandy and Lizzie ran into the kitchen to pack their food.

Mandy got a plastic pitcher, opening a packet of grape Kool-Aid and adding a cup of sugar and cold water from the icebox. They never had any ice, but that was okay; they didn't think about it much.

Lizzie wrapped bologna sandwiches in waxed paper, and half of the chocolate layer cake, potato chips, slices of cheese, and stick pretzels. Mam said they could have apples, too, but Lizzie wrinkled her nose. Mandy took one, though. Debbie didn't like apples, either.

Now they were all set, so after Debbie appeared on the porch, lugging a heavy package with both arms, they carried everything back up to the hay house. They pushed and shoved, pulled and grunted, getting all the bulky packages into their little house.

After they had pumped air into the mattress, it was actually very nice inside. The evening air had cooled the barn, and the little house was so secluded, yet had a secure feeling, because it was a house inside a barn. Dat and Mam's house was close, so there really was nothing to be afraid of during the night.

After they had everything in order, it was time to have their baths, then get their nightgowns on before they actually retired for the night.

Dat shook his head in disbelief when he saw the girls. "You look like you went through a threshing machine!" he said.

"You know what, Dat? We have a mattress that you blow up with an air pump. It's Debbie's," Mandy said happily.

"How are you going to see?" Dat asked.

"With flashlights."

"Just so you don't have any matches."

"We don't."

After their baths, they scampered up the stairs, diving into the tunnel for the last time. They stuck the flashlights into cracks between the bales of hay and had perfect "electric" lights. They spread a sheet across two bales of hay for their table, spreading all the food on it before sitting down to enjoy their delicious picnic supper. Debbie ate a big piece of chocolate layer cake, washing it down with grape Kool-Aid, before she ate a sandwich.

"Mmmm!" she said, closing her eyes as she licked the vanilla icing from her fork. "Your mom makes the best cake in the world."

Lizzie and Mandy agreed, because it really was the best. They ate so much cake and drank so much Kool-Aid, they could not believe the cake was almost all gone by bedtime. They told stories—true ones and made-up ones—until Debbie told a story that was so scary, Lizzie told her she was going to go sleep in the house if she didn't stop it. She told her Amish people didn't let their children hear such scary things, which wasn't entirely true, but it made her stop.

They played tic-tac-toe on an old composition book and told some more stories. Lizzie told Debbie about the time Emma was riding Dolly and her hair caught in a tree branch, dragging her from the pony, where she hung until her hair ripped out.

Debbie didn't believe it. She said Lizzie was telling her a "fib," and Lizzie didn't know what a fib was, but was afraid to tell Debbie, because she would think she was stupid. So she just said she was not telling a fib. Before she fell asleep, she wondered if a fib was a lie.

During the night, Lizzie opened one eye and checked the alarm clock beside the air mattress. Twelve o'clock. Everything was so quiet, you couldn't hear any creaks, or breezes, or cars on the highway. That was because they were in a hay house inside a barn. It was a good feeling, all cozy and quiet, so Lizzie drifted off to sleep again.

Quite unexpectedly, she was jerked awake by Mandy sitting up and coughing terribly. Lizzie took a deep breath in alarm, and her throat felt like sandpaper. She tried to take another breath, but could do nothing but cough. She rolled off the air mattress and lay on her side, rasping and coughing. Debbie sat up, looking bewildered, rubbing a hand across her eyes, before she started sneezing uncontrollably, then she burst into ter-rified sobs.

"I feel horrible," she choked.

"I can't breathe," Mandy whispered, her voice rising to a panic.

Lizzie was terrified. She had never felt so close to panic in her whole life. The air in the little house was so stifling, it felt as if someone was sitting on her chest. She rolled over and struggled to gain composure.

"We have to get out of here!" she said.

"Well, what is it? What's wrong?" Debbie squeaked, her eyes shining white in the semi-darkness.

"I don't know. I . . . I guess it's the hay," Lizzie said, then she started another coughing fit.

Debbie cried. Mandy sneezed and their pitcher of grape Kool-Aid dumped over. Pieces of hay swam in the sticky mess and the edge of the quilt was thrown across it and slowly turned lavender as it absorbed the sticky juice. The whole adventure had turned into a terrible nightmare, as they struggled to keep from coughing.

"I . . . I can't make it!" Debbie gasped.

"The dust is so thick!" Mandy cried.

"Can we make it out through the tunnel?" Lizzie asked.

"No," Debbie said weakly. "I feel like throwing up."

Lizzie was stung into action, thinking about Debbie fainting or throwing up on the quilts. They already had a big mess with the spilled grape drink. She got up and tried to push a hay bale away so they could climb through, but was overtaken by a fit of coughing. She gasped, weakly trying to regain her breath.

It felt as if there was dust in her nose, mouth, and ears. Every time she took a small breath, it hurt her throat and chest. She must do something and do it soon. But if she pushed out one bale, what would keep the roof from collapsing? She would have to try. Carefully, clutching her flashlight, she shone its beam up and down the walls. If she could find a bale that didn't have too much weight from the other bales, she could try and push it out.

Choosing one she thought would work, she shoved with all her strength. Nothing happened. Debbie and Mandy started coughing, ending in weak little gasps. Lizzie kicked against it with all her might. The bale stayed where it was.

"We have to crawl out, Debbie," she said firmly.

"I ca-an't," Debbie wailed.

That left only one thing. Lizzie looked up, the beam of the flashlight playing across the roof of the hay house. She found a bale on the farthest corner, against the roof, and pushed against it with her waning strength. She kept pushing, grunting, and coughing, until it tumbled free, falling to the barn floor outside. A section of the roof caved in, loose hay and boards, creating twice as much dust. Lizzie sneezed and shook her head to clear it, then ran against another bale, pushing it to the barn floor. A large section of the roof collapsed, covering their table and all the leftover food with a thick layer of hay and boards.

Debbie screamed; Mandy cried out in alarm.

Lizzie kicked out another bale, and she could see the outline of the open barn door and the wonderful night sky, stars shimmering in the distance.

"Come on. Hurry up! Give me your hand!" Lizzie commanded. They scrambled to the opening, falling over boards, hay, and the table, and stepping into sticky grape drink. They piled out on the hard barn floor, still coughing, gasping great breaths of the cool night air.

"That was not one bit funny!" Mandy said softly, between gasps of air.

"What happened?" Debbie asked.

"I suppose it was too dusty," Lizzie said.

They crept quietly down the barn stairs, creeping slowly into the kitchen. They tried to not wake Mam and Dat, because they didn't get enough sleep with the twins. They turned the faucet at the sink open only half-way and drank glass after glass of cool water. It felt so good on their raw throats.

Quietly they tiptoed to Mandy's room, tumbled into the bed sideways because there were three of them, and fell asleep as soon as their heads hit the pillow. All except Lizzie. She folded her hands across her chest and whispered a prayer: "Denky, Gute Mann," meaning a simple thank you to the Good Man, which was a Dutch way of expressing God to little children. The Good Man had surely watched over them, because they could have suffocated.

In the morning, Dat explained to them about the lack of oxygen. That was what caused them to wake up, when the oxygen level became too low. Mam shook her head worriedly, saying that was the end of sleeping in the haymow. Debbie giggled when Lizzie said Dolly would have a treat in the coming winter: grape Kool-Aid hay with vanilla icing.

chapter 12

Building the House

The sawmill and pallet shop at the foot of the ridge hummed long hours, producing load after load of pallets. Dat said he was not used to making so much money—it worried him, kind of. Mam laughed happily, saying it was time to start building the house, because the twins were outgrowing their crib, and they certainly did not have room for another.

So they sat together, evening after evening, their heads bent over plans for their house. It would be built on top of the flat basement roof, with a porch out the front on top of the basement porch. They would need only a story and a half, meaning there would not be an upstairs with an attic. Only an upstairs with two dormers built out from the roof, allowing four upstairs bedrooms under the roof. The space between the rooms and the roof would be well insulated, too, being used as a cubbyhole space to store attic things.

The large kitchen along the side of the house toward the barn, and the living room along the front, in a big L shape, was the plan they finally agreed on. There was one small bedroom for the twins, and a large one for Mam and Dat. They would keep the washing machine in the basement, and would have two full bathrooms then, one downstairs and one upstairs. It would be a nice house, Lizzie was sure of that, because Dat was a good builder.

One day a huge orange lumber truck chugged its way up the drive to Lizzie's house. They unloaded lots of lumber, some wide boards and some narrow ones. Before the day was over, Uncle Eli and his boys and Dat and some of his workers from the pallet shop were sawing and pounding nails.

Mam's cheeks were flushed, and her eyes were sparkling with excitement. Emma was squeezing lemons on the lemon juicer while Mam took tray after tray of peanut butter cookies from the oven. The men would need refreshments, she told Lizzie, hurrying between oven and table.

Just as the sun was sliding below the mountain, the men put away their toolboxes and sat on the soft grass, pushing back their sweat-stained straw hats.

"Well, Melvin, looks like you got the hotel started," laughed Uncle Eli.

"Oh, now, you know I'm not building a hotel," Dat said, shaking his head, clearly flustered.

"Of course not," Uncle Eli said. "You just need plenty of room for your second pair of twins."

Everyone laughed, and Dat looked a bit more flustered, then he laughed along with everyone else.

Mam called from the house and the men sat on lawn chairs on the porch after they had washed up in the laundry room. Mam served filled paper plates with large homemade rolls filled with tangy beef barbecue, ice-cold fresh-squeezed lemonade, potato chips, and peanut butter cookies. The men ate hungrily because it was so late.

Lizzie leaned against the block wall of the basement porch and watched the men eating. She had never seen any person take bites as huge as one of the pallet shop workers. She did not know his name, so she wondered vaguely if he was a giant. His hands were bigger than the paper plate he was holding, and his beef barbecue sandwich was gone in three bites. Three! Lizzie was fascinated. She wondered how many more sandwiches he would eat, watching carefully as he got up, helping himself to two more at one time.

Mam couldn't afford to feed too many like him, Lizzie decided. They would spend all the money for the house on food if they didn't watch it. She kept staring at the large man wolfing down his sandwiches until she felt an elbow jabbing her ribs. She turned to see Mandy watching her worriedly, motioning to her to come along.

Lizzie turned and followed her.

"Lizzie, you have to stop staring at that man," Mandy whispered.

"Why?"

"Because."

"Well, Mandy, I've never seen anyone eat so much."

"He can't help it."

"Did you see him eat his first sandwich? Three bites! Three!" Lizzie hissed.

"You have to stop staring at him," Mandy said.

"I can hardly help it."

They wandered back to the porch, listening to the men's conversation. Lizzie cast sidelong glances as the large man selected and downed five peanut butter cookies, with glass after glass of lemonade.

.   .   .   .   .

School had started, so Dat was under a lot of pressure to have the house "under roof," as he said, before the snow flew. The girls went off to school every morning, while Mam cared for the twins and cooked meals for the men who helped Dat build the house. Emma was clearly under plenty of stress, too, coming home to a sink filled with dirty dishes, and the house strewn with toys, baby bottles, diapers, and loads of unfolded laundry on the kitchen table.

One evening, after Mam had a tableful of men to cook for, the house was such a mess that Emma burst into tears of frustration. She threw her lunchbox on the table, ran into her bedroom, threw herself on her bed, and cried.

Lizzie looked up from her after-school snack of cold leftover meat loaf with ketchup, chewing methodically.

"What's wrong with Emma?" she asked.

"Close your mouth when it's full of meat loaf, Lizzie. She's just upset because everything is such a big mess. It's no wonder. If you and Mandy would help more around the house, she wouldn't feel quite so responsible. All you do when you come home from school is eat and read the comics in the paper. You're lazy, Lizzie. You're actually getting quite overweight and you are *lazy*." Mam's voice was red with frustration and anger, as her voice became louder.

The meat loaf that had been so delicious a moment earlier turned to sawdust and stuck in her throat. Lizzie was shocked. She felt hot all over, her face burning with humiliation.

"I don't mean to be rude, Lizzie. I know I'm losing my temper. But you need to shape up, helping Emma and me more over this time. We're building a house and this house is for you, too, so your duty is to help along with everyone else."

Lizzie did not say one word. She couldn't. She supposed what Mam had told her was true. She was fat and lazy. The truth hurt so badly, Lizzie felt like crawling under her bed and never coming out again. She would stay under her bed until she died and turned into one big dust ball; they would never know what had happened to her.

Well, she could change, she supposed. But first she could resent Mam for a while. She wasn't going to eat or talk for a very long time. So long, in fact, that everyone became so worried they would crowd around her with ice cream and whoopie pies, begging her to eat. They would take her to a doctor and he would prescribe all kinds of good food.

She blinked her eyes rapidly to hold back hot, angry tears of shame and resentment. She got up, stalked into the bedroom where Emma still lay across the bed, yanked open her drawer, and got out a clean apron. She tossed her school apron aside, tied on an everyday one, and stalked back to the kitchen.

She started throwing dirty dishes out of the sink, slamming plates on the countertop as hard as she could. She would show Mam and Emma who could get work done around here. She held the bottle of dish detergent upside down and squeezed, producing mountains of white, frothy bubbles. The rinse water was foamy with soap when Mam came to the kitchen to heat water for formula.

"Lizzie, how many times do I have to tell you? Don't use so much dish detergent!" she said.

Lizzie didn't answer. She turned away from Mam, blindly looking for more utensils. *Just go away,* she thought. *Go away and leave me alone.*

"Lizzie?"

She didn't answer. The twins were both crying so Mam knew there was no use trying now. Lizzie would just have to pout.

And pout she did. The only thing that took her mind off pitying herself was the pounding and sawing overhead. Their house was fast becoming a real house, yellow lumber being raised in walls, rising up from the roof of the basement home.

She finished drying every dish, slamming them into the cupboards, and wiping the countertop spotlessly.

Emma was folding laundry, her eyes red-rimmed from crying. Lizzie grabbed the broom and started sweeping long, furious strokes across the glossy hardwood floor of the living room. Jason's farm animals were all strewn across the floor, mixed with sections of plastic fences. Lizzie just kept sweeping, pushing all his toys along into a big pile, catching stray diapers, bottle caps, dust, and wood chips. After she had everything in a huge pile, she started sifting through it, separating toys and dirt.

Emma kept folding laundry, casting furtive glances in Lizzie's direction. Mam was in the bedroom, settling the twins for a much-needed nap, so Emma was watching, hoping Mam would not see what Lizzie was doing.

Lizzie was picking out the farm animals and throwing them in a container, dirt and all. After that, she got the dustpan, scooping up bottle caps, diapers, and all, dumping them into the wastebasket.

"Lizzie, you can't throw diapers away!" Emma said, not being able to be quiet one moment longer.

Without a word, Lizzie fished around in the wastebasket, producing two diapers. She threw them on the clean laundry pile.

"Lizzie!" Emma grabbed them, flinging them toward Lizzie. She grabbed them and, without saying a word, marched into the bathroom and flung them into the clothes hamper.

Suddenly there was a horrible sound from the rooftop. It was like a shout, but it was mixed with a wailing sound. The thing that struck terror in Lizzie's heart was the fact that it sounded like Dat.

Lizzie's eyes opened wide and she stared at Emma. Emma stared back at Lizzie, then they dropped what they were holding and dashed to the doorway.

Lizzie's heart was in her throat as they raced around the incline to the back of the house. There they found Dat kneeling beside the limp form of Jason, his face a reflection of shock and disbelief.

Emma reached them first, and she extended both arms to Dat, trying to take Jason from him. "What happened?"

Dat lifted tear-filled eyes, his mouth working to control his emotions. Uncle Eli and the boys crowded around, trying to see what had caused Dat to cry out like that.

"He fell. He fell backward, tripping over a two by four and fell. Straight down on his head," Dat moaned.

Jason did not cry. He just lay in Dat's arms, his face white and pallid, sweat oozing from his upper lip. Dat bent his face low, murmuring, calling his name, rubbing a hand across his cheek, trying in vain to rouse him.

"Should we call an ambulance?" Uncle Eli asked, trying to be calm.

"I don't know. Lizzie, get Mam."

Lizzie threw a terrified glance at Jason's still form, then she raced back to the house, bursting through the kitchen door, yelling for Mam.

Mam dropped to her knees beside Dat after she hurried out of the house behind Lizzie. She stroked Jason's

cheek, but let Dat hold him, asking questions rapidly.
Yes, definitely, they must see a doctor immediately if he
was not responding. She hurried to get cool water and a
soft cloth, which she laid on his forehead.

Jason's curly hair was soon wet from the cloth and his
perspiration. His long lashes lay on his pale cheeks, his
chest rising and falling. His pulse was good at the wrist,
but he would not wake up.

Lizzie chewed her lip and wrung her hands. Now
Jason was going to die; she just knew he was. Probably he would. Oh, horrible thought. She was sorry for
everything she ever did wrong—thinking he was ugly
when he was a baby, teasing him—and endless thoughts
of bitter remorse flooded her head. How many times had
she made Mandy take him to the bathroom when she
was too lazy? Mam was so right. She was fat and lazy,
just a miserable selfish person.

Just when Lizzie thought she could no longer endure
the suspense of not knowing whether Jason would live
or die, or if it was her fault, he jerked all over, quite vio-
lently. Lizzie muffled a scream, and Emma wrapped her
arms tightly around her waist, questioning Mam with
her eyes.

Mam's cry was involuntary, as she reached for her
son, gathering him close in loving arms. Tears ran freely
down her cheeks, as Jason clung to her neck, crying
great, rasping sobs.

Ivan and Ray turned away, because they were too
big to cry, but Uncle Eli and Dat cried with Mam and
Jason. Emma bent to touch his curly head, but she drew

back in alarm. "Mam!" she gasped.

They all looked, shocked to see a huge purple, black, and blue lump swelling from the side of his head. Lizzie had never seen anything like it. The bruise was so big, Dat said he must definitely see a doctor, but Mam told him if a bruise or lump is on the outside, they should be fine. She would watch him and if he became nauseated and threw up she would take him to see a doctor.

So that was the end of the day for the men. No one felt like building a house after Jason fell, Uncle Eli saying it was time to go home.

Dat and Mam sat weakly on rocking chairs, Mam holding Jason with great tenderness. Dat got him a cool drink of grape juice, which he downed in three big gulps. Then he touched the lump on his head, saying seriously, "I fell *hard* on my head from our new house!"

Everyone laughed, the tension ebbing away, seeing him sit up and talk and remembering what had happened. He was going to be alright, which was such a relief to Lizzie that her knees felt shaky and weak; she crumpled on the couch, laughing unsteadily.

By the time the evening was over, they only had leftover meat loaf sandwiches and grape juice for supper, because Mam was too tired to cook. Lizzie ate only a few bites, and drank lots of grape juice, because it was less fattening.

That evening, when Emma set the alarm clock properly as she always did, climbed into bed, plumped her pillow, rolled over, and said, "G'night," Lizzie didn't answer. After a while, she said, "Emma."

"What?"

"Do you think I'm fat?"

"Ach, Lizzie, it's mean to say someone is fat. I'm not thin, either."

There was silence as Lizzie stared wide-eyed into the darkness. It was not a nice thought, but Mam wasn't very kind. How could she be so mean?

"Emma?"

"Hmm?"

"Mam likes you a lot better than me, doesn't she? I mean, she likes me as good as you can like a fat, lazy person, but she likes you a lot better, not just because you're thin and you work harder, but she really, really, really likes you a whole pile more than me."

"Lizzie, now stop it. You know that's not true."

Lizzie sat straight up. "Emma, I know what's true and what isn't. Don't you try and tell me. Mam said I am overweight and lazy, so that's exactly what she thinks of me. And I don't care."

Lizzie plopped back down on her pillow, snorted, and twisted and arranged herself in a comfortable position, before she said, "G'night."

"Lizzie."

"What?"

"You can't go to sleep thinking that. Mam would never love one of her daughters more than the other. It's just that you *could* help better since the twins are born. There is about three times as much work now as there was before they were born."

"See?"

"See what?"

"I tried to tell you. What do we want another baby for? And then she goes and has two."

"You think it's her fault? God gave us those babies."

Lizzie snorted again, before her breathing became deep and even, and she dreamed there was a water balloon tied to her skirt.

.   .   .   .   .

The squirrels were busy storing hickory nuts in the old oak tree along the fencerow beside the new house. The air was gray and cold, with dry leaves rattling crisply in the sharp air.

There was a truck parked beside the new house that said "Robinson's Flooring" and two men carried a roll of linoleum up the steps to the front door.

Mam and Aunt Mary had been varnishing and sanding all week, doing doors, trimwork, and hardwood floors. The house was beautiful. Lizzie was so amazed at the smooth walls and the windows that you could lock so tightly that there was not a smidgen of air coming through any cracks.

Emma had a room of her own now. It was painted blue, with blue linoleum on the floor. Lizzie and Mandy shared the front dormer room, looking out over the road toward the neighbor's house. Their room was painted bright pink. That had been Lizzie's idea, but after the paint was on, she sincerely wished she would not have picked that color. But they had it now and Mam was not going to change it, because they had chosen it themselves.

After Jason had fallen, Lizzie did try to be more helpful. She also watched what she ate, especially when Mam was around. But it was hard. Often, when Mam was upstairs varnishing and Lizzie had to watch the twins, she ate two whoopie pies. Once, after Mam had made creamsticks, Lizzie ate four. Creamsticks were homemade doughnuts, but instead of being round with a hole in the middle, they were cut in an oblong shape. After they were deep-fried, Mam cut a long slit on the top, filled it with creamy vanilla icing, and put golden caramel frosting on the top. They were the very best thing in the world of desserts, and Mam didn't make them very often, because they were so much work, with two different kinds of icing and all.

So Lizzie learned quickly that it paid to be careful what she ate around Mam and Emma, but it didn't matter if they were busy and couldn't see her. Because painting, varnishing, going to school, and having two new babies was all extremely stressful, nothing made Lizzie feel better about her whole upside-down world than a a good whoopie pie or doughnut. It was so comforting.

After everything was finished and the moving was over, she had also learned another valuable lesson. It was better to help Emma and Mam work while there was plenty of work to be done; then when she was finished they treated her with more respect.

Mam did not lose her temper, and only once was Lizzie's weight mentioned. That was when Mam saw an ad in a magazine for a new kind of diet soda. She looked at the ad, then gazed at Lizzie, who was nibbling on a chocolate chip cookie. She got up, showed her the ad, and asked kindly if it would help her reduce if she bought some for her.

Lizzie shrugged her shoulders. "Does it taste good?"

"Probably."

Lizzie didn't say much. That evening she told Mandy she was very fortunate to be so thin.

"You're not fat."

"I am."

"Not to me, you're not."

Lizzie sighed, content to know Mandy loved her. They were all settled in the new house, winter was coming, and they had a warm room upstairs, even in cold, windy weather. Lizzie supposed turning twelve wouldn't be too bad, as long as she had Mandy and a few whoopie pies.

chapter 13

Ping-Pong

They loved their new house. It was so spacious, with plenty of closets, cupboards, and places to store every-thing neatly. Mam even had a closet in the hallway upstairs, which she filled with clean sheets, pillowcases, quilts, and blankets.

The new hardwood floor in the living room was so sleek and smooth, Lizzie could hardly keep from sliding on it. If you wore knee socks and ran across the kitchen, you could slide clear over to the other end of the living room. Mam caught them doing it once, and that was the end of that.

Even the doors and the woodwork gleamed. Mam had done so much sanding and varnishing, her arms and shoulders were sore every evening for weeks. But now it seemed as if her efforts paid off, because everything looked so nice. The old green sofa stood at one end of the living room, and the blue platform rocker, Mam's bureau, and library table along another wall, but it was still too empty. They just didn't have enough furniture.

So one evening Dat and Mam went to an auction in a faraway town with Uncle Eli. Emma was a bit nervous keeping the twins by herself, so Esther came to stay with them. Lizzie tried hard to stay awake, waiting to see what they bought. But she fell asleep before they came home, and was surprised to see a new sofa and matching chair, almost the same color as the old sofa. They had also bought a few end tables.

It looked so different, much cozier now. Mam spread her large braided rug in front of the sofas. Lizzie and Mandy promptly sat on the new sofa, patting the pillows and smiling at Mam. It was a happy time, settling into the new house just as the weather turned cold. They didn't have to worry about not having enough money now, which was so nice for Dat and Mam.

The basement that had been their house was now just a basement. Everything they didn't really need was stored down there—things like old chairs and tables, or dressers with broken drawers. There was a woodstove in the basement, too, that helped keep the floor warm upstairs.

And one day, Mam was reading the newspaper, when she said, "Girls, listen to this: 'Ping-pong table. In very good condition. One hundred dollars or best offer.'"

Lizzie looked up. "What's a ping-pong table?"

"Surely you know, Lizzie."

"No."

"Well, it's high time you girls learned. I'll call this number and offer them seventy-five."

"Aren't you going to ask Dat?" asked Emma, looking up from her crocheting.

"Oh, he won't mind. He loves to play ping-pong." And with that, Mam was off to the phone, hurrying down the driveway to the neighbors across the street.

"Boy!" Emma said, dryly.

"I'll say," Lizzie agreed.

"She really must want that ping-pong table." Emma resumed her crocheting, her needle flashing in the glow of the gas lamp. She was crocheting an afghan in blue colors for her new room. Lizzie envied Emma's abilities at sewing, embroidering, and now, crocheting, but she didn't have the patience to sit with hand sewing like Emma did. It wasn't that she hadn't tried, especially embroidering. Mam loved to buy cute iron-on transfers of little houses or animals in cross stitch for the girls to embroider. Even Mandy was patiently instructed how to tie a knot at the end of the thread, how to thread the needle, and how to separate the strands of embroidery floss.

Lizzie could never see any sense in the way they made embroidery thread. Why did they put all those strands together in

one thick thread if you had to separate them anyway?
Why couldn't they put only two together? Because that
was always her greatest frustration to begin with — separating those strands. You held a piece up and pulled
it carefully apart, but it always tangled in the end, and
no matter how you twisted and pulled, nine times out of
ten, it was stuck in one hard little knot at the bottom.

Mam told her over and over, if she would use shorter
pieces of thread, it wouldn't happen as often. But Lizzie
never changed the length of her thread, because what
was the use? If you used shorter threads, that's all you
got done — threading your needle.

Then there was the matter of the lazy daisy stitch.
Mam was a great teacher for things like that, and she
slowly swung her thread up and out around, catching it
at a certain angle, so that it made a perfect loop. If you
made a bunch of those loops around a French knot, you
had a perfect daisy. That was another source of irrita-
tion, that French knot. Who in the world was the inven-
tor of that stitch? You could make a middle of a daisy a
lot easier by just stitching over and over in one spot, but
Mam said it didn't look right — it was too sloppy.

Lizzie couldn't see the difference, so she never
learned the French knot, which made Mam pull her
mouth in a straight line and her nostrils flare, but she
didn't say anything. Lizzie knew she irritated Mam —
she could tell by her nostrils — so she never enjoyed
hand sewing too much. She always tried when Mam
bought new patterns, but usually it ended up in the
bottom of the sewing basket, only half finished, and

Lizzie was outside somewhere, while Emma and Mandy completed theirs.

Watching Emma crochet, Lizzie wished she could learn, too, but she sure wasn't going to ask anyone to teach her. For one thing, she was thoroughly left-handed, and for another, she would tire of it too quickly.

Mam hurried up the steps and into the kitchen, waving the paper with the telephone number on it. "We got it! They'll deliver this evening! Net, paddles, and all! This will be a big surprise for Melvin!"

Emma looked up and smiled. Lizzie asked Mam if it was fun, and Mandy said the basement was a mess. So they all hurried down to the basement to clean up, leaving plenty of space in the area that used to be the living room, for the new Ping-Pong table.

When Dat came home for supper, Mam was flushed and beaming. She could never keep a secret very long, so before they had a chance to say anything, Mam blurted out, "Melvin, guess what?"

Dat was washing up in the bathroom, but he peeped above the blue towel he was using to dry his face and said, "Now what?"

"We're getting a ping-pong table tonight!"

"Hah-ah!" Dat said, in disbelief.

"Oh, yes! They're delivering it from close to Marion for seventy-five dollars and it was advertised in the local paper for a hundred!"

Mam turned to the table with a steaming bowl of chicken stew and dumplings, while Emma poured water into the plastic drinking glasses.

"Wonder if it's any good?" Dat asked.

"We'll see. I'll beat you good and proper, Melvin!" Mam said, her eyes twinkling.

"If I remember right, Annie, I skunked you last time we played!" Dat told her, laughing.

'Skunked?' Lizzie thought. That had to be some childish game. Dat and Mam sure were acting simple about it. Skunked?

"What do you mean, 'skunked?'" she burst out.

"Oh, that's a term you use when one person has eleven points and the other has only one or two," Mam said.

"So . . . Dat was a lot better than you, right?" Lizzie asked.

"Oh, it just happened. He can't beat me like that all the time," Mam assured her.

They all sat still, "putting patties down," or folding their hands on their laps as they bowed their heads in silent prayer, something they did before and after every meal, as all Amish people did. Lizzie was so busy thinking about ping-pong, she forgot to say her prayer, till Dat lifted his head. Then she said quickly, "Is it hard to learn?"

"I'm sure you forgot to say your prayer, Lizzie," Dat said soberly.

"She never does hardly. She told me once," Emma sniffed.

"Emma, I do!"

Everyone looked at Lizzie, but Mam was busy filling everyone's plate with steaming chicken stew. There were

large chunks of chicken, white cubes of soft potatoes,
orange carrots, peas, and slivers of onion and celery
floating in a thick, creamy sauce. There were specks of
black pepper, and little soggy pieces of dark green pars-
ley in it, too. But the best part of all was the mound of
fluffy white dumpling on top. Mam plopped half of one
on each plate, spooning gravy over it. Cold macaroni
salad and thick slices of homemade bread with butter
and peach jam completed their meal.

Lizzie was so hungry and everything tasted wonderful, even the macaroni salad. Emma didn't eat very much
anymore, picking daintily at her dumpling with her fork.
She didn't eat any macaroni salad, saying it was too fattening with all that mayonnaise. Lizzie took a huge bite
of dumpling and gravy, chewed thoroughly, and looked
at Emma with narrowed eyes.

"Mayonnaise isn't fattening."

"It is."

"No, I know it isn't."

"Lizzie!"

"It isn't." Lizzie took a large spoonful of macaroni
salad on her plate, her second helping, before taking a
large bite.

Mam watched her sideways, wondering when
Lizzie would ever accept responsibility for her eating
habits. She was getting to be quite overweight, and
Mam wished many times she wouldn't eat quite as
much. There was such a thin line between hurting her
feelings and helping her eat less and more healthful
foods.

"Lizzie, mayonnaise is one of the most fattening things you can eat," Dat said.

"Who said?"

"I don't know. I guess everybody just knows—it's quite a common fact."

Mandy jumped up, opened the pantry door, and came back with a jar of mayonnaise. "One hundred calories for one tablespoon!" she announced. "See?"

"That's a lot of calories if you're dieting," Dat said.

"I'm not on a diet!" Lizzie said loudly.

"No doubt," Emma muttered.

"Mam, Emma is being mean," Lizzie said.

"Emma," Mam said.

So Lizzie ate a large piece of pumpkin pie for dessert, free of guilt, because it seemed as if Mam was on her side. That one piece was not quite enough, so when they were clearing the table, she ate another piece, only smaller, when Emma wasn't looking. That left kind of a yucky sweet taste in her mouth, so when she took the pie back to the pantry, she got a handful of stick pretzels from the jar. After that she drank a large glass of water, and felt miserably full. She would have to stop eating so much, she thought.

They were not yet finished with the dishes when a pickup truck drove up the driveway and stopped. There was a dark green table with white lines around the outside and one straight up the middle propped up on the back.

"It's here!" Lizzie yelled.

So Dat and Mam bustled out the door, down the steps, and helped unload that huge table, which came in

two parts. There was a small green net to clamp on each
side, two red paddles, and two blue ones. The paddles
were round with a short wooden handle. The surface of
the paddle was rubbery, with little dots all over it. Lizzie
loved the feel of the smooth wooden handle, wondering
if she would be good at this.

After Dat wrote a check and thanked the English
man who brought the table, he showed the girls how to
hold the paddle properly. It was not at all as Lizzie had
imagined. You had to hold the round, rubbery part in,
and the wooden handle out.

Mam had to give the twins their bath and settle them for
the night, so Emma helped her while Dat fed the horses.

Lizzie and Mandy tried to bat the little white plastic
ball back and forth, but they hardly ever got it right.
Usually, one bat and it didn't go ever close to where
they wanted it to go, until they were bent over laughing
so hard. They would never learn, it seemed.

But when Dat and Mam were both able to play,
Lizzie was fascinated. The ball went back and forth
almost faster than her eyes could follow. It flew low over
the net, always hitting the table before being slammed
straight back. Mam's eyes sparkled, her arms flew fast,
and her hand gripped the ping-pong paddle until her
knuckles turned white, and her mouth was held in a
steady line. She moved faster than Lizzie had ever seen
her, with her feet almost dancing to keep up with Dat's
furious pace.

Just when Lizzie was positive she could no longer
take the suspense, Mam yelled, "Melvin!"

Dat yelled, too, and slapped his knee in triumph. He had hit the ball to the very corner of the table and it had gone down over, but touched it lightly, meaning it was Dat's point. If the ball had cleared the table, it would have been Mam's point.

Dat certainly did not "skunk" Mam that game, because Mam won, twenty-one points to Dat's eighteen. Mam's cheeks were so red, and she was laughing, running over to open a window and saying it was much too warm in this basement. Jason clapped his hands and squealed with excitement, running off with Mam's paddle until she caught him, pretending to smack his little pants' seat with it.

They played three games before Mam gasped and said that was it, she was too tired for one more game. Dat had laughed, begging her to play one more, but she said it was high time to put Jason to bed.

So Dat played patiently with Emma, teaching her the proper way to serve, telling them all the basic rules of playing ping-pong. Lizzie felt a bit overconfident about playing with Emma. Usually she was superior to her in sports, so she figured it wouldn't be long before she was the best ping-pong player as well.

Night after night, as soon as the dishes were done, they lit two gas lamps, hung them on hooks in the basement, and played. They improved as the weeks went by, until Mam said they would soon be as good as she and Dat.

But Lizzie was in for a big surprise where Emma was concerned. She was fast and accurate, with seemingly

more control over her paddle than Lizzie had. This was
all hard for Lizzie to comprehend, and her pride was
battered horribly. She could not beat Emma, no matter
how desperately she played. The thing was, Emma always returned the ball. No matter where Lizzie hit it, to
the left or right, low or high, Emma returned it.

It was frustrating. Lizzie was not always a good sport,
so some evenings they ended up yelling at each other,
until Mandy tattled, or Mam heard them, making them
stop, come upstairs, and go to bed.

One evening Lizzie tried to tell Emma the reason she
won was because the gas lamp cast a glare on the ta-
bletop. So Emma said they would switch sides, if that's
what it was. That seemed a bit strange, although Lizzie
would never admit it. After that, she became so determined, she hit the ball in the net so often that Emma
"skunked" her, two to eleven, meaning Mandy was
allowed to play while Lizzie watched.

It was too much. Emma was looking at her in that
superior way of hers, trying to mask it with a look of
genuine kindness and concern. She looked so . . . so
plain *good* that Lizzie started crying in annoyance. She
didn't try to hide it, either, lashing out at Emma bitterly.
"You cheated!"

"I did not. How could I?" Emma asked, shocked, then
she looked at Mandy and they both burst out laughing.

That was Lizzie's undoing. Her temper took complete
control of her common sense, and she charged after both
of them, yelling at the top of her voice. "You're both so
mean to me!" She caught Emma's arm and smacked the

ping-pong paddle down hard on her shoulder. Mandy made a beeline for the stairs. She leaped up to the top, opening the door and banging it shut behind her.

"Ouch!"

"You and Mandy think it's funny when you win!" she yelled.

"Lizzie, you better not hit me again. You big baby. I never heard of anyone being such a poor sport. You know what's wrong with you? You're used to being the best at everything, always. Now you can't stand it if I am better at ping-pong. You get so desperate, it's no wonder you can't win. If you would calm down and stop thinking you *have* to win every game, you would be a much better player. Mandy is better than you!" Emma finished.

Lizzie was crying, sniffing loudly, snorting, and blowing her nose in a crumpled paper towel she had found on the floor.

"You just like Mandy better, and don't even try. I know how you two stick together," she sobbed.

"Eww! Lizzie, don't use that dirty paper towel!"

"I will if I want to."

Emma shrugged her shoulders, watching Lizzie crying on the sofa. Suddenly, Emma could stand it no longer. She sat down beside Lizzie, touched her knee and said, "Lizzie, listen to me."

"What?"

"Why do you have this thing about nobody liking you? That gets really old. You claim Mam likes me better than you, and now you're saying me and Mandy

stick together. You know that's not true. It's always
you and Mandy doing things together, not me. Now
you even sleep with her in the same bedroom, and I'm
always by myself. You know I like you just the same as
I always have. Mam gets impatient with you sometimes,
but Lizzie, she has reason to be. All you do is . . ." Emma
hesitated, because she couldn't say what needed to be
said.

"Eat! Just say it, Emma. I'm fat and lazy. Go ahead,
say it!" Lizzie burst out.

"No, seriously, Lizzie, I honestly don't think you like
yourself right now—that's why you feel as if no one likes
you. Your weight does bother you, only you won't admit
it."

"I'm not that fat, Emma."

"But you are."

Lizzie looked steadily at Emma. Emma looked steadily back.

"See, Lizzie, Mam doesn't mean to be unkind. She's
so busy with the twins right now, and wrapped up in her
own little world. So why don't you and me write each
other a diet every day? You write what I can eat, and
I'll write what you can eat! That would be fun! Do you
want to?"

There was a long pause. "Hm-mm."

"Why, Lizzie? You're just not yourself anymore.
You're not even *happy*!"

"Are you allowed to have *any* mayonnaise on a diet?
Emma, I mean this—serious—I can't eat sandwiches
without it."

"No, Lizzie, you can have mayonnaise. Instead of eating three sandwiches in your lunch, try taking one. You can have all the mayonnaise you want on one sandwich."

Lizzie thought about this long and hard. Emma watched anxiously as Lizzie blinked, chewed her lower lip, and stuck a straight pin in and out of her dress.

"Lizzie, don't."

"What?"

"Don't jag yourself with that pin."

"I have a rash from doing it."

"Let me see."

Lizzie showed her.

"Lizzie!"

"I guess it's a nervous habit."

"Why are you nervous?"

"I dunno."

They sat in silence before Lizzie said. "Okay, Emma, you may write me a diet for tomorrow and I'll write you one. Only don't make it too strict, or I won't stay on it anyway."

"I won't, Lizzie. This is going to be fun!" Emma beamed.

Lizzie didn't say anything. After a while she said, "I'm only twelve, Emma."

"Twelve is old."

"Is it?"

"Yes, it is. You're getting older." Emma nodded her head wisely.

Lizzie sighed. But secretly, she was pleased. Emma was such a dear, worrying about her. She really, really cared. Suddenly she leaned over, put her arm around Emma's shoulder, and squeezed. "Thanks, Emma."

"Now you can never say I don't like you, Lizzie. I do."

The funny thing was, Lizzie's ping-pong ability improved drastically after that, because she wasn't so desperate, just as Emma had said.

chapter 14

The Fire

The moon soared above the ridges and the mountain, as the Glick family slept peacefully in their new home.

In the pallet shop, sparks were smoldering on damp sawdust in the diesel shanty to the north. The diesel had been running hot the previous day, so that they had to slow production by shutting down and fixing the situation. Before Dat went home that evening, he sifted through the sawdust, sweeping it away, making sure there were no smoldering sparks. He had not done it quite thoroughly enough, because there were a few live ones burning very low in the farthest corner. A slight breeze fanned the bit of heat, rolling a few pieces of sawdust into some oil-soaked shavings, which ignited immediately, erupting into a steady flame. It gained momentum rapidly, licking at the walls of the diesel shanty, snaking its way across the oily concrete floor

until it reached the diesel itself. That was when the fire
exploded into a raging inferno, fed by the diesel fuel,
shavings, lumber—whatever the greedy tongues of the
fire could reach.

Dat and Mam were awakened rudely by a desperate banging on the aluminum storm door in the kitchen.
"*Melvin!*"

Dat leaped out of bed, followed by Mam, grabbing at
the neckline of her nightgown. They saw the sickening
orange glow in the kitchen window above the sink, even
before the neighbor man yelled hoarsely, "The pallet
shop is burning!"

Mam would never forget Dat's terrified cry of despair.
She heard herself echoing his cry, although she wasn't
really aware of making any noise at all. The shrill wail
of the fire sirens blasted through their veil of unreality,
jerking them to cruel acceptance. This was happening;
there was nothing anyone could do to stop it.

Upstairs, Emma opened one eye, aware of a strange
glow outside. Even her sheer white curtains glowed yellow. She sat up abruptly, turned to look out, and opened
her mouth in a scream of fright, then covered her face
with both hands and whimpered. Then she started praying to God to help them all.

Lizzie was jerked awake by Emma's scream. Without
knowing what caused anyone to sound like that in the
middle of the night, she leaped from her bed.

"What? What?" Mandy cried.

"I don't know! Come with me!"

They groped their way to the staircase, the orange
glow from Emma's room telling them there was a fire

somewhere. Downstairs, Dat was hurrying out the door with the neighbor man. Mam was trying to light the gas lamp, and Emma was gasping with horror.

"Mam! Look!" she pointed.

They all watched helplessly as a fuel tank exploded, sending flames leaping as high as the ridge. There was a dull boom and black smoke poured out of the broken, burning tank. There was clearly nothing to be done — even the firefighters were defeated. They kept the surrounding woods soaked well with strong water pressure from the hoses; otherwise, they watched Dat's pallet shop and Uncle Eli's sawmill go up in smoke.

Everyone who lived in the neighborhood was awake. Lights were turned on in the English neighbors' houses, with groups of people coming to comfort Mam with a kindly arm around her shoulder, or words of encouragement.

Debbie, Jeanie, and their mother came over in their pajamas, with coats thrown across their shoulders. Marlene was so kind, telling Mam if there was anything she could do, to be sure and let her know. Mam's eyes filled with tears, but she bit her lower lip, acknowledging her kindness with a nod of her head.

Aunt Mary came through the dark night, and she cried with Mam. It was quite a devastation for both families. Aunt Mary was always so worried about things, wondering why God allowed this or that to happen.

"It's just like you imagine hell to be," she said earnestly.

"Oh, yes," Mam agreed.

"Maybe God let this happen to remind us again what happens to sinners when they die," Aunt Mary said, clucking her tongue in consternation.

"We-e-ll," Mam said.

Lizzie listened, wide-eyed, as she watched the flames crackling and leaping, smoke billowing up over the ridge. She wondered why Mam said her "well" so long and drawn out. Maybe she didn't agree quite wholeheartedly. Lizzie didn't know how hell looked, but she supposed something like that. God seemed very harsh at that moment, and she shivered, then put the thought behind her.

"We'll never be able to play on the ridge. It looks as if the pine trees are burning," Debbie wailed.

"The firemen will watch it," Emma said.

"I hope the pine trees don't burn. That would be so sad, I can't bear to think of it," Lizzie said, quietly.

Mandy said nothing, standing in the kitchen, her

luminous green eyes blinking. She looked so pale and
slender, shivering in her thin nightgown. Lizzie took pity
on her and got a flashlight from the pantry before running upstairs to get her heavy housecoat. She brought it
down and held it out to Mandy.

"Here, Mandy, put your housecoat on. You look so
cold."

Mandy smiled, gratefully slipping her hands in the
sleeves, and wrapping the housecoat around her thin
frame. "That was nice."

Lizzie smiled and squeezed her hand. The fire continued to burn, but somehow, it didn't seem quite so bad. It
was a huge loss, but they had each other, and that was
what mattered most.

Mam and Aunt Mary decided to make coffee and hot
chocolate, sandwiches, and cookies for the firefighters.
The neighbors brought bread, cheese, and sandwich
meat. Mam used up what she had on hand, and before
long, they had a huge stack of sandwiches cut diago-
nally, put in a square plastic container. Cookies of every
kind were piled on trays, and gallons of coffee and hot
chocolate were steaming on the wood-burning range.

They set up folding tables and chairs in the basement,
and as the clock struck four o'clock in the morning,
weary firefighters and neighbor men, acquaintances,
and friends dropped in and had a cup of hot, steaming
coffee or hot chocolate. They all offered their condo-
lences, until Mam's cheeks were so red, it was alarming.
Her eyes looked almost glazed; she was so tired. Lizzie
knew it had been late before she got to bed, and now she

appeared so exhausted that Lizzie could hardly see how she could keep going.

Mam hurried over, touching her shoulder. "Lizzie, listen. You and Mandy had better go back to bed for a few hours before you have to get up and go to school. You'll just be too tired if you don't. Try and go to sleep. Pull the blinds in your bedroom and close the door."

"Do we have to, Mam?"

"Yes, you can hardly keep your eyes open."

Grudgingly, they obeyed. In the kitchen, they stood to watch the fire a while. It was not burning quite as fiercely, but the sparks and flames were still raging. It seemed hard to grasp, this fire happening so suddenly in the middle of the night. What if it happened in a house?

Lizzie lay awake for quite some time. She wondered if it would be safe to jump off the roof if a fire burned beneath the upstairs. What was the distance from her windows to the ground? If she jumped, she'd probably break a leg, whereas if she stayed in her room, she would probably die. So, yes, jumping would be best. Still, if you really thought about it, you could land on your head if you jumped, then you'd be dead, too, so what was the gain?

Sleep completely eluded her. She was wide awake, although she was so tired she was miserable. She sighed, flipped on her back, and stared at the ceiling. The thing was, a fire could start anywhere. Hadn't the neighbor man said sparks could smolder for a very long time? What if the woodstove in the basement exploded? Did woodstoves explode? They probably could.

She was going to have to tell Mam in the morning that she was very sorry, but she could no longer sleep upstairs in her bedroom. It simply was not safe. Furthermore, the stove in the kitchen had a loose door in the front, and Dat was going to have to fix it, that's all there was to it.

Another thing — Uncle Aarons' chimney fire. She had heard Uncle Eli tell Dat there was no use trying to get away from cleaning out the chimney every year. Uncle Aaron was too sloppy with that. Lizzie couldn't remember ever seeing Dat on the roof cleaning out the chimney at all. Well, she would have to see to it.

Somebody should sleep in the basement. Dat could. She would say something to Mam about that, because two things were enough for Dat, fixing the stove door and cleaning the chimney.

.   .   .   .   .

After the pallet shop fire died down enough, the school children were allowed to go see the damage. They approached the black, smoking mess with a dreadful feeling. Even Danny had nothing to say.

There were heaps of black and gray clumps of ashes, twisted and charred forms of steel that used to be diesels, fuel tanks, and nailers. Even the forklift stood like a grotesque statue of charred gray metal, still smoking, all the rubber melted in a sticky mess. There were mounds of blackened nails, smoking hot roller tables, and tools. It was awful to see, remembering the thriving, industrious shop it had once been.

Dat walked over to them, his eyes drooping with weariness. His face was pale, and there were streaks of black on his forehead. Lizzie thought he looked sad and older, more burdened, as she watched him get out his handkerchief and wipe his brow.

"Looks like a mess, doesn't it?" he said, shaking his head ruefully.

"Sure does," Emma said.

"How are you ever going to clean this all up?" Danny yelled.

"Oh, we'll get a big bulldozer, as soon as it's cooled down and haul this stuff away on dump trucks," Dat answered, looking down at Danny.

"Daddy said he can still use a bunch of his stuff," Danny said.

"Yes, the firemen did a good job with his sawmill, no doubt," Dat answered, surveying the charred remains of Uncle Eli's sawmill.

Lizzie stood speechless, Mandy beside her. She twisted the hem of her apron in her hands, wishing with all her heart Dat would not need to go through this. Now they would not have any money again. Who would pay for the new shop and all the new equipment? Then what would keep that shop from burning like this one? She felt quite overwhelmed with fear of the future, questions she could not figure out by herself.

She caught Dat looking at her. She searched his eyes, and he smiled. Not a spontaneous happy Dat smile, just a tired little smile that seemed to reassure her.

"Dat?"

"What, Lizzie?"

"Who is going to pay for the new shop?"

"We have fire insurance. The Amish fire tax."

"Do they build the new shop?"

"We'll have frolics."

That was a huge relief to Lizzie. They would not have to be dreadfully poor again, and Mam and Dat would not need to sit up at night arguing.

· · · · ·

So they had frolics. Every day groups of men arrived to help, toolbags in hand. They poured new concrete, erected huge wooden poles, set beams and rafters, and pounded nails through the sheathing on top. A brand new silver roof, and new white siding, sliding doors, new windows, and almost before Lizzie could believe it was possible, they had a new shop.

Dat had spent many hours setting up the equipment for the old shop, and now Lizzie felt sorry for him, starting all over again for the new one. He looked tired, staying in the shop till late hours every evening.

Mam was tired, too, and upset more often. The twins did not sleep well at night, because they were teething, so Mam had double duty—caring for them at night and cooking and baking big meals for hungry men during the day. She spoke often of how nice it would be if Emma was out of school so she could help. But every day they trudged to school, feeling sorry for Mam and Dat.

Lizzie was walking behind Edna and Emma, thinking how life just wasn't always good. Just when everything was going really well, the pallet shop had burned. Mam was tired and grouchy, making Lizzie much more aware of all the work to do around the house.

This winter was not fun, so far. The air was cold, but there had been very little snow. They couldn't go sled riding and it wasn't cold enough to go skating. It was just one boring day after another—going to school, doing lessons, coming home, and working nonstop. Lizzie wished it would start to snow and keep on snowing for a few days, then blow as hard as was possible, or something exciting.

Well, not really. The fire had been enough excitement of that sort, but that was not "fun" exciting. Another thing that bothered Lizzie a lot was this thing of growing up. The older you became, the more responsibility was yours—fold laundry, sweep the living room, do dishes—there was no end. And those twins; they were a mess. Often Mandy and Lizzie were not allowed to do one fun thing unless they put them to sleep. So they would give them their bottle, rocking, rocking, rocking, until Lizzie thought she would get sick from sheer boredom.

About the time one would nod off, the other one started crying, waking the sleeping one. So she never changed her mind too much about babies. They were a bother. They kept you from doing everything you wanted to do. She hoped sincerely they would never have any more babies. Six children were enough.

By the time they reached school, her hands were numb with cold, she was in a depressed state of mind, and she had only one sandwich in her lunch. The only bright spot of the day was how thickly she had spread mayonnaise on the one lone sandwich.

chapter 15

Double Happiness

Dat had a new spring in his step this morning, because they had received a letter stating that Doddy and Mommy Glick, Uncle James, and some of the aunts and other relatives were coming on Saturday. They had already helped rebuild the pallet shop, but they wanted to help Dat with the new diesels. Doddy Glick was very good at that sort of thing.

But the best news of all—Marvin and Elsie were coming along. Lizzie and Emma were very happy to think of seeing them again.

"Emma, I bet you anything I'll be ashamed of Marvin," Lizzie said, as they washed dishes together.

"I know what you mean. He'll soon be fifteen!" Emma said. She threw a fork back into the dishwater. "That isn't clean."

Lizzie washed it again, chattering on happily about

the upcoming event. "I hope Mommy Glick brings a chocolate cake with caramel icing," she said.

"Mmm!" Emma agreed.

"It seems long till Saturday!"

Mam said from the pantry, "Oh, no, it doesn't. You know how particular Mommy Glick is. We have some corners to scrub before they get here."

"Like what?"

"This pantry, for one thing. We had so much food given to us over the fire, I don't know how in the world to organize this mess in here. Some of these jars of canned food need to be carried to the basement and—"

"I'll do it!" Lizzie broke in.

"What? Are you sick? Oh, my goodness, Lizzie offers to *do* something!" Emma gasped, clapping a hand to her forehead in mock disbelief.

Mam's laugh rang out from the pantry. "Emma!" she said, good-naturedly.

"I will; I'll organize the pantry," Lizzie said. She set to work immediately. First, she carried the extra boards for the table and set them in the middle of the kitchen. She gathered up bags and boxes of canned goods, blue granite canners, stainless steel buckets, old plastic containers, empty quart jars, containers of flour and sugar, oatmeal, and noodles. There was seemingly no end.

Mam told her to get a bucket, helping her fill it with hot water and a good brand of lemon-scented soap, and Lizzie began. It was actually fun, because the pantry was, as Mam had said, a mess.

She scrubbed and scoured the shelves and the walls.

She clenched her tongue between her teeth, her hair became quite scraggly, and the hairpins in the back of her head loosened, causing her covering to slip to the side. She got scouring powder from beneath the sink in the kitchen cupboards, bustling back to the pantry and scrubbing black marks with a vengeance.

She did not see Emma hide her giggles, or Mam raising her eyebrows behind Lizzie's back. She was seriously cleaning. It was amazing what a difference she could make in this pantry.

Lizzie stored the blue granite canners on the top shelf, along with the jar lids and other canning items. They would not be needed till summer. Mam helped her dispose of old things like bread crumbs gone bad, some questionable bread flour, a cracked plastic container, and a bag of sunflower seeds that Mam laughingly told her must have come from the Civil War.

Lizzie loved Mam when she became a bit silly. They separated the donated canned goods, laughing about some of the odd-looking contents in the jars. Mandy helped carry tray after tray of canned items to the basement, where Mam put it in the proper space.

After everything was finished, the pantry did not look like the same place. Lizzie's heart swelled with happiness when Mam praised her efforts sincerely.

"It was fun!" she said.

"I can't figure out what crawled over you!" Emma said, using a favorite phrase of the family.

"Maybe Mommy Glick!" Lizzie responded.

.   .   .   .   .

When Doddy Glicks arrived very early on Saturday morning, they told Mommy Glick what Lizzie had done. She threw up her hands and laughed, examining the pantry thoroughly. Sure enough, she had brought a chocolate cake with caramel frosting and a large yellow bowl of cornstarch pudding. She brought two mince pies for Dat, and oatmeal cookies.

Marvin had grown at least six inches. The girls were actually too shy to say hello to him, because he looked almost like a sixteen-year-old boy who was allowed to "run around" with the youth. Elsie didn't look much different, although she had grown as well.

"Your house is so nice!" Elsie said, smiling and touching the woodwork.

"We really like it," Emma beamed.

While Mommy Glick and Mam got coffee break ready, Dat, Doddy, and Marvin visited, while Uncle James took a tour of their barn. Elsie exclaimed about their rooms, the twins, and how much everyone had grown. They talked about school and how different their Mennonite school was compared to the one here in Jefferson County. They were having another big Christmas program.

Lizzie became a bit wistful about that. She so loved their Christmas programs when she was in first and second grade, with lots of plays and different parts. She felt almost jealous of Elsie's school, but she didn't say anything, mostly because that would not be polite.

They were sitting in the basement when Marvin joined them. "Hey, what are you doing?" he said, grinning.

"Marvin!" Lizzie said.

"It's good to see my nieces," he said, smiling a genuinely broad grin.

"You seem so big and old!" Emma said.

"I am!"

The girls giggled.

"Hey, you know what? On the way up here, over here, or wherever you live way out here in the mountains, you know what I saw? An upside-down tractor and trailer!"

"Not upside-down. Just lying on its side!" Elsie corrected him.

"It *was* upside-down, Elsie. I can still see all four wheels sticking up!"

"Marvin, it wasn't," Elsie said quite severely.

Emma and Lizzie stole sideways glances at each other, hiding their grins. They were still the same Marvin and Elsie—that was one thing sure.

"Anyway, a tractor and trailer has eighteen wheels, not four," Marvin corrected himself. "But what I can't figure out, how could he get himself in that position if there was no snow or ice? Do you suppose the driver fell asleep? He could have had a heart attack and fallen over dead in his truck."

"Marvin, you don't have to know," Elsie said.

"I know. But still . . . that was something to see! Whose ping-pong table?" he said, all in the same breath.

"Ours," Lizzie said proudly.

"Can you play?"

"Sure!"

They had just started playing, Lizzie realizing she had
a formidable opponent, when Mam called them for coffee break. Marvin was fast and accurate and had accu-
mulated five points to Lizzie's two.

They raced up the stairs, helping themselves to hot
chocolate and a handful of oatmeal and molasses cookies. There were also bought doughnuts from the bakery
in Marion. Mam had bought them the previous day,
saying she was just so sick and tired of baking. These
doughnuts were lighter than homemade ones. It seemed
you could eat three and still hadn't started. But Lizzie
didn't take three. That was because she had learned to
watch what she ate. Emma had helped her to understand that you couldn't go through life eating anything
and everything you wanted. So she carefully selected
one sugared doughnut and one oatmeal cookie. That was
all.

Doddy Glick teased the girls, telling them it looked
as if they had plenty to eat here in Jefferson County.
"You need to be out baling hay and milking cows on
a farm. That would get rid of some of your 'shpeck!'"
That meant it would help them lose weight. But he was
not unkind, having a twinkle in his eye when he said it.
Lizzie tried to stand up straight, pulling in her stomach
after he said that, but only for a while. She forgot about
everything except the joy of being with Marvin and
Elsie once again.

Marvin had to go with the men to the pallet shop after
break, so the girls played ping-pong a while before they
sat on the old sofa and chairs in the basement and talked.

They had plenty to talk about, living so far apart. Elsie told them about the teacher they had, who smacked the children's hands with a ruler if they whispered. One little boy quickly pulled his hand away and the ruler came down on his desk, breaking into three pieces.

Emma put her hands to her mouth and squealed, her eyes opened wide. Mandy giggled, and Lizzie said, "Hah-ah, Elsie! Then what did she do?"

"She got really upset then," Elsie said, taking a deep breath and launching into her story. They listened with rapt attention as Elsie related other stories of misconduct and punishments that occurred over the course of the school year.

They talked about their school, and swimming in the river. Elsie shivered, saying she couldn't see how they could like swimming in that awful river.

Suddenly they heard a great commotion upstairs. Mam was actually shouting, saying, "Oh, my word! This is just no sense! What are you doing here?"

There was such a loud fuss—men's voices mixed with women's laughter—that Lizzie and Emma just looked at each other. It sounded a lot like Doddy Miller and Aunt Vera!

They slid off the couch together and took the stairs two at a time, throwing the door open and standing together, peering out.

"There they are! Just like two rabbits! Come on out. Hello, hello," and Aunt Vera hurried over to shake their hands quite rapidly. "My, how you've grown! You girls are growing faster than a cornstalk in July. Do you help your mom good? Sure you do. Lizzie, I declare you're bigger than Emma. Yessir, you are. Stand here once." She pushed them together, back to back, triumphantly announcing, "See there? What did I say? Now, Mousie, you better let Emma catch up." She laughed at herself, before saying, "Remember, Mousie? You were so little we had to shake the blankets out to find you. Yes, we did. Didn't we, Dat?" she said, turning to Doddy Miller.

Doddy Miller came over, leaning on his cane. He had aged alarmingly. His smile and handshake were feeble, and his hands shook all the time, even if he wasn't shaking hands.

"Yes, Vera, she was tiny. Hard to believe. My, how you've grown. And there's Mandy."

They all turned to see Mandy and Elsie in the doorway, shyly peeking out at all the commotion.

"Now whose girl is this?" Vera asked, turning to Elsie.

Mommy Glick was smiling, saying, "That's our youngest."

"Really? You still have one that small? Well, I'll be. She looks like you, doesn't she now? Where are these twins? You know, we haven't seen them yet. I told Homer that's enough of that stuff, right now. We're going to go see these twins. Then when we heard about this pallet shop burning, we just came as soon as it suited. This is our busy time at the lumberyard. Firewood and coal. Yessir, Homer lives over there. Never at home. Sometimes I take supper over, sometimes Leroy does. Always something. Always something. Now, where are these twins?"

Mommy Glick was laughing openly, and Mam laughed with her. Aunt Vera was so fussy, but a real delight, talking and laughing nonstop. When she spied the twins, she threw both hands in the air and shrieked.

The twins were sitting side by side on the sofa, propped up with pillows. They were wearing freshly laundered pale blue dresses, and their blue eyes were lined with heavy black lashes. Their dark hair was thick and glossy, just as soft and silky as a bird's wing. KatieAnn had a small white pacifier in her mouth, and Susan was playing with a string of beads.

"Awww, Annie!" For once in her life, Aunt Vera was completely speechless. It was of short duration, though, as she soon regained her speech.

"Now I have never in all my life seen anything so cute! Are you sure they're real? Didn't you get them mixed up at the hospital? 'Course . . ." she paused. "I'd say they look a little bit like Emma did. That hair! It's so thick. And shiny. I can't get over this. I better sit down—I'll have a heart attack, next thing I know."

Uncle Homer smiled his slow, quiet smile, his eyes crinkling at the corners, shaking his head in disbelief as he said, "Isn't that something?" That's all he said.

Lizzie's head was whirling. This was actually the biggest surprise, to have Doddy Miller and Uncle Homers coming when Doddy Glicks were here. Mam was so flushed and excited, assuring them there was more than enough food to go around for dinner. They had come all the way from Ohio and were staying till Tuesday, which thrilled Emma and Lizzie.

Aunt Vera picked up Susan, holding her while she rocked back and forth quite furiously. Susan looked a bit bewildered, but she did not cry, actually enjoying her frantic ride. Vera had only two children, so she wasn't as used to babies as Mommy Glick was. But it was Vera who watched the twins while Mam and Mommy Glick finished preparing dinner.

Doddy Miller had brought Swiss cheese and Trail bologna, which was always a specialty from Ohio. He also had a fresh bag of round pink candies that tasted exactly like Pepto-Bismol. He always gave these to the girls, and they always thanked him, but never really ate any of them. They just didn't taste good, although they never told him.

Uncle Homers had brought plenty of food as well. Lizzie thought of her well-organized pantry, hoping sincerely Mam didn't throw everything in there any old way.

Lizzie discovered the fact that Doddy Miller was planning on staying a while. He might even stay permanently, because he loved the mountains here in Jefferson County, and since Mommy Miller had passed away, he had no real reason to stay in Ohio. Lizzie was worried about him, though. He was so very much older looking, much weaker in his legs, thinner, and so much more feeble.

He was on heart medication, Aunt Vera assured Mam, but there was no doubt about it; he was losing out.

Mam's eyes filled with tears as she watched her father leaning heavily on his cane to sit in the living room. But she controlled her emotions, turning to Mommy Glick and smiling.

"Well, since we're all here together like this, we'll just add more water to the soup, throw everything together, and have a good meal."

But Lizzie knew Mam would have plenty of good food for everyone. She always made more than enough when company came, so Lizzie figured there was no need to put water in the soup. They probably weren't planning on having soup to begin with.

When the men returned at lunchtime, the table was spread almost the entire length of the kitchen. Heaping platters of fried chicken, mashed potatoes with browned butter running down the sides, noodles, filling, and homemade baked beans with plenty of onion and bacon filled the table. There were also small glass dishes of coleslaw and red beet eggs, and, of course, those horrible little olive green saccharin pickles. Lizzie couldn't understand why Mam had to ruin a perfectly good company meal with those pickles.

Mam had made homemade dinner rolls, too. Instead of putting the bread dough in ordinary bread pans after it had risen, she oiled her hands well, pinching off small pieces of dough and shaping them into a round ball. She plopped them into square cake pans, adding more oil on the bottom of the pans first. Then she slid the pans back on the countertop and let them rise again, before baking them until they were golden brown and greasy looking on the top.

When they were cool, Mam could break them apart into individual rolls, although they looked like a bumpy cake when they were taken out of the oven. They were the best thing ever. You took a roll and broke it in half, spreading butter thickly on one side, and strawberry jam on top. They were so warm and soft, the bread melted in your mouth, leaving a sweet, buttery aftertaste because of the jam.

Lizzie ate two, but she could easily have eaten three or four. She hoped there would be a few left over, to eat in her lunchbox at school. But, of course, there were none left after the meal, which kind of upset Lizzie, because it would take her a long time to persuade Mam to bake them again.

Aunt Vera could hardly finish her dinner; she was talking so much. Doddy Glick laughed and laughed at her. He just couldn't help it, Lizzie thought. It was such an entertaining meal, listening to Vera banter with Doddy. They were both smart, and loved to tell interesting stories.

"I'll tell you one thing. You mark my words. Things are going to get bad. We're absolutely sure to have another depression. You watch," Aunt Vera said, shaking her head. She stopped talking long enough to take a bite of fried chicken, wipe her mouth, and swallow, before she started again.

"Remember the Depression? Sure you do. You're older than I am!" At this, Doddy Glick protested wholeheartedly. Mommy Glick smiled, and Uncle Homer shook his head, chuckling.

"You didn't have food like this then. You kept your chickens for the eggs—no chicken to eat. Beans. We ate a lot of pole beans. Annie, remember? No, you were just a little girl back then. How could you remember?" she went on.

Mam laughed. "Oh yes, I remember. Mam made us dresses from chicken feed sacks. We only had two or three dresses, one for school and a few for everyday or Sunday. We almost never had any meat to eat."

"Or eggs," Aunt Vera broke in. "You took your eggs to town, hoping to make enough money to buy flour and sugar. Yessir, we did! But the thing is, people aren't happier nowadays, even if they have a lot more money. We were happy as polecats, weren't we, Annie?"

Mam smiled and acknowledged that fact.

Lizzie looked at Elsie and smiled.

"Is she always so fussy?" Elsie asked.

"Oh, my, yes. Sometimes she talks more than this!" Lizzie said proudly.

"She's funny!"

"You should hear her sometimes!"

Watching Mam take away the dishes to prepare the

table for dessert, Lizzie thought happy little thoughts of thankfulness, mostly for all the good food on the table, and everyone who was there.

She loved all the relatives, on Dat's side as well as Mam's. They were very different, but the same in many ways, although there was no one like Marvin and Elsie. Since they lived here in Jefferson County, she supposed Edna and Debbie were just as dear, but Marvin and Elsie had lots of good memories for her.

She leaned over and said, "Emma says I act like Aunt Vera sometimes."

Elsie giggled. "I never heard you talk that much!"

Lizzie giggled back. "I'd love to be like her. There's nobody I like to listen to more than her. It gives me a warm, cozy feeling when she says 'Apps-olute-ly.'"

They hid their smiles behind their hands. Aunt Vera saw them and said, "Now, look at that. They're laughing at me. Yes, they are. Mousie! Now mind!" And she laughed.

Lizzie's eyes shone across the table, conveying all her love and admiration, Aunt Vera catching it and smiling back, returning all of Lizzie's love.

Relatives were better than bought doughnuts, Lizzie decided.

chapter 16

Driving Bess

Spring came to Jefferson County, clothing the ridges and mountains in a new, light green veil of color. The bare branches of the trees didn't really have leaves on them, yet everywhere Lizzie looked, the pale green color shone through. She supposed it was new little leaves pushing through the red buds of the trees.

The air was soft and new, after the April rains had washed away all the dirty snow and mud. Mam said Mother Nature did her spring housecleaning, too, with the wind and the rain.

Mam opened the windows of the house, letting the fresh breezes blow through. She washed curtains and bedspreads, quilts and rugs—even the doilies on the dressers. She washed walls, swept spiderwebs, and washed windows inside and out until they sparkled.

The girls had to help in the evening, bringing in the clean curtains and bedsheets, babysitting the twins so Mam could finish a room, or starting supper if it got really late.

Mam didn't even have time to go to town for groceries, so one evening she asked Dat if the girls could drive Bess to Malone, the small town a few miles before the town of Marion, where the supermarkets were.

Dat had bought Bess from Uncle Eli. She was an old black mare that was safe for Mam to drive. At the same time, he had bought a secondhand springwagon, just like the pony springwagon he had built for the miniature ponies, Teeny and Tiny, except it wasn't nearly as fancy. It was just an ordinary springwagon for a horse, painted plain black with no ornate gold scrollwork.

The difference between a buggy and a springwagon was the roof. There was no roof on a springwagon. Just a box with sides and one seat with a back on it. There was a dashboard on the front, so you wouldn't fall off behind the horses' feet. The seat was up higher than an ordinary buggy, so it was quite thrilling to ride in.

Emma and Lizzie were hardly ever allowed to take Bess by themselves, mostly because of Mam. She was afraid one of them would fall off, or they couldn't handle Bess. Dat always said something like, "Phsaw!" a bit like a snort.

"These girls are easily old enough to drive Bess to Malone. She's such a 'plug.'" That was Dat's word for a slow, lazy horse, which he had no patience for. Red was his horse, head held high and trotting along so briskly he had to keep a firm grip on the reins.

So that was how it all came about on Saturday morning. Emma and Lizzie were allowed to hitch up Bess to
the black springwagon and drive to the small town of
Malone to buy groceries.

Emma was taking her own shiny black purse, and
Mam gave her the money and shopping list, which she
folded carefully in different compartments of her wallet.
They put on freshly ironed coverings, pinned securely,
and black aprons, which were dressier than their gray
everyday ones.

Mam told them the springwagon had no lights on
it, so they had no turning signals. If they wanted to
turn left, whoever wasn't driving had to extend their
arm straight out to the side, in case there was a vehicle
behind them. That was so the person would know they
were turning in, and he would not try to pass from
behind, perhaps hitting them if he was unaware of their
turning.

"That's too embarrassing," Lizzie muttered.

"But you have to, or I won't let you go!" Mam said
sternly.

"We will," Emma assured her.

Dat had put Bess's harness on before he left for the
day's work at the pallet shop, so all they had to do was
slip on the bridle and hitch her to the springwagon. Bess
was so docile, she hung her head meekly, opening her
mouth obediently as soon as the steel bit of the bridle
touched her teeth. They backed her easily between the
shafts, fastened the leather straps used to pull the buggy,
and clipped the snap shut on the backhold straps.

Emma was allowed to drive on the way to town, so she fastened the rein attached to the bridle. Unwrapping the reins, Emma stepped back, checking every buckle and snap to make sure Bess was hitched up properly. She climbed up beside Lizzie, lifted the reins, and clucked her tongue, telling Bess to go. Bess stood there, quite content not to move an inch. They giggled.

"Come *on*, Bess," Emma said, slapping her lightly with the reins. So they started off at a slow walk down the gravel drive, turning right before Bess fell into her gentle, rocking trot.

This was wonderful. Lizzie took a deep breath of pure exhilaration. Sitting way up high on this wooden seat, and the horse so far below, with the warm breeze flowing through her hair—this was her idea of a fun thing to do on Saturday. It was much better than helping Mam clean house all day.

They went past Uncle Eli's place waving to Edna, who was raking the yard.

"Where are you going?" she shouted.

"To Malone for groceries!" Lizzie yelled back happily.

"Lucky!" Edna answered.

They waved again, and passed the shoe store where a new Amish family was moving to from Ohio. They had an odd name that Lizzie couldn't remember.

"When are those people moving in?" she asked Emma.

"Don't know. Soon," Emma answered.

Bess trotted on, down a small winding hill. Emma drove with her left hand, applying the brakes with her right. The brakes were a block of heavy rubber that rubbed against the steel rim of the wheel, pushed back and forth by a lever beside the driver. You had to push the lever out of one notch and push it into another, however you wanted the brakes to be, only a light pressure or a hard one, depending on how long and steep the hill was. Brakes were a very good thing on a buggy. They always made Lizzie feel more secure. If a horse wanted to run and keep on running away, you could always apply the brakes, which made it much harder for the horse to get out of control. So Lizzie could rest easy, hearing the grinding sound on the back wheel.

They passed Hetrick's pond, which was shining blue from the sky's reflection. Small green grasses grew in profusion, with the yellow color of the dandelions and the purple of the wild violets adding a colorful touch, much like an artist's palette. There was a blackened spot in the middle of the grass and dandelions, remnants of the bonfire that burned night after night in winter.

"Makes you feel like going skating!" Lizzie said.

"You wouldn't get very far," Emma said dryly.

Lizzie lifted her head, laughing. Birds twittered and chirped, flying in little arcs overhead, wheeling and dipping, either catching insects or busily gathering material to build nests. There were clumps of cotton candy clouds, as they called them, drifting lazily far above the birds. The sun shone warmly, caressing their backs with its warmth.

"Here we turn in," Emma said.

"Do I have to stick out my arm?" Lizzie asked.

"Mam said to. Of course!"

"That's so dumb."

"Come on! I'm turning!"

Lizzie swiveled quickly to see if a car was approaching from behind. Sure enough, a pickup truck was fast closing in on them, so there was nothing for Lizzie to do but extend her arm, holding it straight out and as rigid as she could.

Emma pulled on the right rein, and Bess clopped steadily to the left, gravel spitting out from under the steel rim of the wheel. As soon as they had turned, Lizzie clapped her arm securely to her side, her face flaming.

"That's so stupid, Emma. I'm not going to do it one more time."

"We don't have any turning signals, Lizzie. Stop being so thick-headed."

Lizzie didn't answer. She was going to have to talk to Dat about putting turning signals on the springwagon. It was just too embarrassing holding out your arm. It would be her turn to drive on the way home, so Emma would have to hold out her arm. She hoped sincerely a vehicle would come from behind, and Emma would see how it felt. But she said nothing.

Bess slowed to a walk, pulling them up a steep hill. Emma relaxed, letting the reins hang loosely, sitting back against the seat.

"Boy, she's slow. If she'd be going any slower, we'd be backing down this hill. Make her walk a little faster, at least," Lizzie said.

"You're just like Dat," Emma said, laughing.

Dat had told them where to tie the horse when they reached town. They were not supposed to cross the main highway that went through town. There was a hitching rack across the highway from the little general store under a large maple tree. Emma had gone with Dat to Malone, so she knew where it was, only she had never parked there herself. They were a bit nervous as they approached town, with more traffic on the road. Cautiously, they turned in to the hitching rack, expertly driving straight up to it before they stopped.

Bess came to a halt, happy to have reached her destination. The minute Emma loosened the reins, she lowered her head gratefully, rubbing her nose against the steel pipe. Emma slipped the neck rope around Bess's neck, tying the other end securely around the steel pipe.

Dat had shown both of them the right way to tie a knot in a horse's neck rope, so that the horse could not get loose and run away. It was a knot that only pulled tighter if the horse jerked on the rope. Emma could tie it properly, but Lizzie was still a bit unsure of herself.

She didn't tell Emma, though, because she didn't need to know that.

Emma grabbed her purse, and they walked to the highway. Looking both ways, they dashed across when there was no traffic in sight.

The bell above the yellow wooden door tinkled when Lizzie opened it. Actually, it was quite noisy, more like a jangling, and it startled them both.

"Good morning, girls!" A small round man approached them, his white teeth flashing under a coal black mustache. His head was bald, with a ring of black hair surrounding the shiny dome of his head. He was wearing a clean white apron over a red-striped shirt. Lizzie thought he looked exactly like a picture in her Mother Goose book of a grocer in a store.

"Good morning!" they answered in unison.

"Fine morning, eh?"

"It is," Emma said.

"If you need any help finding your things, let me know."

"I will." Emma propped her purse on a shelf, extracting her wallet and finding the grocery list. "Butter and margarine first," she muttered, heading toward the coolers lined up along the back wall. She kept finding items written on the list, so Lizzie decided she didn't need to tag along with her; she'd find some other things to look at.

She checked out the candy display, selecting a Fifth Avenue bar. Mam always let them buy a treat, and these candy bars were her absolute favorite. Sometimes it was

hard to decide between a Fifth Avenue and a York pep-
permint patty, but usually the Fifth Avenue won over.
They were so rich and chocolaty and crumbly. After you
ate one, you could eat another one right after it—that's
how good they were.

She wandered over to the magazine rack, selecting
one and flipping through it. She loved to look at all the
fashionable girls in magazines. They were so fascinating, with long, shining blond hair, wearing all kinds of
beautiful clothes. She wondered how it would be to look
like that. When she was a little girl, she longed for high-
heeled shoes. She did anything in her power to attain a
pair of shoes with heels on them. She was still intrigued
by beautiful women dressed in fancy clothes and shoes
that clicked when they walked, but she knew there was
no way she could be like them.

For one thing, she was Amish, and Amish people
dressed plain. She didn't think about it very much at this
age. She was happy to dress in the clothes Mam made,
pin her covering on, and go. There was a lot more to life
than trying to get Mam to buy her a pair of high heels.

Being Amish kind of settled that sort of thing. To look
so nice was beyond her reach. It was quite unattainable,
so she admired the girls in the magazine and was actually fascinated by them, even wishing she was half that
pretty, but it didn't make her feel disobedient or discon-
tented. That was just how life was if you were Amish,
and Lizzie did not wish to be anything else. The secure
circle of family and friends was quite fulfilling, and
besides, she could never hurt Mam and Dat by telling

them she was going to be English now. Her parents had often told them there was nothing wrong with English people being English. They were raised that way, and lots of them were good Christian people. So Lizzie never thought English people had to be Amish in order to get to heaven. God loved everyone, Mam said.

"Lizzie!" Emma hissed. "Get over here and help me."

Lizzie put the magazine away and hurried over where Emma was placing items in a small grocery cart. She looked a bit flustered, her note wrinkled, and her pen poised to cross off another item.

"I can't find vanilla," she said.

"I'll get it." So Lizzie walked up and down the aisles twice, checking all the shelves, but could find no vanilla extract. So she walked up to the counter and asked the grocer if he had any.

"Vanilla?" He wrinkled his brow, and Lizzie was quite alarmed to see his whole head slide back. It seemed as if the skin on top of his head was loose when he did that.

"Yeah, I've got that somewhere." He hurried around the corner of the counter, his portly frame careening around a stack of boxes. "Here. Here you go. Right here by the rest of the baking supplies."

"I'm sorry. I must have missed it," Lizzie said. She carried it triumphantly back to Emma, holding it direct-ly in front of her face.

"I asked."

"Did you? Boy, you have nerve!" Emma said, amazed that she had enough pluck to ask the storekeeper. Lizzie just smiled.

They found everything on Mam's list, and were ready to check out, when Lizzie spied marshmallows. They reminded her of Rice Krispie treats, which she just loved.

"Emma, let's get marshmallows and Rice Krispies to make Rice Krispie candy," she begged.

"No, Lizzie, it's not Christmas. That's about the only time Mam makes that."

"It doesn't have to be Christmas."

"No."

"Yes."

"Lizzie, no. Now stop it. I'm not buying them."

"I'm going to, then." Lizzie marched back to the cereal, grabbing a box of Rice Krispies and three bags of marshmallows. She threw them in the cart, her mouth in a determined line, her eyes flashing.

"Lizzie! Get them off the bread. You're smashing it." Emma flung the Rice Krispies out, setting them on a shelf. She fairly threw the marshmallows out as well. So Lizzie calmly gathered up the items and held them to her chest, walking behind Emma the whole way to the counter. She was so bossy. Lizzie didn't even have a chance. She was hungry for Rice Krispie Treats, and Emma could just give up this time.

"All done?" the storekeeper asked, sticking a pen-

cil behind his ear. How he balanced that pencil behind
his ear was quite beyond Lizzie, but she guessed if the
pencil stayed there his ears were pretty tight to his head.
Maybe that was why his hair fell out.

Emma loaded everything on the counter. The cash
register pinged, adding up every item. Lizzie clutched
the Rice Krispies and marshmallows until she was finished, then she stepped forward and put them on, too.

"Making Rice Krispie treats, are we?" the storekeeper
said, smiling. "I love them things."

"Me, too!" Lizzie beamed enthusiastically.

There was not one thing Emma could do. Not one.
Lizzie could tell she was aggravated by the way she
sniffed and lifted her chin, but that was alright. She was
going to have to give up.

Emma paid the bill, putting the change carefully in a
little compartment of her wallet for Mam. See, she had
plenty of money, Lizzie thought.

The storekeeper had his helper help them across
the street. The man could hardly push the cart up the
bumpy drive to the springwagon. Lizzie was terribly
embarrassed. She wished Emma would say something,
anything, to make a conversation, but she didn't. Lizzie
thought of things to say, but they all sounded too sense-
less. She was relieved after the last bag had been loaded,
and he said, "Have a good day, girls."

"You, too," Emma said.

"We will," Lizzie said.

They untied Bess, and Lizzie took her turn on the
driver's side. Bess backed away from the hitching rack,

then walked slowly down the drive toward the road.

"Put your brakes on," Emma said.

"She can hold it. This isn't a steep hill," Lizzie replied.

Bess stumbled, and the reins flew out of Lizzie's hands. Emma muffled a shriek, but Lizzie stood up quickly, reaching across the dashboard and grabbing them back as fast as she possibly could. She pulled back hard on them, saying, "Whoa!" She looked right and left, before pulling out on the road that led home.

"You're not fit to drive. I *told* you to put the brakes on," Emma said loudly, thoroughly frustrated at her driving skills.

"She didn't fall."

"She could have; she stumbled."

"But she didn't fall."

Bess fell into her slow and easy trot, and Emma turned around, finding two boxes of chocolate milk and a bag of potato chips.

"Here."

"You got chocolate milk? Good!" Lizzie loved store-bought chocolate milk, because it was so creamy and sweet, almost like a milkshake. The perfect thing to eat with it was potato chips, all greasy and salty.

"Mmm!" Lizzie took a long drink and smiled at Emma. "I didn't know you got chocolate milk."

"That's because you were too busy watching the storekeeper's ears. Lizzie, you were staring at him so much that I was embarrassed."

"Well, Emma, he didn't notice. I was trying to figure out how in the world that pencil stayed behind his ear.

What kept it from sliding down?"

"It was probably stuck in there pretty tight."

Lizzie crunched a potato chip and thought about that. Ears were funny things. Some boys' ears were so big they stuck out from their hair, parting it at the side. Other people hardly had any ears that you could see. Mam always said people with big ears were kind, and people whose ears were small were stingy and mean.

Dat said that was an old wives' tale, a myth, but it wasn't with the storekeeper. His ears were big and he was a very kind man.

She pulled on her own earlobes. "Are my ears big?" she asked.

Emma turned to look. "Mmm, kind of. You have long earlobes. Watch where you're going."

Lizzie watched the road, glad that one part of her ears was big. She wasn't always kind, just sometimes. Nobody was kind all the time, not even Doddy Miller. Once he had scolded them for coloring sloppily in their new coloring books, which Lizzie never forgot. Doddy Miller's ears were huge.

Emma started singing, and Lizzie joined in as soon as she finished her potato chip.

"Over the river and through the woods,
To Grandmother's house we go."

It was a Thanksgiving song in the spring, but it fit for today, and their song rang out as Bess clopped steadily homeward.

Billy

"**L**izzie, you're going to have to give up," Dat said firmly.

Lizzie swallowed the lump rising in her throat, looking at Dat with mournful eyes. "But, Dat . . ."

"No. This pony is completely blind now. She can't even tell the difference between light and shadow at all anymore. Watch." Dat held Dolly's halter with one hand, waving his other one swiftly past her eyes. She didn't even flinch. "See that?"

Lizzie nodded her head. Mandy stood beside her, nervously pleating her sleeve with her fingers, her big green eyes full of sympathy.

"Dat, some people drive blind horses," she volunteered.

"Yes, Mandy, they do. But Dolly is past the age where she can even pull the cart very far. You girls don't ride her much, and she just stands in her stall. Her legs hurt her all the time, because she has arthritis. See those painful knees?" Dat asked, bending down to run a hand expertly across a swollen joint.

Dolly flicked her ears, but stayed quiet, her head bent as usual. There was no doubt about it—she was hardly a healthy pony anymore.

"Well, what happens now? I mean, if we do have to get rid of her soon, what happens? She can't be hauled in a horse trailer like ordinary horses. Her legs would never hold up," Lizzie said.

"Oh, she'd be alright. She'd be a killer," Dat said.

"A *what*?" Lizzie asked, horrified.

"A killer. It means she'd be sold for her meat. They use horse meat for pet food. She's at the end of her rope, Lizzie. There's no use trying to keep her," Dat said.

"But nobody is going to kill her. That isn't right!" Lizzie wailed.

Dat sighed. He opened Dolly's door to her stall and patted her rump. She stepped painfully into her straw-filled box, stopping just inside the gate.

"She'll never know what happened. They do it as swiftly and painlessly as possible. She'll be put down, and never feel a thing. Actually, it's kind to put her out of her misery," Dat said.

Lizzie sighed, looking at the rafters overhead. She watched cobwebs swinging between them, pieces of hay twirling around as the breeze caught them.

Poor Dolly. She could not imagine life without her. She was such a sweet-natured, faithful pony. They had gone on so many rides in the cart, tied her to hitching racks, and untied her again, clopping briskly home with nothing to worry about. Now they would have no pony.

"You have Bess to drive," Dat reminded her, as if reading her mind.

"I know. But she's not a pony."

"I'll tell you what. We'll get another one. If Dolly leaves next week, I'll look around for a decent pony for you girls to drive."

"Not a wild one!" Mandy said.

"Maybe a little wild," Dat said, his eyes twinkling. "One you can hardly hold back!"

"Like Red!" Mandy squealed, clapping her hands.

Lizzie did not say anything. She didn't smile or join in the conversation, because if she did, Dat would think she was happy about selling Dolly, which she most certainly was not. What did it matter to let her stand in her stall and eat? At least she was alive. The thought of her being made into pet food was more than she could handle. *Probably Jim Zeigler's cats will eat Dolly*, she thought. That horrible slimy stuff from a tin can they fed their cats. The whole idea was just sickening.

Lizzie stalked out of the barn, her posture showing her rebellion. *If he has to sell Dolly, I won't be friendly about it, that's for sure,* she thought. He could at least let her eat oats and hay this summer yet, feeding in the pasture, standing under the apple tree swishing her tail at the flies. She didn't even want another pony. It wouldn't be Dolly.

Mandy caught up with her, touching her sleeve. "Lizzie, why are you acting so childish? It's best to sell her," she said.

"Mandy, I know it is. I just can hardly bear to think of it. She'll be killed!" Lizzie lamented.

"We'll get another one," Mandy consoled her.

There was yard to be mowed that evening, so Lizzie started while Mandy helped Emma with the dishes. The grass was thick and long, so she had to use all her strength to push the reel mower through the thickest spots. Back and forth, back and forth she went, until her face was quite red and perspiration trickled down her spine. She loved to mow grass, so she kept going, in spite of becoming too warm.

She had just turned around on the farthest side of the lawn, when a truck slowed and rattled up the drive. It was a black and silver truck, pulling a matching horse trailer. Lizzie's heart sank, then thudded thickly in her chest. Already! Dat had made plans to sell her, so soon, and only told them a few hours ago.

She did not know what to do. She couldn't help load her and she couldn't watch. She hadn't said good-bye to

Dolly at all. How could she go out to the barn now with Dat there?

She'd just mow grass. She set her jaw firmly and plowed through the thickest grass, never glancing in the direction of the barn. On she went, determined not to cry. When she could no longer bear it, she glanced over, just in time to see a hesitant, bewildered old pony being led up the ramp.

Dropping the lawn mower, she ran blindly toward the house. She couldn't go in to Mam and Emma, so she ran to the side of the house away from the barn, and flung herself down behind the chimney. She pulled up her knees, laid her head on them, and wrapped her arms around her legs. Moaning, she cried softly, tears mixing with perspiration, her hair sticking to her forehead. She had never felt quite as forlorn in her life, except maybe when Teeny and Tiny, the miniature ponies, had been sold. But in a way, that was different.

They could stay alive, their new owner being a kind, older gentleman. Dolly was simply going to die. It was quite the saddest thing she could ever think of happening on a beautiful evening like this. The sun was just above the mountain, making everything seem golden. The spring breezes were warm, just lovely. It was the time of year when you could open your windows in the evening and it smelled of lilacs and violets, warm summer grasses, and freshly tilled soil.

Sighing, Lizzie wiped her eyes, dug a Kleenex out of her pocket, and blew her nose fiercely. Fresh tears overflowed when she thought of poor Dolly, struggling

to keep her balance in that trailer, speeding down the
highway to some awful building where they killed her
and turned her into pet food. She hoped every dog and
cat that ate their food that was part of Dolly got sick and
died. Especially the cats.

She bit her lower lip, trying to stem the flow of tears.
She thought about going in to the kitchen right now,
and telling Dat he was cruel. He was. He could have let
Dolly live for a while yet. She couldn't go telling Dat
what she thought, because he wouldn't like that. Amish
children are taught to obey, respecting their elders, so it
was really out of the question. But she was not going to
be nice anytime soon.

She got to her feet, wiping her eyes with her tattered
tissue. When she got to the
kitchen, Dat was stand-
ing by the counter

talking to Mam. She walked stiffly past them, sniffing, her nose held higher than usual, and did not say one word to them.

She had the satisfaction of hearing Mam say, "What's her problem?" and Dat said quietly, "Dolly."

Good. So he knew how badly she felt about losing her. Good for him.

· · · · ·

Time has a way of erasing grief and sad feelings, Lizzie found out. She didn't think much about Dolly as spring turned into summer and they all began playing on the ridge again.

Their cabins of the previous summer were in absolute shambles, ripped black plastic, rusty pallet nails, soggy pine needles, and broken boards, making the whole Lovely Acres seem a bit sordid.

Every afternoon when their work was finished, they all went to the ridge with plenty of food and Thermos jugs of ice-cold water or tea. Mam bought diet soda for Lizzie, and she shared it with Mandy in their little house.

As the summer temperatures soared, the ridge lost some of its charm, mostly because of the stifling heat. They spent their afternoons at the river as long as the heat prevailed.

One evening at supper, Dat told the girls a man named Bill Werner was bringing a pony for them to see. Dat shook his head and laughed, saying, "He said this little guy has spunk. He's not sure if you girls can handle him or not."

Mam frowned.

Mandy's eyes opened wide, a forkful of mashed potatoes halfway to her mouth. Lizzie just looked at Dat, her
eyes narrowing.

"We're getting a new pony?" Jason asked.

"We'll see," Dat said.

"Melvin, I sure hope you don't get a pony that's dangerous. These girls aren't as strong as you are," Mam
said, a bit sternly.

When a horse trailer pulled in later, Lizzie dashed
down the steps and out to the barn, Mandy at her heels.
She was so excited, she forgot about being shy around
the driver of the truck.

"Dad here?" he asked, coming around to the back
of the trailer. He had long blond hair and a mustache,
with a cap pulled low over his eyes. He had a big wad
of chewing tobacco in one cheek, making it difficult for
him to talk. He spat to the side, a long stream of dark-
colored liquid landing an unbelievable distance away.

Lizzie swallowed, feeling a wave of nausea come up
into her throat. Mandy whispered, "How can he spit
that far?"

Lizzie shrugged her shoulders. She forced herself
to look at the driver, then she said, "He's around here
somewhere."

Dat rounded the corner of the horse trailer, saying,
"Hello there!"

"Bill Werner." The blond man stuck out his hand. Dat
grasped it and they shook hands, quite furiously, Lizzie
thought.

"Pleased to meet you," Dat said. He looked so little
compared to this tall, blond giant that Lizzie almost
pitied him.

"Here he is. We'll let you see him and see what you
think. He ain't no ladies' pony. These your daughters?
Dunno. Dunno." He shook his head.

Lizzie's heart raced as the door was let down. There
was a clanking and rustling as Bill Werner walked up
the ramp and loosened a grayish brown pony. They
came down the wooden ramp so fast, Mr. Werner had to
hold back the pony with all his might.

"Whoa there. Watch it now," he said.

And there he was. This pony was so beautiful, Lizzie
gasped before clapping both hands to her mouth. She
hadn't meant to make an audible sound, but she just
couldn't help it. He was perfect. A Shetland pony in
grayish dapple color, except he was a bit brown, too.
His heavy mane and forelock were the color of oatmeal,
his neck was arched, his perfect ears pointed straight
forward, and his nostrils quivered with excitement. He
picked up his dainty forefeet before putting them down
impatiently.

Dat walked around the pony, and Lizzie could see he
was every bit as excited as she was. He gave a long, low
whistle. "He sure is a nice-looking animal."

Lizzie thought he sounded a little conceited. Why
couldn't he say "pony" instead of "animal"? Maybe he
was too excited and felt a bit carried away.

Dat pulled away the pony's lower lip, checking his
teeth to see how old he was. That never made any sense

to Lizzie, although she had seen it done lots of times. Dat had tried to explain the procedure to Lizzie once, about the length and shape of the teeth, but she didn't think it could be a very accurate way of telling a horse's age. Some horses might chew harder than others, so it was hard telling if you got a four-year-old or an eight-year-old. You just had to trust the papers, stating the age.

They talked about age, where he was raised, who broke him, and on and on about seemingly endless boring subjects. Lizzie wished Dat would try and hitch him to the cart, but he didn't. Instead, he sent Lizzie to the house for the checkbook, wrote a check, and talked on and on about more boring subjects.

Finally, he led the pony back to Dolly's stall. He snorted and shied, prancing around, bouncing on his feet as if there were springs in them.

At last the English man left, the trailer rattling behind the truck, down the drive and out the road.

Dat turned to Lizzie.

"Are you going to hitch him up?" Lizzie asked quickly.

"Do you want to?" Dat asked.

"Of course!" Mandy shouted.

So they got the pony from his stall. Dat asked the girls to come up with a name. They thought of lots of names, but none of them really suited him, until Dat suggested "Billy." That was a nice-sounding name and not hard to say or with too many syllables or too fancy.

So Billy he was.

For as nervous as the new pony was, he did fairly well. Dat had to adjust so many straps that Lizzie

became terribly impatient. The girth that went around
his stomach was too loose, so he had to adjust that. The
bridle was too long, so he had to loosen and tighten four
buckles. When they finally had him between the shafts,
he wouldn't hold still long enough for Dat to climb into
the cart. He told Lizzie to hold his head, meaning the
bridle, but to stay to the side, because he wanted to
break loose so badly.

"Better let me go by myself the first round," Dat said.
His eyes were shining. He had no fear of ponies, loving
the challenge of trying out a new one. Lizzie hoped she'd
be allowed to go along after he had run him a while.

Lizzie held firmly to the bit, and after two attempts,
Dat clambered into the cart. He found his seat the
instant Billy lunged, and they were off, down the gravel
drive, then turning on to the hard road, the wheels sliding on the macadam.

And then, Mandy and Lizzie stood beside the fence
laughing helplessly as Dat's straw hat flew off his head,
and the pony went trotting down the road faster than
anything they had ever seen. They could do nothing but
hang on to the fence and bend over double from their
laughter.

What was so funny, the pony didn't trot like other
ponies. His feet went so fast they whirred like a wheel.
His little hooves went "blip-blip-blip-blip" so fast, it just
created a giggle, even if you didn't feel like giggling.
They couldn't watch Dat turn around, because he drove
the pony out of sight, but when they saw him coming
down past Uncle Eli's place, they started laughing again.

"I never saw a pony run like that!" Lizzie gasped.

"He's never going to make the turn into the drive-way!" Mandy screamed, clutching the neckline of her dress.

And he didn't. Dat was holding back as hard as he possibly could, but Billy lowered his head, tucked his mouth under, arched his neck, and ran. Dat finally got him slowed down enough to turn around, making the turn into the drive from the opposite direction. His hair stuck out in a wild circle and his beard was split in the middle, where it had blown back. He was laughing, his eyes shining, and when Billy slid to a stop, he shook his head.

"This pony is crazy!" he said, shaking his hands to restore the feeling.

"Can I go along this time?" Lizzie asked.

"Look at that! He isn't even puffing one bit. He's one tough pony," Dat said with a laugh.

And he wasn't. He looked quite unfazed, just like he had a nice long walk.

When it was Lizzie's turn, Billy started off with the same powerful lunge. Her head flew back, and for a wild instant, she felt as if she was falling off backward. They slid around the corner before starting down the road. The wind rushed in Lizzie's ears, and the world zoomed past almost as if she was in a vehicle. But the thing that caused her to laugh so much was the pony's little dappled rump. His tail was so thick and heavy, and with each tiny step, the hairs on the tail all jiggled up and down. The britchment that went down the sides of the rump bounced up and down so fast, it almost made her dizzy.

Blip-blip-blip-blip. Faster than any pony Lizzie had ever driven, the little hooves were placed on the road, pulling the cart steadily behind him. When Dat could get him slowed down enough, they made a short turn on the road. Then Billy knew he was headed home, and he burst into another level of speed.

"You want to drive?" Dat shouted.

Lizzie looked up at Dat, questioning his decision.

"Can I?" she asked.

"Sure you can."

He handed over the reins. When Billy felt the slightest release on the bit, he surged forward. Lizzie was afraid, but she wouldn't tell Dat. She simply hung on to the reins with every ounce of strength.

That was when she discovered the joy of driving, really driving, a fast-moving pony. There was a feeling of oneness with Billy, as if they were attached, and he could feel every move of Lizzie's fingers. It was a wonderful sensation. She had never felt so powerful, so afraid, and so exhilarated all at one time.

"See? You can handle him," Dat said gleefully.

"You think so?" Lizzie asked, about to burst with happiness.

"Sure!"

Lizzie could not get him stopped to turn in the driveway, so they drove on past before turning him around. They slid sideways to turn but made it safely to the barn. Mandy was jumping up and down with Jason beside her, wanting the next turn. Lizzie shook her hands, as she said, "You better let Dat drive, Mandy!"

So that was the beginning of the "Billy" era. He was quite a pony. There was actually a time when Lizzie thought she was glad Dat had made the decision to sell Dolly. Billy was much more fun to drive, although they were not allowed to hitch him up on their own for many weeks. Dolly was still precious to Lizzie, but only in her memories. Billy was the one she loved now. He soon learned to nicker for them in the morning, just like Dolly had always done. And he was a much better-looking pony.

Debbie was afraid of Billy at first. She would not go for a ride, and neither would Edna. Even Uncle Eli shook his head, telling Dat he wouldn't pay fifty cents for that piece of dynamite. Uncle Eli liked his horses to be fat and dependable, certainly not the type you couldn't trust. Mam wasn't very happy about Billy, either. She told Dat the girls would not be able to hold that pony, and if they had a wreck, who was going to pay? He was going to keep on with these ponies till someone got hurt, or far worse, killed. Aunt Mary clucked her tongue, saying she didn't know why they didn't just send him to be made into dog food right away, too.

Dat laughed good-naturedly and caught Lizzie's eye, and she laughed back. There was not one thing wrong with Billy. He had excellent stable manners and the girls could hitch him up by themselves—though not without thudding hearts and nervous stomachs at first. He just

loved to run as fast as he could and he didn't like to
be held back. So they drove him all over the place by
the time the summer was over. Down to the river, past
Hetrick's pond, around the sawmill and pallet shop,
wherever and whenever they had a chance. Mam even
let them drive him to the dry goods store that was three
miles away, which was actually six miles going there and
coming back.

And still he did not pant. Dat said he could probably beat any other pony's endurance he had ever seen,
which only made Lizzie love Billy more.

chapter 18

A Part of Growing Up

Lizzie could tell that there was going to be a special church service, because a group of young people had been going to instruction class all summer.

Mam had explained it all to Emma and Lizzie, and they were instructed to take this very seriously. Dat was even becoming more strict. Every Sunday morning when they did not have church services to attend, he told Emma, Lizzie, and Mandy to come sit with him in the living room. There he had four German Testaments, which he distributed to them. It was a time of seriousness, devotional, which was a bit new, something to get used to.

Dat read from the Scripture, Emma read the verse after his, and so on. Reading the German language was a bit more difficult for Emma, so it took her longer to read a verse. German had always been easier for Lizzie, so she zipped through her verse, her reward being a sincere smile from Dat. As Mandy faltered through hers, Lizzie noticed Mam's unhappy expression. Now what had she done wrong? Evidently something, by Mam's drawn eyebrows and stern mouth.

On they read, with the exact same results—Dat's smile, sighing impatiently if Emma missed a word, until Mam opened her mouth, then closed it again before she said something.

"Melvin, I can hardly stand it. Emma and Mandy are trying to read just as well as Lizzie. You need to have more patience with them. If Lizzie can read so much better than the others, why does she have to read at all? She knows everything there is to know about German."

Dat stared at Mam, looking a bit subdued afterward. Lizzie felt like running out of the room and never reading a word of German ever again. Her feelings were terribly hurt. She had always been proud of her German reading ability. Emma did lots and lots of other things so much better than she did, just not reading German.

That's just how Mam is, Lizzie thought. *She always likes
Emma so much better than me. I'm not going to talk to Mam
for so long she'll know she hurt my feelings.*

They finished their session of German reading, Dat
telling them they were free to do whatever they wanted.
It was an in-between Sunday, meaning a day their district
did not have services. All Old Order Amish have church
services in the home only every other Sunday. This is an
old custom to allow ministers to visit other districts.

Emma and Mandy wandered into the kitchen for a
snack, but Lizzie went straight up the stairs to her bedroom. There she flung herself on the bed, stuck her face
in her pillow, and pitied herself. She had planned on
crying, but the tears wouldn't come, probably because
she was more angry than hurt. After awhile, she felt a bit
silly, so she got up, smoothed her dress, and wondered
what she could do to worry Mam. She didn't care what
Emma said; Mam always took her side. Emma never did
one thing wrong. Mam should be glad she had a daugh-
ter that could read German so well. If she'd be a boy,
she'd probably be a preacher or a deacon, then Mam
would be so happy to hear her read German in church.
She ought to be ashamed of herself.

She couldn't figure Mam and Dat out lately. Everything the girls did they were scolded for, saying you
don't do this, and you don't do that. It was starting to
work on her nerves. She knew it had something to do
with the group of youth who were joining church. It was
a very serious thing, but Lizzie had a hard time understanding why it had to be different at home.

Oh, Mam had explained it well, and Lizzie could grasp what Mam told her. She said these young people felt they were sinners, needing to be baptized, which represented their sins were washed clean because Jesus died for them on the cross. The whole summer they were learning how to live a new life, trying to live the way that Jesus taught. They learned the rules of the church, promising to obey and help build the church as well.

Mam even had tears, telling them all this, and Lizzie could tell Emma took it very, very seriously. But the whole thing depressed Lizzie to the point of tears. That would not be fun. They had to be so careful. What if they said or did one thing wrong ever again in their life? And if they grew into old people, imagine the hopelessness of their situation, unless they all stayed at home and read their Bible almost continuously.

Mam read her Bible a lot, teaching the girls as well. Emma read her Bible every evening before she blew out her kerosene lamp, but Lizzie wasn't even sure where her Bible was. Mam would have a fit if she knew. Lizzie never told anyone, but the Bible scared her a lot. It just seemed too holy, too righteous, and too impossible to follow. She often wished she wouldn't feel that way, wondering if it was normal. Emma said the Bible comforted her, which was beyond Lizzie's understanding. That made her feel so guilty, she could never, ever tell Emma how she felt.

She heard steps coming up the stairway, so she slammed her door shut. Nobody had to find her.

"Lizzie, are you in there?" Mandy called.

No answer.

"Lizzie?"

She still didn't answer.

The steps turned, the sound ebbing away, before starting down the stairs. *Good. She can go play with Jason.* She rolled over, searching for a book to read. She had read them all so many times she hardly knew what to read anymore. If only Mam could find more Trixie Belden books, but they were getting harder to find. Lizzie just loved those books, about teenagers not much older than she and Emma solving exciting mysteries, some of them even a bit dangerous. They were all interesting, good clean books that Mam approved of. They weren't allowed to read just anything. Black Stallion books were good, too, but she only had a few of them. Besides, the last one she had read was about a huge colony of bats living in a cave. They were called vampire bats. If one of them bit a horse or a human being, the bats gave them a disease called rabies which caused you to lose your mind, dying a slow, painful death.

After Lizzie had read that Black Stallion book, she would not go outside after dark. There was an electric pole light at the corner of their yard, which was actually the neighbors'. Every night in the summertime, there was a cloud of insects whirling around the pole light, and often bats swooped in among them. Dat had often told Lizzie they didn't have rabies, only on very rare occasions. Bats also have radar that warns them of an approaching object, which makes them steer clear of it. Lizzie told Dat these vampire bats are thirsty for blood, and they'll sit on horses and drink their blood. Mam said she should quit reading those Black Stallion books if she was going to be afraid of bats and said very likely none of it was true.

Marvin had told her quite often that once a bat flew into Rachel's room and sat in her hair. Rachel screamed and screamed, picking up the horrible creature and throwing it against the wall with all her strength, where it slid to the floor, quite dead. That one was very likely rabid, or why would it have become tangled in Rachel's hair? Evidently the radar was not working, meaning it had already lost its mind. So Lizzie remained unconvinced, refusing to go out at night for a very long time.

There was her Tom Sawyer book, which she had read countless times. But that one was boring now, so she kept looking. *My Friend Flicka*. Oh, that was a different one. She had only skipped through that one the first time. She was so happy to have something to read. Rearranging the pillows, flipping on her back, she opened the book and began to read. She was soon transported out West on a horse ranch, working alongside this family who owned a great herd of horses and cattle.

She was quite unaware of anything out of the ordinary until she heard her name being called quite anxiously. It sounded as if it came from the yard outside. She listened a while, but didn't answer. Then she heard someone at the foot of the stairs.

"I *did* look up there!"

"Well, where could she be? Lizzie!"

It was Mam, and her voice sounded as if she were close to tears. For an instant, Lizzie felt like remaining quiet, but her conscience made her do what was right. Putting her book aside, she yelled, "What?"

"Where *were* you?" Mam asked weakly. Lizzie could hear the great relief in her voice. "We looked all over the place for you."

"I was up here."

"Then you didn't answer when I called you the first time," Mandy said.

Lizzie didn't answer.

"Come on down now, Lizzie. We're having a snack," Mam said.

Lizzie sat up and fixed her hair and covering a bit, checking her face in the mirror, before starting downstairs. She was so pleased that Mam was worried. That was so good for her, because now she would be more careful what she said, and like her every bit as much as Emma. She would talk to Mam now, after all.

Dat and Jason were making popcorn, the smell making Lizzie hungry. Jason squealed, jumping up and down when the popcorn started making pinging noises against the lid. Mam had made a pitcher of ice-cold chocolate milk, and there were pumpkin whoopie pies and blueberry pie. Lizzie sat in a chair, smiling at Emma, feeling so happy because everyone had been worried.

"Where were you, Lizzie?" Mam asked.

"In my room."

"What were you doing?"

"Reading."

"Didn't you hear us looking for you?"

"Hm-mm."

"I bet you did," Emma said.

"No, not until someone was calling for me in the yard." She unwrapped a pumpkin whoopie pie, taking a huge, soft bite. The icing stuck to her cheek, and she wiped it away with her hand. Mmmm. Mam made the best whoopie pies.

Suddenly, out of the clear blue sky, Mam said very seriously, "Lizzie, I know why you went to your room. It was because you were angry at me, and you were pouting. That is just an awful habit of yours, and I certainly hope you get over that childish whim before you get older. I did not mean to hurt your feelings about reading German. I just meant to remind Dat to have more patience with Emma and Mandy. That was not fair to them. They cannot help it if they can't read German as well as you can."

Lizzie stared back at Mam, chewing a mouthful of whoopie pie. There was nothing to say. So what if Mam always knew if she was pouting? At least, just for this once, she had been absolutely worried.

"Well?" Mam questioned, getting no reply.

Lizzie shrugged her shoulders.

The popcorn was ready, and Dat poured it into a huge stainless steel bowl, adding salt and melted butter. Everyone took their own colorful plastic dish and dug into the bowl, shaking it down, piling more on top to make the dish heaping full. That was Lizzie's favorite Sunday snack. The buttery, salty popcorn, washed down with cold chocolate milk. It was amazing how you could have a whole mouthful of popcorn and the minute the chocolate milk hit it, the popcorn all dissolved and went to nothing. Kool-Aid, iced tea, or water did the exact same thing. She supposed if they were English and drank Pepsi, it would dissolve popcorn, too. That was because popcorn was mostly air.

"Where's church next time?" Emma asked, around a mouthful of popcorn.

"At Levi Kanagys," Mam said.

See? There Emma talked with her mouth heaping full and Mam did not say one word about it. That's why I pout, Lizzie decided.

"It's a baptismal service," Dat said.

"I know."

"Do you know what that is?" Dat asked.

"Mam told us," Lizzie said quickly.

"Did you understand?" asked Dat.

"Mm-hmm."

"I wondered, though," Emma broke in, "if someone's sins are all forgiven when they are baptized, what happens when they sin again?"

"That's a good question, Emma," Dat said. "Actually, that's when the power of Jesus' blood goes into effect. After you profess to believe in Jesus, you become one of God's children, and your sins are forgiven when you repent, praying to be forgiven. That happens over and over again as we go through life."

Oh, Lizzie thought. *So that's how it works.* Well that made everything seem much more possible. It wouldn't seem quite as dangerous joining church if you had a chance of making some mistakes afterward.

"How old do we have to be when we decide to be baptized?" Emma asked.

"Not yet, Emma. You need to feel the need to become a better person, and you're only thirteen. In some churches they're baptized at a very young age, but we believe it's alright to wait until you're a bit more mature," Dat replied.

Lizzie wished they'd stop talking about all this serious stuff. Everything had been strict enough around the house lately. It just gave her the blues. She didn't know why things had to change when you became older.

"You girls probably think Mam and I have become a bit hard on you of late. We don't mean to be, but watching the youth join church this summer and seeing how fast you're growing up, kind of puts a fear in us. Like we want to do all we can to help you girls be the mature young women you should be, before you join the youth and go to the singings Sunday evenings," Dat said, so soberly that it sounded as if there were tears in his voice.

That was nice, what Dat said, Lizzie decided. She believed him, and felt like trying hard to please Dat and Mam in everything. But that was enough now.

"Let's go for a walk, Mandy," she suggested.

So they tied on their head scarves and thin coats, stepping out into the early autumn afternoon. They turned into the field lane beside the house, kicking large brown hickory leaves as they started out. The whole lane was littered with acorns, big ones and little ones—even some double ones.

"Acorns are the cutest things," Lizzie said, bending to pick up a few. "These little things on top look like a hat."

"Let's gather a bunch to put in a bowl."

They picked out only the nicest ones, those that still had their "hats" on. Their pockets bulged with them, so they put a bunch in their coat pockets. They continued their walk up the gradually sloping hill toward a lone, craggy pine tree that stood way on top. Smooth hay fields stretched on each side of them, and the little group of houses by the highway looked like a village on a greeting card. Samuel Renno's farm was to the left, the red barn standing in contrast to the colorful mountain. Their white house and silver windmill, with the adjoining sheds and corncribs, made quite a picture. Lizzie just loved it here in Jefferson County. She often noticed the beauty of the area.

Lizzie plopped down by the pine tree to look at the view. Mandy sat down beside her, and they said nothing. The wind sighed in the pine branches, reminding them of the ridge.

"I miss the ridge," Mandy said quietly.

"Me, too."

"I don't know what got into Mam and Dat," Mandy said fervently. Her big green eyes searched Lizzie's face worriedly. "I mean, we used to be more carefree or something."

"I know what you mean. But you know what? They could start by telling Emma not to chew with her mouth full. See, Mandy, that's why I go pout. Mam doesn't understand, but she likes Emma a lot better than me. I am *always* being scolded for something; Emma never is. Her mouth was completely full of popcorn and do you think she got scolded? Oh, no."

Suddenly Mandy sat bolt upright, her green eyes flashing. "*Lizzie!*"

Lizzie was surprised into speechlessness.

"You act so childish. You know you heard me knock on your door when you were upstairs in your room the *first* time. You should be spanked. Who do you think *Dat* was favoring when he gave you that *nice* smile every time it was your turn to read German? You are the one who was Dat's pet, then. It's always that way when we read German. It was so good for you what Mam said. How do you think me and Emma feel when you're rattling off your verse twice as fast? You know what's wrong with you, Lizzie? You're childish and jealous. You're so jealous of Mam and Emma, it's a wonder your face doesn't turn green. You can just be mad at me if you want to, but for once in your life, you're going to hear it. You know we have a nice Mam and Dat. They would never favor one of us over the other. Get it out of your head!"

Lizzie stared at Mandy, her mouth open in disbelief. *Mandy!* Quiet little unassuming Mandy. Lizzie was shocked, then ashamed. She felt so ashamed, she didn't say anything for a very long time. Mandy was sifting pine needles through her fingers, her chin on her knees. The trucks and cars droned far below them on the highway, and the breezes played with the pine branches above them.

"You had better think about it, Lizzie. I hate when
you don't talk, and you do it more and more often."

Lizzie looked up at the sky. She blinked her eyes and
chewed her fingernails. She thought about what Mandy
had said. Pouting was her way of getting back at Emma
or Mam. She never felt like pouting because of Dat.
Maybe pouting was just jealousy. Maybe she just wanted attention, like a three-year-old.

"I don't know why I pout," Lizzie said miserably.

"I do."

"You don't."

"Yes, I do. You pout so everybody will get worried
and think, *Oh, now what did I do to hurt precious Lizzie's feelings?*"

"You don't know."

"Mm-hmm, I do."

Lizzie cast a sideways glance at Mandy. She started to
smile before she said, "Mm-hmm, I do!"

Mandy flopped back onto the soft pine needles and
burst out laughing. Lizzie put her head on her knees and
laughed with her. The laughter was a wonderful healing
of all the bad feelings that had been pushing their way
between them, maybe even the whole family.

"So, I'm childish," Lizzie gasped. "Why don't you
spank me?"

"I'm going to," Mandy said, rolling over and preparing to smack her. But Lizzie was off, running down the
hill as fast as she could, with Mandy in pursuit. They
came to the thick hickory leaves before Lizzie rolled into
them, her breath coming in painful gasps.

Mandy delivered a few good blows on Lizzie's legs, before she stopped to regain her breath, too.

"Whew!"

"Whew!"

"That was fun!"

"Let's hitch up Billy!"

"Let's do!"

They were up and running, Lizzie's sides aching. She felt so very much better, running around outside, just being twelve years old again. She forgot all her petty little jealousies, thinking instead how Emma and Mandy must have felt when she sat there absorbing Dat's praise.

It was sad, having to worry about the responsibilities of growing older, but she could still have Mandy and Billy. As long as things didn't get too serious, she supposed she could handle it.

chapter 19

The Renno Farm

Mam and Dat did not buy their milk at the store in cardboard or plastic containers like some people. They thought it was much too expensive, so Lizzie and Mandy—or sometimes Emma, if she wasn't too busy doing something else—would walk down to the highway where there were a group of houses. They would turn to the left instead of going straight across and walk along the highway for a short distance until they came to the Renno farm.

They were never allowed to drive Dolly or Bess, and certainly not Billy after they had him, because they would have had to pull out onto the highway on the other side, and Mam said it would be far too dangerous, with all those trucks on the road. So they had to walk, carrying the little tin gallon jug with a lid on top, to have it filled with milk from the milk cans in the cooler.

It was a job, just an ordinary everyday chore they didn't dislike, but weren't too excited about, either.

On Saturday morning, Mam and Emma were cleaning, as usual. Lizzie was supposed to be helping more than what she was actually getting accomplished. The main reason she wasn't getting more work done was the Saturday morning paper. She kept reading the comics, or trying to get a bit of crossword puzzle done if no one yelled at her. It wasn't that Lizzie was being rebellious; she was actually in quite a good mood.

But cleaning just wasn't very interesting, with Emma going ahead and doing most of the important things. She almost always went over Lizzie's dusting, clucking her tongue in that annoying way, which meant *"Lizzie, why don't you grow up and dust as well as I do? You will never learn, no matter how often Mam tries to tell you"*. This morning was no exception.

Lizzie found the paper when she cleaned out the magazine rack, and since it made her too tired to hold the paper while sitting in a chair, she spread it on the floor, her chin in her hands, her knees bent, and the rest of her sticking up in the air. She was not bothering anyone or being in Emma's way, just innocently reading the paper, while Emma took the furniture polish and sprayed it on the dust mop. She began swishing it vigorously along the glossy hardwood floor until she came to Lizzie and stopped.

Lizzie saw the dust mop out of the corner of her eye and looked up. "What?"

"Move."

"Go around me."

"Move, Lizzie."

"No."

"I'm going to tell Mam. Mam!"

Lizzie didn't even stand a chance. *Emma didn't even give me time to move out of her way*, she thought.

"Mam!"

"What?"

"Look at Lizzie!"

There was silence as Lizzie got to her feet, quite guiltily. She was expertly folding the paper in half, then in fourths, before placing it back in the magazine rack. Her sentence, however, was handed to her quite promptly.

"Lizzie, you are too old to be lying in the middle of the floor reading the comics while Emma does all the work. I don't know what to do with you if you don't help better with the cleaning. Mandy is even cleaning the basement all by herself and there you are," Mam said, her hands on her hips and her cheeks quite red.

"Well, what shall I do?" Lizzie asked.

Mam sighed. "Why don't you and Mandy go for milk and then you can both clean the basement when you get back? I need milk for the cornstarch pudding I'll be making."

"Okay," Lizzie agreed. "I'd rather go for milk than clean any day."

"That's not hard to figure out," Emma snorted, picking up dirty socks and shaking dust fuzzies off them before putting them in the clothes hamper.

"Too bad we're not alike," Lizzie sang out, watching Emma's stiff back entering the bathroom door.

Emma turned around and told Lizzie there was no way she was ever going to be fit to be a wife if she didn't learn to clean her house while she was still young.

Lizzie ignored her, although she knew what Emma said was true. For one thing, if she was married, it would be her own house and her own stuff. That would be entirely different. Here, as soon as one room was cleaned, Jason got all his toys out again, and the twins pedaled around in their walkers. You could never tell if it was cleaned or not. When she had her own house, there would be no babies. She didn't like them.

So Emma just didn't have to worry one bit about her housecleaning abilities. What about the pantry before Mommy Glick came, huh? But she didn't say it, knowing Mam was in no mood for the girls' bickering this morning.

Lizzie yanked open the basement door and yelled for Mandy. "We have to go to Samuel Rennos for milk!"

"I'm not done yet," Mandy replied.

"I have to help you when

we get back," Lizzie told her.

So they set off, head scarves tied securely, their coats
snugly buttoned around them. There was a stiff autumn
breeze, making them bend their heads, their skirts whip-
ping around their legs. Lizzie told Mandy it was time for
Mam to buy tights—winter had to be close behind this
cold wind.

After they turned left on the highway, the wind hit
them from the side, but it was easier to walk, because
it didn't push quite as hard against them. They looked
both ways before crossing the busy road, trucks hum-
ming past them as if they were little specks. It was much
safer to walk out here, Lizzie thought. They could never
get Billy to stop and wait until all the traffic was past.

The big gray farmhouse was close to the road. There
were two porches, one on the side, and one on the
front. There was a fence made of fancy wire all the way
around it, which Lizzie always thought was an excellent
idea. How would they keep their little children off the
road otherwise?

They opened the yard gate, hurrying up the sidewalk
to the south porch. They could smell a faint good odor
before they knocked and opened the door.

"Come on in," said Sylvia Renno with a smile. She
was a dark-haired, portly woman in her thirties who had
a big family, with children of all ages. Her kitchen was
small, with long, narrow windows letting in plenty of
sunshine.

There was a large black range against the farthest
wall, the stovepipe looming up behind it like a big black

soldier. The oven door of the wood-fueled range was partly open, and Lizzie could see long, low pans of shelled corn roasting inside.

So that's what we smell, she thought. The children were seated on chairs or benches, holding large yellow ears of corn, shelling them with their hands, the kernels plunking into a huge stainless steel bowl.

One of the older girls was churning butter in a glass churn. It was a large churn, with wooden paddles hanging from a metal lid. There was a handle attached to these paddles, and when she turned the handle, the paddles went back and forth, back and forth. The milk in the jug made a funny, slapping sound. Lizzie almost pitied the milk, seeing it never had any rest. About the time it was pushed to one side of the churn, it was pushed back. No wonder it just gave up and became butter.

"So you need milk?" Sylvia asked, wiping her hands on a dish towel.

"What is all the corn for?" Lizzie asked, her curiosity overcoming her good manners, as she forgot to answer her question.

"The corn? We're roasting it for cornmeal. After it's finished roasting, we'll take it to the mill and have it ground. Doesn't your mother make fried corn mush on cold winter mornings?" Sylvia asked.

"Sometimes," Lizzie answered. "But we never roast our corn. Is it field corn?"

"Oh yes, just the good, heavy ears. It makes the best cornmeal."

"It smells good in here," Lizzie said.

Sylvia pulled on her coat, tying her head scarf as the girls followed her out the door. She opened the milkhouse door, pulling it shut behind them so the wind would not swing it out of her grasp.

"That's some wind," she remarked.

The interior of the milkhouse was painted a metallic gray. The concrete floor was damp and cold, with a ring of water around a metal drain in the middle. There was a big concrete trough along one wall, where huge steel cans of milk were set in ice-cold water. The air smelled fresh and damp, with a faint scent of soap, making it seem clean.

Sylvia reached up on a peg in the wall and deftly got down a rubber mallet with a sturdy wooden handle. It looked like a hammer, except it was much heavier. She banged it against one side of the lid, and then the other. A few more taps and she could easily lift off the heavy steel lid. She reached across the trough, getting down a shiny stainless steel dipper, which she used to stir the milk. That was because all the cream rose to the top of the milk, no matter if it was in a huge container like this, or a small plastic pitcher. That's just how milk was.

After stirring it well, she dipped about six dipperfuls directly into the small jug, which she balanced expertly on the edge of the milk can with one hand.

Lizzie asked her what would happen if the little jug of milk dumped into the cold water.

Sylvia laughed, saying they would have to drain it, clean it well, and refill the trough. She was always careful, and it had never happened, although she wasn't saying it never would.

After paying for the milk, Lizzie asked if they were allowed to set the jug on the milkhouse floor and look at the animals before they left.

"Samuel's in the field husking corn, so yes, you may," she said. "Just be sure and close the milkhouse door when you leave."

They thanked Sylvia, who returned to her work in the kitchen. They opened the door to the cow stable. There were no cows in it, being all out at pasture, but the girls could see where the cows were tied to be milked.

The cow stable was as clean as the milkhouse, with fresh straw for the cows to stand in. The middle aisle was swept spotlessly, and lime was spread on it to make it look nice and smell clean.

Here in Jefferson County the Amish people did not have milking machines and big tanks to keep their milk. They milked all their cows by hand, keeping the milk in cans, so they had smaller herds of cows.

Lizzie loved this farm even more than Doddy Glick's farm. It was exactly like a child's picture book of farm animals. Besides the cows, there was the horse stable, containing stall after stall of gentle brown Belgian work-horses. They were tied in their stalls, tossing their heads and making the chains rattle up over the wooden beam. They munched on some leftover wisps of hay, gently blinking their huge eyes, their black eyelashes sweeping softly over their eyes. Lizzie would have liked to stand there for hours, watching these wonderful, kind-looking animals.

There were pigeons cooing somewhere overhead, but no matter how long Lizzie stared up into the beams of the ceiling, she could never find them. Mandy said they were probably higher up, in the haymow, under the roof.

Beside the big barn, there was a smaller shed built on, where there were about twenty pigs — big pink creatures with snouts that were never still. A pig could hold perfectly still, not even blinking, and its snout kept right on moving, either right or left, up or down. Some of them were lying in the dirt, sound asleep, only an ear twitching occasionally. Others were snuffling around their feed trough, although there was no feed in it.

"Wonder why Samuel Renno doesn't feed his pigs more often?" Mandy asked.

"I don't think you feed pigs all they want. They'd eat until they die, I think," Lizzie mused, although for some reason that didn't seem right, either. Then she remembered. Doddy Glick's pigs that were in a pen with the steers had feeders they pushed open with their snouts. Any time of day or night, they could push on these lids

and put their head underneath, eating all the feed they wanted.

"No, Lizzie . . ." Mandy started.

"Oh, I know! Now I remember. Doddy Glick's pigs! I guess these pigs just have to be hungry until Samuel Renno does his chores," Lizzie said.

They found a pen of sheep, which had heavy coats of wool all over them except their faces. They leaned in over the fence, trying to touch them, just to see what the wool felt like, but they always turned sharply and dashed away on their skinny little legs. Lizzie thought they must weigh an awful lot to be carried around on those dainty hooves, unless the only thing that made them look so fat was all the wool on their bodies. They were really strange-looking creatures.

Before they picked up the milk jug, they found the chicken yard, with colorful chickens scratching in the dust. The wind caught their tail feathers, looking as if they could blow away across the fence and into the wild blue yonder. It didn't seem to bother the chickens at all; they just went about their business, pecking in the dirt and dust.

On the way home, Lizzie sighed. Imagine how that would be. They would go to the henhouse for eggs, fry their own cornmeal mush, and have all the milk they could possibly want for their own use. She was sure Sylvia baked all the bread for the family, too. They would butcher the pigs for ham, bacon, and sausage.

She wanted to be like Samuel Rennos so much that she wished she could turn back time and be like Laura Ingalls. That would be a lot better than buying bread at the store, and never making butter or anything like that. They would store their onions and pumpkins in the attic, just like Laura Ingalls did. She was going to have to talk to Mam and Dat about living more like Samuel Rennos.

Dat could at least buy a cow and Mam could churn butter. Lizzie would be so excited to milk a cow. She was almost certain Dat would know how, and he could teach her.

The little tin milk jug felt heavy after they crossed the highway, so Mandy took a turn carrying it.

"You're really quiet. This wind is pushing us home!" Mandy said with a laugh, pretending to run.

"I was just thinking. I'm going to ask Dat to buy a cow," she said.

"Why?"

"We should churn butter, roast corn, and have pigs to butcher."

"What is wrong with you? If we get a stinking old cow, I don't want to milk her. You wouldn't either, Lizzie. I guarantee it."

"Yes, I would. You know I would. I'd enjoy that. I'd even churn the butter!"

Mandy said something that sounded a lot like "Humph!" but Lizzie wasn't quite sure.

The wind almost tore the screen door out of their hands as they reached the kitchen door. Panting, they set the jug on the table before they took off their scarves and coats, hanging them carefully on the proper hooks, remembering it was Saturday morning and Mam and Emma had just finished cleaning.

"Mam, you're going to have to ask Dat to buy a cow," Lizzie said, brushing back her windblown hair.

Mam looked up from scouring the sink. She frowned as she took notice of Lizzie's wildly blown hair. "Lizzie, your *hair*! How many times did I tell you to comb it in tighter? You look like a genuine . . . I don't know what," she trailed off wearily.

"It was windy. Mam, you have to ask Dat if we can get a cow," Lizzie repeated, undoing hairpins as she fixed her hair.

Mam wrung out her dishcloth, hanging it on the wooden rack beside the sink. She smoothed her wet hands across her apron, then she sat down on a kitchen chair.

"Do you use conditioner on your hair, Lizzie?" she asked, trying to be patient and kind. Lizzie knew that tone of voice very well.

"No, it smells bad."

"Now, Lizzie, it doesn't. If your hair doesn't start staying in better, you're going to have to use hairspray or something."

"Oh, no, Mam." Lizzie shook her head from side to side. "Lavina and Esther told Emma hairspray causes your forehead to break out in big pimples. Do you want me to walk around with flat hair and big, ugly, red pimples, or woolly hair?"

Mam narrowed her eyes, pulling her mouth down in a strict expression, but before she accomplished it, her mouth and nose twitched in a funny way. She threw up both hands and burst out laughing helplessly. She laughed and laughed, until she took a Kleenex and wiped her eyes under her glasses, and said, "Lizzie!" in the most endearing way.

Lizzie was delighted. She laughed with Mam, although she wasn't sure what was so funny. Emma and Mandy laughed just to hear Mam.

"Now, why do you want a cow?" Mam asked, still smiling. She lifted one of the twins from her walker onto her lap.

"Samuel Rennos' farm is so cozy. Did you know they use field corn and shell it and roast it, and have their own cornmeal for fried mush? Anyway, they churn butter, too, and it's all so much like pioneers. Like Pa and Ma, Laura, Mary, and them."

"You think a cow would make our barn and house cozy?" Mam asked.

"Sort of."

"Who would milk her?"

"Me. Did you ever milk a cow, Mam?"

"Oh, my, yes. I used to be a 'maud' here in Jefferson County as a young girl, and I certainly did. I milked five or six cows by hand every morning and evening. I know exactly how to milk a cow."

"Does Dat?"

"Oh, I'm sure Dat can milk."

"Well, then . . ."

"A cow would be nice. We could get a little Jersey. They give rich milk and not as much as those big Holsteins," Mam mused.

"I'll churn butter," Emma said. "I always wanted to live in an old farmhouse, so churning butter goes right along with that, too. And quilts—I have to learn to make quilts."

Dat was quite unprepared for his wife and all the girls to meet him at the door, begging him to buy a cow, of all things! He always thought he wouldn't be able to understand women—now he was sure he wouldn't.

chapter 20

The Cow

And so Dat bought a cow. As cows go, she was a very nice one. A small brown Jersey, with huge, dark eyes framed with heavy lashes, a dished face, and a wet black nose that was so much cuter than those Holsteins, in Lizzie's opinion. Her bones were small—even her legs and feet were delicate for a cow.

Dat gave her the most comfortable stall, where Dolly had been, so he didn't need to make a new feed box. There was one there, low enough for the cow to reach easily. She looked quite content, standing amidst all the loose, clean straw, swishing her tail and chewing her cud. That was, after she was tired of walking around her new stall and mooing. Dat said she was probably mooing for her calf, because she had just been "fresh."

"What in the world does that mean? If she was fresh, does that mean she's stale now or what?" asked Lizzie.

"No, no. That is just a term for saying she just had a calf. Now she'll have plenty of milk for a while."

"Oh."

Lizzie wasn't too sure about this cow, although she said nothing. For one thing, she didn't like the smell of her. She smelled a bit sour or something. She also had this annoying habit of sticking her tongue in her nostrils, which was just disgusting. Horses and ponies would never do that. She was positive once she learned to milk her, she would like her a lot better, because, in a sense, she was disappointed. Lizzie wished the cow wouldn't smell sour and act so dumb.

When it was almost suppertime, Dat told the girls to come along if they wanted to learn how to milk. They also needed to think of a name. Most cows were named Bess or Mollie or Spot, he said, but they already had a horse named Bess.

"Spot is a dog's name," Mandy said.

"Not always."

"It is in the lower grade reading book."

"I guess you're right. Okay, no Spot or Bess. What's wrong with Mollie?"

"'Mollie is a girl's name," Emma said.

Nothing Dat suggested suited the girls at all. Somehow, it seemed hard to name a cow, and the poor cow never did have a name. She was always "Cow," or in Pennsylvania Dutch, "Coo," or "De Coo."

That first evening they were fully planning on naming her, but the more the girls looked at her, the less they felt like naming her. She was just such an ordinary cow; it seemed too grand to give her a name.

Dat pulled up a small stool on the right side of the cow and pushed it up against her so far that Lizzie was afraid he would crawl under her.

"Dat, she's going to kick at you!" Lizzie warned.

"Nah," Dat said, self-confidently.

WHAM! The cow's hoof flew through the air so quickly, it was a blur, but the sound of her hoof hitting the stainless steel bucket assured them all that she meant business. No one was going to milk her!

Dat grabbed the stool, stood back, lifted his hat, and scratched his head. "Boy! She must be used to a milker. Whoa, girl." Dat smoothed his hand across her back and down her sides, talking to her in soothing tones. He stayed well back from that right hind foot, Lizzie noticed, so she was sure he wasn't perfectly comfortable with her.

He eased carefully onto the stool again, gingerly grasping the cow's teats to pull the milk out. She stepped over, whacking her tail hard on Dat's head, sending his straw hat flying across the stall. The girls gasped, just sure that her next move would be another resounding kick.

"You better watch it," Lizzie warned him.

"She'll be alright," Dat said. He started milking slowly, pulling gently, until the cow seemed to be holding still and allowing it to be done.

"Here's how you do it," he said. "One teat on each side. First the front ones, then the back ones. Don't pull too hard, or she won't let her milk down. If she doesn't let her milk down, you can pull all you want, but you still won't be getting much milk."

The cow seemed to be settling down, being reasonable, although she would not eat the feed Dat put in her box. Lizzie thought she didn't look too relaxed, and, sure enough, just as Dat thought she would let her milk down, she crow-hopped away again, leaving Dat sitting in the middle of the box stall, looking as silly as he felt.

Dat got up quickly—so quickly, in fact, that Lizzie knew he had had enough.

"Dumb cow!" he shouted. He hurried around to the other side, pushing her none too gently to the place where she had been. "Now, whoa!" he yelled.

He clapped the small stool beside her, firmly grasped the teats, and started to milk. He was not taking any more monkey business. The girls hid their giggles behind their hands, rolling their eyes to each other, so Dat would not see or hear them. He was not happy. The cow was definitely not enjoying this either, turning her head to look back at Dat as if to say 'Why don't you go get a milker and stop your stupidity?' She turned to the feed box, snuffling around in the feed before licking up a mouthful with her tongue.

Now, thought Lizzie, *she'll be fine. She's relaxing enough so that Dat can finish milking her.*

He was milking methodically now, so he called the girls over to watch. They all slipped quietly into the box stall and held perfectly still, as the cow let down her milk. It was like magic. Suddenly, the milk came down into the bucket so thick and fast, the milk that was already in it became foamy. Instead of a thin stream that made a hissing sound, there was a heavy, thick stream that made a dull, swooshing sound.

"See? She's letting down her milk!" Dat said. "Now, when the milk slows down, that means you are about finished. But you need to be very careful to get the last bit of milk, because if you don't, she could get mastitis, which is a bad thing. The milk gets all lumpy and curdly and she hurts when you milk her."

Lizzie felt sick to her stomach. Eww! Cows were not near as cute and "Laura Ingalls-y" as she had thought. *Stinky old thing,* she thought, but did not say it, because she was the one who had wanted the cow. She wished with all her heart she had never seen this strange creature.

But the cow was there, and in time Lizzie learned to milk her. Mandy always went along and sometimes helped milk her, but mostly, the responsibility was Lizzie's.

Mam taught the girls to take a clean cloth and attach it on top of a glass gallon jar with clothespins, set the jar in the sink, and pour the warm, foamy milk through the cloth to strain it. She always fussed and scolded if there was any straw or dirt in the bucket, so Lizzie had to be careful to keep the milk as clean as possible.

After the milk had been strained, it was cooled in the mechanical cooler in the basement.

Mam bought a butter churn and the girls helped make the butter. That was fun at first, but became extremely boring after the first few weeks. You could turn and turn and turn that handle, and the milk sloshed around in the churn, looking exactly the same way it always had. The girls learned to take turns if their arm became tired, but as a rule, churning was a wearisome task.

Mam loved the homemade butter to cook with. She said it made the best browned butter for noodles and mashed potatoes. It had a more pungent odor than store-bought butter or margarine. Mam always shaped the butter into a nice, clean bowl with a tight lid on it, and had a wide knife to take out a scoopful whenever she needed it.

The longer Lizzie milked the cow, the more relaxed she became. So relaxed, in fact, that she and Mandy would often have an avid conversation when they entered the barn. Lizzie would throw a scoopful of cow feed in her box and grab the stool from the wall, kicking some clean straw around the back end of the cow. She would flop down on the stool, sit on it, bend over, and begin to milk with sure strokes. The cow was accustomed to the girls and never made much fuss. She had kicked once or twice, but it was never anything serious. Lizzie had soon found out if she kicked or didn't act calm and docile, there was something she did wrong, like digging her fingernails into a tender area or something.

So it all worked out well, after they learned to trust each other, till one cold winter evening when Lizzie was about halfway through the two back quarters. Without warning, up came the cow's right hind leg in a vicious kick, hitting Lizzie squarely on the knee, then stepping solidly into the bucket of milk.

Lizzie yelled as the stool flew out from under her and she sat down hard. She grabbed her knee, but saw the overturned bucket with all the milk trickling away.

"Ow! Ow!" Lizzie cried, turning to crawl away before the cow stepped on her. She put her injured knee down, putting weight on it without thinking, and great searing spasms of pain exploded in her knee. She screamed, and Mandy joined in, while the harassed cow danced a jig in her stall.

"You have to get the bucket!" Mandy cried.

"I can't!" Lizzie sobbed.

So Mandy made a brave dive for the bucket, before the cow would trample it again. She opened the gate, her big green eyes rolling in fright, watching the cow, with Lizzie crying and yelling "Ow! Ow!" in the corner.

"Lizzie, you have to get out! Right now! That cow is mad! She's going to tramp on you!"

"*Help me!*" Lizzie yelled, her face fire engine red and every vein in her neck sticking out.

Mandy made another heroic dive, helping Lizzie to her feet as the cow watched belligerently in the corner. With Lizzie's arm around Mandy, they made their way out of the barn. Mandy latched the gate quite firmly before they made their painful way to the house. Halfway there, Lizzie told Mandy she could not make it, and sat down in the snow.

Mandy was quite hysterical. "Lizzie, *get up*! You can't sit there in the snow like that! *Get up*!"

"No! It hurts!"

Lizzie resumed her wailing, so Mandy cast one wild-eyed look at Lizzie before dashing to the house. She returned promptly, with Dat buttoning his coat and clapping his hat on his head.

"What is going on? Get up, Lizzie!" he said.

"I can't. My knee hurts too bad," she answered.

"The cow kicked her, Dat; I told you," Mandy said.

Dat knelt down in the snow, gingerly touching her knee. "Ouch! Ow!" was Lizzie's response.

"Let's see if you can bend it. Come, let me help you up." He took both Lizzie's hands, pulling her to her feet, but she could put no weight on that knee. She tried to bend it, but found it too painful. So with Mandy on one side, and Dat supporting her with an arm around her waist, they slowly made their way to the house. Lizzie's face was quite pale, her mouth clamped in a straight line, as she tried to endure the pain without yelling.

Mam was inside the door, a very serious expression on her face. "Melvin, do you suppose she broke it?"

Dat shrugged. "She sure can't put any weight on it."

Even Emma was concerned. She hurried to bring the
blue hassock and a clean, soft pillow for her leg. Lizzie
eased into the platform rocker, and Dat gently lifted the
injured leg onto the pillow.

"Does that hurt too much?" he asked.

"N-no."

Mam went down on her knees, gently touching the
knee, asking Lizzie to bend it, and looking at Dat with
worried eyes. "I wonder."

Lizzie probably could have bent her knee if she wasn't
quite so afraid of the pain. It definitely was starting to
feel better than it had, but she didn't say so. She hoped
very much it was broken. She had always wanted a cast,
because it would draw so much attention. She would
have to go to the hospital and get piles and piles of get
well cards. All her friends would want to sign their name
on the cast. She would just sit there and give them mark-
ers, smiling prettily (but a bit painfully) and everyone
would pity her and love her very much.

"Now see what you can do," Dat was saying. "Just try
and bend it for me, to see whether you broke it or not."

So Lizzie obediently pulled up her leg, which really
went quite well, considering the amount of pain it had
caused her.

"Good!" Mam said.

"You're lucky, Lizzie," Emma said.

"I don't believe it's broken. Probably just bruised
rather badly," Dat said, with a sigh of relief.

"I'll get my elastic bandage and wrap it real good,"
Mam said, hurrying off to find it in the bedroom drawer
where she kept her bandages.

Lizzie didn't say anything, because she was too disappointed. She doubted if she'd ever break anything in her entire life, the way this was going. She always just bruised or sprained ankles and knees. Well, if it wasn't broken, she sure wasn't going to sit in this chair very long; that was one thing sure.

Mam returned with the roll of Ace bandage, which was a beige-colored fabric that was soft and elastic. It was Mam's answer for every ache and pain, so Lizzie gritted her teeth while Mam wound it gently around her aching knee. It didn't even hurt very much, but no one was going to find that out now, as long as she could get all this attention. Besides, someone was going to have to finish milking that ignorant cow.

"Dat, you have to finish milking," she said.

"What happened? Why did she kick like that?" Dat asked.

"I have no idea. She's just dumb! I wish we never would have gotten that smelly, ugly cow!" Lizzie burst out.

"Who wanted her?" Emma called out.

"Who thought it would be all 'Laura Ingalls-y?'" Mandy sang out.

"I still like her—just not if she kicks," Lizzie defended herself.

So Dat went to finish the evening chores, while Lizzie sat on the chair, her knee aching, and pondered the difference between what seemed all cozy and pioneer-like from the outside. But when you actually had a cow and a butter churn it seemed a lot different. Cows smelled bad, kicked, stepped in the bucket of milk, and had so many other disgusting habits, you could write a whole tablet full. It was the same way with making butter. The task was so tiring, you hated it before you even started. She shuddered, thinking about shooting a pig in the head and butchering it.

She was most definitely not going to marry a farmer. Even to think of a whole cow stable full of huge black and white Holsteins was depressing. Smelly creatures! Then Mam always told the girls they must learn to pray for God's will for their lives. She wondered if it was alright to ask Him to please not make her milk cows, though. There were lots of other ways to make a living that were just fine. Now she wished so much she would never have wanted a cow, because now she just had a brand new concern in her life: how not to ever marry a farmer.

She sank down low in her chair, her brows drawn low over her eyes. The evening was long and tiresome, her knee still throbbed painfully, and her thoughts became steadily more burdensome.

Dat entered the kitchen. "Lizzie, that cow has mastitis. She's just full of infection. You must not have been milking her properly in the back. That's why she kicked like that," he said.

"My hands get so tired," Lizzie said darkly.

"Well, if you don't try and do better, we're going to have to sell her," Dat said firmly.

"Just sell her," Lizzie mumbled.

"What? And lose all my homemade butter? I guess not," Mam said.

So Lizzie learned a very valuable lesson through the cow. Sometimes you had to grit your teeth and do things you disliked, and after a while, it didn't seem quite as bad. Especially if you had no choice.

chapter 21

Doddy Miller

Spring arrived early that year, with lots of warm sunshine at the end of March. Mam said the sun was so friendly you could almost feel its smile. Gardens were put in early, although Aunt Mary said they would have a cold spell in April, which never happened. Every day was warm and pleasant, except for spring showers every now and then.

There was only one thing to spoil that wonderful spring weather. Uncle Eli allowed a bachelor named Joseph Peachey to build a cabin on the edge of Lovely Acres. They were all quite upset about this, but there wasn't much they could do about it.

One evening they all marched back up to the ridge, deciding to ignore Joseph Peachey and his bachelor cabin. Briars had choked out the trail. There were lots of weeds growing along the edge of the pines. Every-

thing was just horribly depressing. Their little huts were
an awful mess, same as every spring. But this year, it
seemed like the magic was gone. It just wasn't fun anymore. They stood around, a subdued group of friends,
with nothing to say.

Danny kicked at the pine needles, stuck his hands
in his pockets, and surveyed the tops of the pine trees.
"Well, what are we going to do?"

"I don't feel like fixing up our cabins this year," Edna
said.

"It isn't the same with that real cabin right here where
we play," Debbie agreed.

"It isn't fair," Lizzie moaned.

"Did you know he catches sparrows and opens their
chests to watch their hearts beat?" Danny asked.

"Who said?"

"Ivan and Ray."

"Huh-uh!"

"Who could be so cruel?"

"He's a strange bachelor."

"Must be."

"Especially if he lives way up here on the ridge by
himself."

"He spoiled our life good and proper."

They all marched back down the trail, singing "Lovely
Acres, Ugly Makers!" as loudly as they could. Somehow, it eased the pain, and they hoped Joseph Peachey
was in his cabin, hearing every word they sang.

It was the same spring Uncle Eli and Dat found out
about a new highway that was being planned. It would

run straight through their neighborhood, past their be-
loved ridge. It was enough to give them the blues.

Uncle Eli and Dat talked with the neighbors, but they
all agreed that there was very little any of them could do.
Once the state decided on a project that huge, everyone
might as well just step politely aside, they all said.

So that was the end of the ridge. Debbie, Lizzie, and
Mandy had a serious farewell talk under the locust tree
in the yard.

"I guess we just have to realize we're growing up,"
Debbie said sadly.

"I guess."

"And changes happen."

"Yeah."

There was silence as Debbie broke off blades of grass, rolling them between her fingers.

"Another thing," she said. "I don't know how many evenings I could play, because of all my homework. Since I'm in high school, I have more and more books to bring home every night, it seems like. Besides, I'm signing up for baseball this spring."

"Are you?"

"Mm-hmm."

"We have to pick raspberries at David Phelp's raspberry field this summer. And work in some other orchard," Lizzie said.

"Do you?"

"Mam said."

"Wow!"

"We're old enough to earn money now, and there's lots of work in these orchards around here."

They wandered into the house, where Mam and Emma were washing the supper dishes.

"We kept your plates of food warm," Mam said.

"Oh, good. We're hungry. Mam, we can't play on the ridge anymore because of Joseph Peachey's cabin. Why did Uncle Eli have to let him build there?" Lizzie asked, peeping under the aluminum foil-covered plate.

"I guess he needed a place to stay. He works for Eli at the sawmill," Mam said, smiling at Debbie as she set a plate of mashed potatoes, gravy, corn, and macaroni and cheese in front of her.

"Mmm!" Debbie said appreciatively. "I love Amish food." She spread a piece of homemade bread with apple butter, then took a bite, rolling her eyes at Lizzie.

Doddy Miller came hobbling into the kitchen with his walker. He had come to stay for a few weeks, before taking up permanent residence at Uncle Aarons' place. His health was failing, his steps becoming shorter, and his balance unstable. Mam told the girls he had hardening of the arteries, which had something to do with his heart.

He was not the same now. His hair and beard were still as snowy white as ever, his eyes were just as brilliant blue, and his nose as big, with all the purple and blue veins running through it. He did not tease them as much and was less talkative now. Sometimes he became irritable, which was very unlike him. So Mam was relieved to know he was moving in with Uncle Aarons. Much as she would have liked to have him stay with them, she had her hands full with the twins, Emma still being in school and all. This was Emma's last school year, so Mam looked forward to having her help at home.

"There's my girls," Doddy said, more quietly than usual.

No one answered, because they were eating.

"What are you doing?" he inquired, sitting beside them, breathing heavily, his hands resting on his walker.

Lizzie told him all about Lovely Acres, Joseph Peachey, the new highway, and Debbie's homework and baseball.

Doddy Miller listened closely, then he smiled, shaking his head. "Sounds to me as if you're going through a bad case of growing up. You're probably at the age where it's just not as much fun playing on the ridge as it was a few summers ago, Joseph Peachey's cabin or not. You're about old enough to quit playing there," he said kindly.

Lizzie buttered a piece of bread and frowned. He didn't know. He probably never did anything that was nearly as much fun as playing pioneers and Indians on the ridge.

"What are you doing tomorrow evening?" he asked.

"Nothing. Why?"

"I'll tell you what. You can push me in my wheelchair up to the harness shop and Andy Byrd's store, and I'll buy you ice cream," he said, his blue eyes twinkling.

"Okay! We will!" Mandy said excitedly.

Andy Byrd had just put in a small grocery store beside the harness shop. He was an older gentleman who was retired and enjoyed visiting with his customers, especially Doddy Miller. He sold all kinds of ice cream, in cones, ice cream sandwiches, or icy, colored, juicy Popsicles. But everyone's favorite was a thick block of Hershey's Neopolitan ice cream, chocolate on one side, vanilla in the middle, and strawberry on the other side. There were two "lids," like two pieces of bread on a sandwich, but they were made with the same ingredients as an ice cream cone, except they were flat.

Andy Byrd would take two of these flat "lids", unwrap a thick block of the ice cream, plop it on top of one lid, and put the other lid on top. It was like an ice cream sandwich, except a lot bigger and much better, because of the three different flavors. Lizzie always ate the strawberry part first, because that was her least favorite, saving the chocolate for last.

Lizzie grinned, telling him they would go.

Darkness was closing the day, so Debbie got up, saying she had to go home and do her homework. "Thanks, Mrs. Glick, for the good supper," she called, waving to Mam as she opened the screen door.

"You're welcome, Debbie," Mam answered.

Lizzie sighed, her elbows on the table, her hands propping up her chin. Doddy Miller watched her, then he asked, "What's wrong, Lizzie?"

"Oh, nothing!"

"Did you milk your cow?" he asked, trying to hide his grin. The cow was a never-failing source of amusement for Doddy Miller, who teased Lizzie about how much she liked to milk.

"No."

"You better go."

"I know." She got up, ready to get down the bucket, when Dat came in the back door, carrying a frothy pail of milk. Lizzie's eyes opened wide. "You milked tonight!"

"You weren't here for supper, so I figured you'd be late. I could milk tonight," Dat answered.

"Good," Lizzie said fervently. "Dat, why did Uncle Eli let Joseph Peachey build his cabin right at the edge of Lovely Acres?"

"I guess he needed a place to live. He's kind of different. I guess he was talking about moving to Montana or some western state. Maybe it was Alaska. I'm not sure."

"I wish he would move to Montana. We can't play on the ridge now, with his big green cabin right there," Lizzie said sourly.

"You could, Lizzie," Emma said.

"I know we could," Mandy chimed in. "It's all Edna and Lizzie."

"It's probably a good idea to quit playing there. You are working in the orchards this summer anyway, aren't you? I doubt if Joseph wants a bunch of children yelling around his property all evening, after a hard day's work at the sawmill," Dat said, washing his hands at the small basin inside the door.

"We were there *first*!" Lizzie said loudly, her eyes flashing.

"Lizzie, he bought some of that land from Uncle Eli. That's his. You don't own Lovely Acres," Emma said, carrying a stack of plates to the cupboard.

"How do you know? If you know so much about Joseph Peachey, why don't you go marry him?" Lizzie asked.

Doddy Miller burst out laughing. He laughed and laughed, tears running down his cheeks, slapping his knee weakly. "Now!" he said, trying to reprimand Lizzie. "Maybe if you like your pine ridge so much, *you* should be the one to marry him."

Lizzie tried hard to look hurt and angry, but she couldn't help smiling at Doddy Miller. She just genuinely liked him, because he never took life too seriously. He could always find the humor in almost any situation, letting petty little worries roll off his shoulders with a good laugh.

Doddy Miller caught her eye, still smiling, as he told

her she'd make a good bachelor's wife, as much as she
loved milking that cow. They'd have all the good milk
and butter they needed.

Everyone laughed with Doddy Miller, then—even
Lizzie. She loved him with all her heart.

.   .   .   .   .

The next evening, they helped Doddy Miller put on
his blue denim "overcoat", as he called a light jacket,
then helped him out the back door, and into his wheelchair. They made sure he had his wallet, because he
could not buy them ice cream without it.

Pushing him through the gravel was impossible,
because the front wheels swiveled, getting stuck in the
deepest parts. Doddy Miller chuckled as they pushed
and grunted, then told them to turn the wheelchair
around. That made a big difference. The large wheels
in the back cut right through the gravel, and in no time
they were on the macadam. They started out at a brisk
pace, then Doddy Miller made them slow down. He said
if a car would come in both directions, they'd have to get
off to the side, and at this pace they'd dump him out.

Aunt Mary was working in her strawberry patch
beside the road, so they stopped to talk a while. Doddy
said he had never seen finer strawberry plants, which
made Aunt Mary very happy. She had a perfect patch
of strawberries, carefully kept in neat rows with plenty
of sawdust in between the plants. Mam never had too
much to say about Aunt Mary's strawberry patch.
Emma told Lizzie she thought Mam was just a wee bit
jealous, because she never tried to raise strawberries.

Lizzie didn't think people as old as Mam and Dat became jealous, but Emma said they did.

After they passed Aunt Mary, they went up the gradual slope to the harness shop. The bell above the door tinkled as they pushed the wheelchair through.

This harness shop was a lot bigger and contained much more than Dat's harness shop had, when Emma and Lizzie were little girls. This harness shop had piles and piles of shoes, boots, and other leather items. There were all kinds of fancy shampoos and lotions for horses, besides halters, neck ropes, saddles, saddle blankets, and just about anything you could think of that pertained to horses.

Lizzie loved the smell of the harness shop, just as she always had. The owner was a young man who was selling it soon to a family named Keim, moving in from Ohio.

The owner greeted Doddy Miller warmly, talking about the pleasant weather, how soon the new family was moving in, and what he was planning on doing. Doddy talked and talked, until Lizzie and Mandy became terribly bored. They wanted to go to the small grocery store and buy ice cream, not stay in this harness shop so long.

The only thing that saved them from becoming upset was a man and his little boy who came to buy a pair of boots. The little boy was smaller than Jason, with the blondest hair they had ever seen. It was almost white. He tried on pair after pair of cowboy boots, clunking proudly down the aisle, but always saying the same thing: "No, not that pair."

Lizzie and Mandy had to hide their smiles, because
the father was definitely exercising all the patience he
possessed. Finally, when he could take it no longer, he
threw his hands in the air, telling his son that was it,
he'd not be getting any boots because they were leaving.
Quickly, the little boy dashed over to the box containing the very first pair he had tried on, picking it up and
holding it against his chest.

"This pair, Daddy!" he trilled.

Sighing and rolling his eyes, his father got the box,
plopped it on the counter, and dug into his hip pocket
for his wallet.

That stopped Doddy Miller's talking, so he turned
his wheelchair and told the girls it was time to go. They
couldn't believe their good fortune, pushing him out
of the shop as fast as they dared, hoping he would not
change his mind and go back to talk some more.

As soon as they arrived at the small grocery store, it
was the exact same thing. The owner and his wife went
on and on and on, visiting with Doddy Miller.

Mandy and Lizzie sat on the wide windowsill at the
back of the store, listening for a while, until they became bored. Then they walked up and down the aisles,
looking at everything that was stacked on the shelves.
They heard Doddy Miller say he had come to buy ice
cream for himself and his two granddaughters, then he
launched into a long complicated history of his threshing
machine.

"Let's go home without him!" Mandy whispered.

"I will if you do!" Lizzie whispered back.

"That would teach him a lesson to hurry up and quit talking. Listen to him," Mandy said.

He was enjoying himself; there was no doubt about it. Gesticulating with his hands, his eyes shining like two blue stars, he was showing Mr. Byrd what happened if some wheel was placed improperly. Then, of all things, Mrs. Byrd asked Doddy if he wanted a cup of coffee, and if he wanted cream with it.

"Oh, no!" Lizzie hissed. "That does it."

She walked quickly to the front of the store, stopping politely beside Doddy's wheelchair without saying anything. When he looked up at her, she said, "Doddy, if you'd buy our ice cream, Mandy and I could eat it. Only if you were planning on buying us some," she finished.

"Oh, yes, of course," he said.

So Andy Byrd laughed, asking the girls what they wanted. Doddy Miller told him, and he placed two ice cream cone wafers on the clean counter, before unwrapping the ice cream and adding another wafer. He handed it to them in a white napkin.

"Thank you," Mandy said.

"Thanks. Aren't you having one, Doddy?" asked Lizzie.

"Oh, yes," he said. "Just as soon as I'm done talking. You go out and sit on the bench a while, and eat your ice cream."

So they did just that, glad to be allowed out of the store. They sat on the wrought-iron bench in the golden spring evening and ate every bite. Ice cream was very special to them, because they had no freezer at home. The times they could have ice cream was when they brought it straight home from the grocery store before it melted.

The ice cream was hard to eat properly. If you crunched the top wafer too hard with your teeth, it broke off and you were left with too much ice cream and not enough wafer. If you ate too much ice cream without the wafer, it was dry and tasteless. So they broke off some of the wafer, using it to dig out the ice cream.

They wiped their mouths with their napkins, and sat a while longer.

"I'm thirsty," Mandy said.

"Me, too."

"Wonder if he's ready to go?"

"Surely by now."

When they were too tired of waiting, they opened the door, the bell tinkling. Doddy Miller looked up to see who was coming in. "Oh, are you still here?" he asked. "I guess we had better leave. I think the girls are all ready to go, their ice cream all eaten and everything."

They pushed Doddy Miller home so fast, his head bobbed up and down and he had to hold on to his straw hat.

"Now, not so fast!" he called back.

So they slowed down a bit, but not very much. Lizzie thought if he could sit there and talk for almost an hour and a half, they could save time by pushing him home as fast as they could. Mam looked questioningly at the girls when they held the door open and Doddy Miller hobbled in with his cane. He was so tired, Mam quickly became concerned.

"Dat, you're worn out! Where were you so long?" she asked, hurrying over to help him remove his hat and overcoat.

"*Talking*," said Lizzie and Mandy, exactly at the same time.

"Now," said Doddy Miller.

chapter 22

Old Mary

Emma and Lizzie sat on the porch, waiting on Edna and Danny to go to school. The air was a bit chilly, but they were ready to go earlier this morning, so they waited on the porch.

A large tractor and trailer came slowly around the bend in the road, pulling a white mobile home. It was a nice one, as mobile homes go, with black trim and black shutters. There was a large bow window on one end, making it look very new and modern.

"Where is that trailer going?" Lizzie asked.

"I know exactly what it is. Remember Janet telling Mam about Jim's old aunt who was coming to live with them?"

"Oh, yes, I remember."

"See, it's slowing down. They're looking for the Zeigler place."

Sure enough, the trailer slowed to a stop in front of their house. Mr Zeigler came out of his garage door immediately, signaling to the driver to stop. They talked a while, but before the girls could tell where the trailer was going to be placed, Edna and Danny came walking up the driveway. They called for Mandy, grabbed their lunchboxes, and joined them.

"Good morning!" Emma said.

"Hey, who's that?" Danny asked, pointing to the tractor and trailer.

"They're going to put that trailer in beside Jim's house," Lizzie informed him.

"Who's going to live there?"

"Some old lady. An aunt to Jim Zeigler."

"All by herself?"

"I guess."

They continued on their way to school, other subjects and interests taking the place of the black and white mobile home and the old lady who would live there. But that evening when they arrived home from a day of school, they were amazed to see the trailer completely set up, with the white skirting neatly put around the bottom. It was nestled between two trees, with a few bushes in the front yard, so it looked as if it had always been there.

The girls asked Mam how they could set up the new trailer so quickly.

"Oh, they're not finished yet. The electrician and the plumber still need to put in water and electricity. I really wonder what the old lady will be like," she said.

"Why?"

"Janet told me she's eccentric."

"What does that mean?"

"Just that she's a bit different. She doesn't conform to the usual standard of things."

"You mean she's strange?" Lizzie called from the pantry, where she was lifting lids of Tupperware containers, looking for molasses cookies.

"Kind of, yes," Mam answered from the sewing machine where she was sitting.

"Well, then we aren't going to be neighborly," Lizzie said, still looking for the cookies.

Mam adjusted the shoulder of a green dress, put it under the presser foot of the sewing machine, and proceeded to treadle, the machine whirring and clunking in its usual rhythm.

"Mam, who ate all the molasses cookies?" Lizzie called.

"Probably you," Mam answered.

"I'll bake some," Emma volunteered.

"Good! Then Lizzie and Mandy can get the laundry off the line and our work will be finished. I'd like to finish this dress, then I made four today," Mam said, returning to her sewing.

Lizzie gave up finding cookies and ate pretzels. She dipped them in mustard, which tasted alright, but not nearly as good as a stack of molasses cookies would have.

"Right, we're not going to be neighborly?" she asked.

"To whom?" Emma asked, peering into Mam's recipe box for the cookie recipe.

"That old lady."

Mam stopped the sewing machine, snipping off the threads attached to the new green dress. "Lizzie, let me explain something to you. We should never decide who we're going to like and who we aren't. Love thy neighbor as thyself, you know. The Bible doesn't say we can only love certain ones. That's everybody. Besides, if you're kind to strangers, we never know when we're entertaining angels unaware. Suppose this old lady was sent by God to see what we make of having her here?" she asked.

Lizzie didn't say anything. She knew how Mam was. When they were small children living in Randolph County above the harness shop, they often had homeless men stop in. They were called tramps, and Mam never turned them away. She always fed them, talking to them as she would to a friend, sending them on their way with a sandwich in their pocket. She often had tears in her eyes as she watched them walk on, wondering what would become of them. Dat was even a bit more suspicious about tramps than Mam was, but he always agreed to giving them a meal.

Emma stirred the eggs into the sugar and butter, saying, "You don't even know what she's like, Lizzie. Maybe she's a cute little lady whom we'll just love to go visit."

"I know. But I'd rather just have Debbie," Lizzie said.

·   ·   ·   ·   ·

They did not have long to find out. About a week later a blue and orange moving truck pulled into the new drive leading to the trailer. Men dressed in navy blue suits with orange caps carried furniture into the trailer. The old lady arrived about the same time as her furniture, in a black car driven by a man who walked bow-legged, like Jim Zeigler.

Emma and Lizzie were watching everything from the front kitchen window. Mam said they had to stay back, because it was impolite to stare out a window at your neighbors, but she didn't get much work done for a while, either. It was just too interesting.

The bow-legged man walked around the car, opening the door for the old lady. At first, Lizzie thought it was a child, until she saw her bent back. She was very small and thin, with her gray hair pulled back tightly into a bun on the nape of her neck.

"She has a 'bob!'" Mandy said in awe.

"She does!" Emma echoed.

Instead of going into the trailer, the man opened the back door of the car, reaching in to pull out a large wire cage. He set it on the grass, pulling another one across the back seat, setting it beside the first cage before slamming the door.

"She has dogs!" Mandy said.

"I think they're cats," Mam said.

Bending down, the old lady opened the door of the cages, letting out five cats. They were ordinary house cats — two black ones and three striped gray ones. She stroked and caressed her cats, holding one up against her face as the others rubbed themselves across her skirt. She did not go into her new home until she had snuggled every cat up to her face.

"Five cats!" Lizzie shrieked.

"And they're all going to live in one little trailer," Mam said, laughing. "Oh, well, she probably has a good vacuum cleaner."

.   .   .   .   .

The old lady had only moved in for a few days before Mam ventured across the road with a loaf of homemade bread and an apple pie. The girls watched as she walked up the steps of the small porch and pressed the doorbell. They waited breathlessly, until they saw the door of the trailer open and Mam stepped inside, the door closing behind her.

It seemed to the girls as if Mam had been gone an awfully long time. Emma was beginning to glance at the clock with a worried expression, Mam walked up the steps to the porch. She was smiling to herself and she didn't have the bread or the apple pie anymore.

"What's she like?" Lizzie asked.

Mam sat down on a kitchen chair, threw her hands in the air, and burst out laughing. The girls laughed with her, just because it was funny to see how much Mam had to laugh.

"Oh, my!" Mam finished, lifting her glasses to wipe her eyes with her handkerchief. "I'm not trying to make fun of her, bless her heart," she said, still chuckling. "But she most definitely is an eccentric! She wants me to bring all of you over so she can meet you. Why don't you put a clean shirt on Jason, Emma? I'll wash the twins' faces."

So they smoothed back their hair, put on clean aprons, and with Mam carrying Susan and Emma carrying KatieAnn, they all walked across the road to the black and white mobile home.

The old lady threw open the door before Mam had a chance to ring the doorbell. Her wrinkled face was wreathed in smiles as she told them all to come in.

She was thin, with a worn housedress hanging loosely from her small shoulders. Her hair was parted at the side, but combed back almost as tight as theirs used to be when Mam rolled it. Her complexion was dark, with a round nose and dark eyes that were almost hidden by puffy folds of flesh. Her teeth were stained and yellow, but she seemed reasonably clean and certainly friendly.

She sat down on the living room sofa, telling everyone to have a chair. Lizzie noticed her gnarled, work-worn hands picking at the folds of her dress, so she knew she must be nervous.

"Girls, this is Mary Nobinski. Mary, this is Emma, holding one of the twins; Lizzie. Here's Mandy; the little boy is Jason; and Susan, here on my lap," Mam said, introducing them all.

"How do you do? How do you do?" Mary said, evidently

quite overwhelmed. She shook her head, as if in disbelief.

"Oh, Missus," she said, her swollen eyes surveying
the children. She kept looking from one to the next, but
made no attempt to hold the babies, touch Jason, or talk
to any of them.

The girls all said they were fine, smiling a bit stiffly,
because it seemed as if she could not meet their eyes.
Her eyes were not shifty or suspicious looking, certainly
not evil or guilty, so Lizzie thought she must be a bit shy,
as nervous as she was.

The trailer was very nice. There was thick blue
carpeting in the living room, with mirrors on one wall,
making the room appear to be larger than it actually
was. The furniture was not as grand as Debbie's mom,
Marlene's, but it was clean and presentable. The dishes
were stacked neatly in the dish drainer on her countertop, and the table was cleared off except for a box of
crackers and Mam's homemade bread. There were lots

of small china figurines, artificial flowers, and little lace
doilies everywhere. Pictures of the crucifixion hung on
the walls, as well as pictures of praying hands and Jesus
in the Garden of Gethsemane. Lizzie thought she must
be a Christian.

The cats were all over the house. They padded around
on the carpeting without making a sound, their eyes
blinking, whiskers tilting first one way and then another.
Cats made Lizzie nervous. She never knew where they
were for sure, until—bang!—there they were. That's
exactly how these cats were. One would quite suddenly
appear at the side of Mam's chair, or leap up on the sofa
beside the old lady, making no sound, not even a whisper. It was creepy.

"So these are all your children?" Mary was saying.

"Yes. Yes, they are," Mam answered.

"You're a busy lady. I can see that. A busy, busy lady,"
Mary went on. She asked Mam to look at the pictures
on her walls, telling her she was a Catholic. Mam smiled
and nodded her head, saying she liked the picture in her
dining room.

"Now, Missus, when I need something at the grocery
store, or if you have anything for me to do, you send
these girls over, and I'll be there. I cleaned schools and
homes for forty-two years. Yessir, I did. Forty-two
years. Hardly ever missed a day of work. Hardly ever. I
washed down walls, cleaned windows, scrubbed floors,
cleaned bathrooms, oh yeah. I don't know much, but I
know how to clean," she said.

"Well, maybe on Saturday morning you can help us with the cleaning," Mam offered.

Lizzie's heart sank. She did not want this strange old person in their house. Why did Mam have to say that? It was alright to love your neighbor and all that, but you didn't have to let them in your house.

Suddenly Mary stood up, reaching down the neckline of her dress. Plastic rustled, and she held on to the belt of her dress as she fished around for something she was searching for. She gave the front of her dress a few good shakes, before retrieving a small plastic bag filled with money.

Emma and Lizzie both knew they were not allowed to look at each other or they would burst out laughing, then Mam would say they were making fun of Mary. But, my!

She searched for quarters with her gnarled fingers, before presenting one to each of them. As the girls thanked her, she beamed with pride, stuffing the small plastic bag down the front of her dress again, adjusting her belt as she sat down.

Then Mam said they must go, but she would be wel-come to come over on Saturday morning.

"Good-bye, Missus," she called, as they all filed down the porch steps.

.   .   .   .   .

From that day on, Old Mary, as they called her, was a fixture in their lives. She was quite a big help, actually She always called Mam "Missus," never using her given name, or even "Mrs. Glick." It was always just "Missus."

Oh, how she loved Mam! She adored the ground Mam walked on, Dat said. Every Saturday morning, exactly at nine o'clock, she would knock on the kitchen door, eager to help clean Mam's kitchen.

She refused to use a mop, saying mops didn't clean a floor properly. She would get down on her hands and knees, with a bucket of hot, soapy water and a thick rag, and proceeded to give the kitchen linoleum the best cleaning it ever had. She would start in one corner, wiping down the baseboard, before scrubbing the floor. On each area of the floor, she'd clean it well once, dip her rag back into the soapy water, and repeat the cleaning the second time.

"Missus!" she called.

"What?" Mam answered from the living room.

"My dress is pulling up, isn't it? How far can you see?" she asked.

"Oh, it's not up very far," Mam replied, trying not to laugh. She never scrubbed the kitchen floor without calling out to Mam, "Missus! How far can you see?"

If she needed groceries, Mam would take her along to town with her driver. She helped her find the items she needed, which Old Mary appreciated very much.

One day Mam came home with a load of groceries. The girls helped her bring in all the bags, while Jason yelled, rummaging through every one, looking for candy. Emma had started putting things in the pantry when Mam started laughing.

"Oh, that Old Mary!" she gasped.

"Now what did she do?" Emma asked with a smile.

"You're not going to believe this. You know how she would never carry a purse? Well, we got to the check-out counter, and I paid for mine first. When it was her turn, she loaded everything on the counter, and started fishing down the front of her dress again.

"The clerk waited patiently, and she shook the front of her dress and carried on the way she does, before finally coming up with her little plastic bag of money. She was a quarter short, so she fished around some more, finally holding the belt of her dress out and shaking, before two quarters fell out from under her skirts, rolling across the floor.

"'There we go,' she cried, chasing the quarters in front of a gentleman who was standing in line. She handed them over to the clerk, whose face was a study in control."

Mam laughed quite easily about things Old Mary did, but never in a mocking or demeaning manner. She loved Mary, respecting the fact that she was a devout Catholic.

She told the girls about Catholic people, asking Mary to show them her rosary beads. She explained the nuns' and priests' lives to them, too.

Lizzie fell silent for a long time after hearing about nuns. Why would you go to some big school and wear a long dress clear up over your head and promise never to marry? That was so depressing that she couldn't think about it very long or it made her too sad. She asked Mam why in the world any girl in her right mind would do something like that.

"Well, Lizzie, I know it's different from what we're used to," Mam said. "But I honestly think if they can

give their lives to God, serving only Him and not themselves, they experience inner peace, more than we
imagine. It's not our way, but we can't look at them as
if that's all completely wrong. God knows, Lizzie—we
don't have to."

"I know," Lizzie said. "But I'm glad I don't have to be
a nun."

"When I was in the hospital with Jason, there was
a group of nuns helping out for the day. I still remember that one girl's eyes. They were so clear and calm, I
decided she had to have the right spirit, to have eyes that
portrayed such peace and contentment," Mam told her.

"You see, we think whatever we can buy or doing
what we want will make us happy, when often just the
opposite is true. Real happiness comes from a meek and
quiet spirit, given up to God's will," Mam said.

Lizzie didn't answer, not knowing what to say. She
thought about her prayer not to marry a farmer and milk
cows. "Does that mean we shouldn't pray for things we
want?"

"Not necessarily. God just knows what we need, so
He doesn't always answer the way we think He should."

"Oh."

That was hard to figure out. If she prayed to please
not marry a farmer, and God thought that would be
good for her, He'd make her. That was just as depressing
as being a nun, so she put all those thoughts behind her,
wandered into the pantry, and found the chocolate layer
cake. She was just cutting a sizable piece onto a small
plate, when there was a knock on the kitchen door.

"Missus!" Old Mary stuck her head in.

"Come on in, Mary!" Mam said.

"Here. You wouldn't let me pay the driver, and I don't feel right. You take this five dollars or I won't be able to sleep. Come on now. Take it, Missus." She shoved the five dollar bill at Mam.

"No, no, Mary. You keep it. I had to go to town for groceries anyway, whether you went along or not. No, I don't want it," Mam insisted.

So Old Mary stuffed the five dollar bill down the front of her dress, saying she wouldn't take her money on Saturday morning for scrubbing the kitchen floor.

Lizzie licked the frosting off the knife before looking at Mary. She was actually cute today, wearing a new aqua blue and white gingham housedress. Her hair, which was usually a bit greasy, was light and shiny, combed back a bit more loosely. Her complexion looked especially dark because of the aqua blue dress, and Lizzie decided she must have been attractive at one time.

Mam patted her shoulder, turning her around, to let her know she may as well leave; the five dollars was hers. So Mary just said, "Oh, Missus," and went out the door and down the driveway, before Mam could see her tears.

chapter 23

Sleeping in
the Playhouse

T he weather turned suddenly
much warmer in October the
year Lizzie was thirteen. So much warmer, in
fact, that Debbie suggested they sleep outside in the
playhouse, one more time before it got too cold.

They were sitting on the front steps, eating a Grandpa cookie with fresh vanilla icing on it. The icing was
actually pink, but that was because Mam had put red
food coloring in it. She was baking them, and Debbie,
Jeanie, Lizzie, and Mandy were all eating their second
cookie. Grandpa cookies were best if they were still
warm, so Mam spread icing on them, making sure they
could all have one. They were actually a sugar cookie, so
Lizzie never did find out why they were called "Grandpa
cookies."

"We could sleep out in the playhouse on Friday evening, because there's no school Saturday," Debbie said.

"If it stays warm like this," Lizzie said, stuffing the last of the cookie in her mouth. Debbie finished hers, wiped her mouth with her sleeve, and looked over at Lizzie.

"How many cookies do you think your mom would let us have?" she asked.

"I don't know. Why?"

"I could eat another one."

"We can ask."

So they all got up and asked Mam if they were allowed another cookie.

"You'll ruin your supper," Mam said, but she was smiling, which meant they were allowed one more.

"Thank you, Annie," Debbie said.

"Thanks, Mrs. Glick," Jeanie said.

Lizzie and Mandy didn't say anything, because it was their Mam and their cookies. But Lizzie was glad Mam made good cookies, so Debbie would like her.

They all sat back down on the steps, eating another cookie, except Mandy, who said she would have to throw up if she ate one more. Lizzie envied Mandy's ability to stop eating after one cookie. She often wished she was thin like her, but could never survive on as little as Mandy ate, or so she thought.

"We'll bring our sleeping bags and pillows," Debbie said.

"We have to ask Mam," Lizzie informed her.

"Why didn't we ask when we got another cookie?" Debbie asked.

So they all got up, and walked across the porch and into the kitchen. They leaned against the table, watching

Mam. Her face was flushed from the heat of the woodstove, as she slid a spatula under a big, round cookie, expertly loosening it from the aluminum cookie sheet. She
flipped them on an old plaid tablecloth that was spread
on top of the plastic one. Emma was spreading the icing
on top of the cookies that had cooled sufficiently, whistling under her breath.

The kitchen was bathed in the yellow glow of the
late afternoon sun. It caught the gleam of the light oak
kitchen cabinets, reflected on the windows, and made
the top of the wood-fired range sparkle. There was a pot
of meat bubbling on the back of the stove, which smelled
almost better than the cookies.

Emma was growing up. She was about the same
height as Mam, and a lot slimmer. She had steadily lost
a few pounds every month, and now she looked almost
like a young girl that went to the singing. It just gave
Lizzie the blues, watching Emma expertly spread icing
on cookies, looking so slim and grown up.

"Mam, may we sleep in the playhouse tonight?" she
asked, turning to look at her.

"Tonight?" Mam asked.

"It's not too cold at all," Mandy chimed in.

"We're not sleeping there tonight," Debbie said. "You
forgot. Not till Friday night."

Mam looked a bit dubious, but she allowed the girls
to sleep there, as long as the weather did not turn colder.
Debbie was thrilled, saying she'd bring Pepsi to drink
and they would make hot dogs on an open fire if Dat
would allow them to.

Mam smiled, listening to the girls' plans. Winter would soon be upon them, so if these balmy Indian summer days lasted, they may as well enjoy them.

So Friday night after the laundry was brought in, folded, and put away, Lizzie and Mandy were free to go.

They swept the playhouse clean, arranging sleeping bags and old quilts and square pillows and oblong ones, anything they might need to be comfortable on a chilly night. The one window was broken out and there was no screen, so they worried about the cold night air coming in.

When Debbie and Jeanie came over, they didn't seem to think the window would be much of a problem. The air was not chilly at all, the decided together, and since the playhouse was close to the low branches of the trees in the fencerow, it was almost like a screen across it.

Debbie brought two sleeping bags, one for her and one for Jeanie. They stored the cooler with cans of Pepsi and ice in the low cupboard, arranged their ketchup and mustard around it, and went to the house to find Dat.

"Now everybody be quiet, and let me ask Dat," Mandy said.

Lizzie did not agree. "Mandy, you know if Debbie asks Dat, we'll be allowed to much sooner."

"I'm not asking," Debbie said, rolling her brown eyes.

"He's not going to let you, Lizzie, 'cause you're always asking to do crazy things," Mandy said seriously.

"Let's just all go in together," Debbie suggested.

They found Dat sitting at the kitchen table, reading the newspaper.

"Dat, we need to ask you a question," Mandy blurted out. "I mean, we're about positive you're going to say no, but would we…"

"Are we allowed to start a fire in the yard to roast hot dogs?" Lizzie broke in.

Dat shook his head. "Not in the yard."

"Where else?" Lizzie asked.

"It's much too dry to start a fire in the yard. You'd ruin the grass, anyway. No, certainly not. Why do you have to start a fire in the yard?" He returned to the newspaper, paging through it as if the conversation was over.

Debbie looked at Lizzie, raising her eyebrows. Lizzie pushed back a strand of brown hair nervously, cleared her throat, and began. "Dat, you don't understand. Debbie and Jeanie are allowed to stay overnight, and we want to have a hot dog roast for our supper. We don't want to cook the hot dogs on top of a pan in here," she said, lifting both hands with the palms up.

Dat put down the newspaper. He looked at Lizzie before he said, "I guess not. You can't make hot dogs on top of a pan."

Debbie giggled out loud, and Mandy slapped Dat's arm. "Where else?"

"I guess if you clear away the weeds and stay away from the trees you can lay concrete blocks in a square and build a small fire. But just enough to roast your hot dogs, and you have to make one for me. I like them burned."

"Thank you, Mr. Glick!" Debbie called back, as everyone rushed to get out the door and start the fire.

First, they found a spot close to the playhouse, but not in the yard. They cleared away all the weeds and leaves, until the brown dirt showed through. Mandy and Jeanie collected kindling from the wood house while Debbie and Lizzie hauled eight concrete blocks from the pile behind the barn. They were heavy, and filled up the wooden wagon almost to capacity. They pulled it across the lawn and arranged the blocks carefully around the dirt area.

"Newspaper!"

"Oh, we forgot newspaper!"

Mandy was off across the lawn, her heels flying, as she dashed up the steps to the kitchen.

"We don't have matches."

"Matches!"

Jeanie raced across the yard, as fast as she could go, her little brown feet propelling her chubby legs. She took the steps as fast as she could, meeting Mandy on the porch. Together they went back to the kitchen for matches.

Debbie crumpled the newspaper, and Lizzie arranged slivers of wood on top. With a few attempts, the match ignited, the flame burning quickly, consuming the newspaper. They waited breathlessly, hoping the wood would catch fire as well, but the paper curled into thin black nothingness, with the wood still lying on top.

"That wasn't so great!" Debbie said.

"Use more newspaper," Mandy said, starting to crumple a sheet. So they tried again, using lots and lots of paper, and only the smallest slivers of kindling. The flame licked greedily at the paper, quickly turning quite hot, and as they all watched anxiously, the kindling turned red, crackling into flames as well.

Lizzie reached for larger pieces of wood, but Mandy grabbed her hand, saying, "Not too much!" So Lizzie added smaller pieces, watching them burn before she added larger ones.

The sun was sliding behind the mountain, casting a shadow across the playhouse and fencerow. But the fire crackled merrily, illuminating their faces with an orange glow. Jeanie backed away, wiping her eyes, waving her arms, and saying, "Make the smoke go away!"

They laughed and went to find sticks to sharpen, then they speared the hot dogs on the end. They all sat around the cheery little fire, balancing their hot dogs carefully, so they wouldn't get burned. All except Lizzie, who was making one for Dat. She held it much lower, until it was burned completely black, then put it on a roll, added ketchup and mustard, and dashed across the yard.

After she returned, she burned another one for herself. Debbie and Jeanie had already eaten one before Lizzie's was finished, but they soon started on the second hot dog. They drank their Pepsi, tears forming in Lizzie's and Mandy's eyes, because they hardly ever drank it. They blinked, trying to hide it, but Debbie laughed at them.

"So, maybe you don't drink Pepsi very often, but your mom bakes!" she said.

It was getting dark in earnest now, and they moved closer to the friendliness of the crackling fire. They ate

hot dogs until they could eat no more, and sat back on the grass contentedly. A few birds twittered good-night to each other in the branches, and the fire died down to red coals.

"Let's tell spooky stories!" Debbie said.

"You say the first one," Lizzie said, suppressing a burp. Pepsi was so good, except it always made her burp, which was embarrassing.

So Debbie launched into a story about two people being lost on a mountain. The story became so frightening, with Mandy's eyes becoming steadily bigger and rounder, until Lizzie could stand it no longer.

"Debbie, I guarantee you that story isn't true," she said, defending Mandy.

"Yes, it is. I saw it on TV."

"That's too scary. You have to say something else."

"Would you rather hear about ghosts?"

"*No!*"

"There *is* such a thing as ghosts," Debbie said.

"That's not true, Debbie. And if you don't quit saying things like that, I'm going to go in and not sleep in the playhouse ever again. I mean it."

That was one thing Lizzie could not think about ever. Ghosts. If there was such a thing as a ghost, the whole world would never be safe, because they could walk through walls. Mam had told her it wasn't true, and she shouldn't worry or think about such silly things. But Lizzie often imagined ghosts walking around out in the cornfield, until she was so afraid she had to hold a pillow over her head to go to sleep.

And now, here they were, sleeping in the playhouse, and Debbie had to bring up that ghost subject. "Let's stop telling spooky stories and go inside in our sleeping bags," she said, rubbing her arms and shivering.

"No, not yet. We didn't toast our marshmallows!" Debbie announced. Jeanie produced a bag of marsh-mallows, and Debbie threw a few sticks of wood on the fire.

Marshmallows were funny things. You could only hold one over the fire for a very short time, before it erupted into a little fire of its own. Then you had to blow on it as hard as you could if you wanted to save any of it at all. The best thing to do with marshmallows was put them between two Ritz crackers with peanut butter on them. But they didn't have any, so they just ate the hot marshmallows off the stick, yelping as it stuck to their mouths, burning their tongues.

"Oh, I know a really scary story. Did you know that in Alaska they found tracks as big as a sofa? They say there's a creature roaming the snowy landscape that's bigger than a house. Nobody knows for sure where it came from or what it looks like. They just know there's a huge creature walking around. They call him Bigfoot," Debbie said.

Lizzie's eyes narrowed, and she slowly swallowed the rest of her marshmallow. She was sick to her stomach immediately. "W-w-where did you hear such a thing?" she quavered.

"My mom saw it in the paper. She was laughing about it, but my grandmother says if there were tracks in the snow, something had to make them."

"It was probably an extra, extra, outsized polar bear," Mandy said sensibly.

"The only thing is, a group of hunters think they saw him, and it's like a huge human looking kind of thing, with a bear's head," Debbie explained.

Lizzie became chilled all over. What an awful thought! She shivered. Surely there was no such thing. She wished she could ask Mam if there was something like that, or if God didn't make all the animals for sure.

"Well, whatever it was, it's not here in Pennsylvania," Mandy said, being very grown up and wise.

Lizzie looked quickly behind her. She thought she had heard a rustling in the fencerow. "I'm going to bed!" she announced shrilly, her eyes darting from one side to the next.

"What about the fire?" Debbie asked.

"It'll burn out—it's not windy," Lizzie called back, already halfway through the playhouse door.

The other girls giggled and laughed, arranging pillows and blankets to suit themselves. Mandy put the marshmallows, ketchup, mustard, and hot dog rolls in the cupboard, checking the ice in the cooler to see if the leftover hot dogs were still cold.

Lizzie rolled herself in an old quilt, turned her face to the wall, and felt quite sick. Wouldn't it be just horrible to see a huge white creature come walking down the road, stopping to peer in the upstairs windows? She couldn't believe it. She tried to think of other things, but her imagination conjured up vivid images of creatures she wasn't absolutely certain did not exist. She wished Debbie would not have said that. That was the trouble with English children. Nothing scared them—not one thing.

Suddenly she sat up, glared at Debbie, and said, "I'm going to go sleep in my room if you don't stop saying those things about creatures and ghosts. None of it is true."

"No one knows for certain, Lizzie," Debbie said.

"Well, I do," Lizzie huffed.

"Why don't you just go to sleep, and the rest of us will play tic-tac-toe?" Debbie asked.

So Lizzie flounced back on her pillow, turned her back, and closed her eyes, while the others pulled up a small table, turned on the battery-powered flashlight, and played tic-tac-toe. They giggled and teased each other so much that Lizzie had to smile in spite of herself. When Debbie pounced on her and pulled off her quilt, Lizzie sat up and pulled her hair. Then they forgot all about Bigfoot and ghosts, having a wonderful time play-

ing games and eating marshmallows out of the bag until
they could no longer stay awake.

When Jeanie's head began to nod and the flashlight
turned a bit dim, they wearily crawled under their quilts
and sleeping bags. With a tired sigh, Lizzie clicked off
the flashlight and they all settled themselves comfortably.

"G'night!" Debbie whispered.

"G'night. Don't let the bedbugs bite," Mandy answered.

"They will in here!" Jeanie giggled.

Silence fell over the playhouse, as, one by one, the
girls drifted off to dreamland. Their shoulders rose and
fell, and small snores punctuated the stillness of the soft
night. The three-quarter moon rose grandly above the
mountain, the shadows changing with a small whisper of
a breeze. A tractor and trailer hummed along the highway, and a bat swooped under the pole light, catching
an unwary moth.

As the girls slept peacefully, two of Old Mary's gray
cats and two of the Zeiglers' white cats prowled in the
dark. As is the nature of cats, they eventually began to
chase each other, racing across the lawn, with two of the
white cats clawing their way up the trees of the fencerow, where they sat, hissing at the unfriendly intruders.
Old Mary's cats were not about to give up the fight.
They started climbing the trees as well.

The girls were terrified to be awakened in one whirl
of a hissing, scratching, and meowing cluster of fighting
cats. They screamed. The cats fought.

Lizzie jumped up, grabbing a pillow and beating the cats, while Debbie grabbed the flashlight. Mandy and Jeanie screamed and cried, while Lizzie danced around the interior of the playhouse, whopping anything that moved with the soft pillow, yelling hoarsely all the while. In the melee that followed, Lizzie accidentally knocked Jeanie's head against the wall with her pillow, which elevated her screaming to an ear-piercing wail. She grabbed her pillow, still crying, and ran home all by herself.

After the cats finally found the door, they all raced in different directions, their hair standing on end. The girls' screams ended in hoarse breathing. They were shaking all over. Lizzie sagged weakly to her knees and Mandy collapsed on top of her sleeping bag.

"What was that all about?" Debbie asked shakily.

"Cats! Jim Zeigler's cats!" was all Lizzie could say.

"Where's Jeanie?"

"She ran home."

"This isn't funny."

"I'm never going to sleep in this dumb playhouse again as long as I live."

"We should have put a screen across the window."

"Let's go in."

"Let's do."

Grumbling, they grabbed their flashlights and pillows, mumbling and complaining their way across the moon-drenched yard.

"Whose idea was it to sleep out there?"

"Yours."

"Hah-ah. Yours."

"Be quiet."

They opened the door quietly, padding silently across the kitchen floor. The old platform rocker was creaking, with Mam rocking one of the twins. She looked so peaceful, half asleep, rocking in the moonlight.

"Who goes there?" she whispered, a smile in her voice.

"Us."

"What happened?" Mam asked, holding the baby to her shoulder.

"Jim Zeigler's cats had a fight with Old Mary's, and they fell through the open playhouse window."

"Right on top of us!"

"Where's Jeanie?"

"She ran home."

Mam started to say something, then sputtered, threw back her head, and laughed softly. The baby on her shoulder shook silently as Mam laughed helplessly. She lifted one hand and let it fall on her knee.

"Ach my, girls. I almost don't want any of you to grow up. There are times in your life that you will never forget. What fun times you have had living here!"

"I guess," Mandy said crossly.

"Yes, I suppose," Debbie said, trying to be polite.

They grumbled their way up the stairs to their rooms, leaving Mam chuckling alone in her platform rocker.

Lizzie lay awake long after Debbie had drifted off to sleep. She put her hands behind her head, locked her fingers together, and stared at the ceiling, watching the pattern of shadows across it.

It was true what Mam said. Her life was carefree, filled with loving friends and family. She didn't want to grow up, either. But she supposed slowing down time was as impossible as harnessing the tides of the sea. You could never tell what lay before you, but she wondered if happiness didn't depend a lot on your eagerness to see what lay around the bend. She suspected the flow of her life was as inevitable as the current of the river.

With a sigh of contentment, she thought her prayer to God before her breathing became deep and even.

the end

The Buggy Spoke Series

by Linda Byler

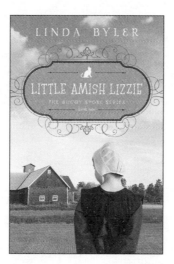

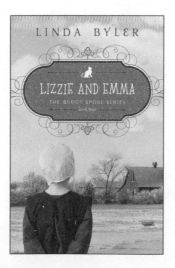

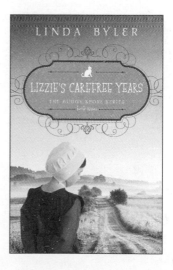